D0407956

Dallas Public Library
950 Main Street
Dallas, Oregon 97338

BAD
MANNERS

BAD MANNERS

MARNE DAVIS KELLOGG

WARNER BOOKS

A Time Warner Company

Publisher's note: This novel is a work of fiction. Names, characters, places, and incidents either are the product of the author's imagination or are used fictitiously, and any resemblance to actual persons, living or dead, events, or locales is entirely coincidental.

Copyright © 1995 by Marne Davis Kellogg
All rights reserved.

Warner Books, Inc., 1271 Avenue of the Americas, New York, NY 10020

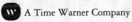 A Time Warner Company

Printed in the United States of America
ISBN 0-446-51836-0

34071156 9-07

For Peter—my heart and the center of my universe.

Dallas Public Library
950 Main Street
Dallas, Oregon 97338

BAD
MANNERS

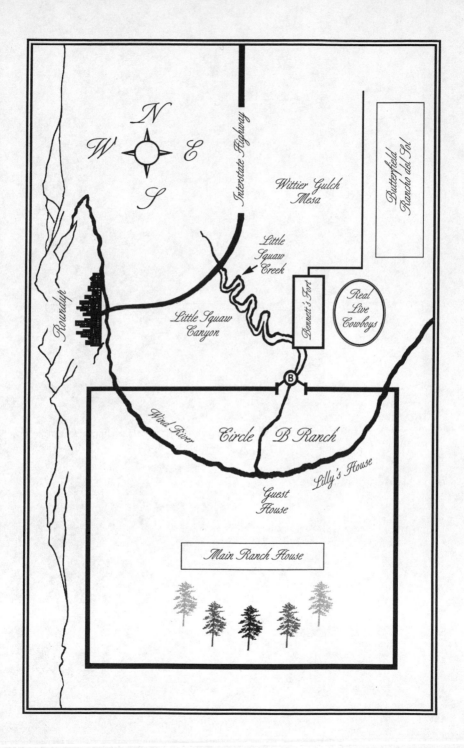

≈ Chapter One

I quit my job as chief of detectives of the Santa Bianca, California, Police Department because I could not bear the thought of seeing pictures of myself and my lover, Edmond A. "Wink" Harrison, chief justice of the California Supreme Court, in flagrante delicto on the cover of the *National Enquirer* as I stood in the checkout line at the grocery store. Or hearing Wink's wife, who had paid some sleaze to shoot the photos and videos, tell all on the *Sally Jessy Raphael* show. I'd rather change jobs than read about my lovers, and believe me, there have been a few, while I'm getting my hair done. I mean, who needs it? And believe me, no one would have noticed for a second that Wink was older, whiter, and flabbier than I was. So I did what any intelligent person would do under the circumstances: I quit. After twenty years on the force.

I submitted my resignation the next morning claiming burnout— unheard of in detective ranks. Cops on the beat burn out when they get passed over for promotion a few times. But detectives? Never. Letting my coworkers believe I had lost my nerve was preferential to letting the truth be known. We all contributed to the smoke screen: I, by pretending to be glad to return to Roundup and the Circle B and full-time cattle ranching. Back to the land. And they, by pretending to be jealous.

I was the first woman in the country to be a chief of detectives, which sounds good but truly was not that big a deal because, as everyone knows, women are everywhere, advancing like wildfire. First, as my father laments, "the tee times go," then the police department. Some girl would have gotten the nod as chief sooner or later, and I'm glad it was me. But since I had been the first, before I left town the mayor gave a testimonial banquet in my honor, and *CBS This Morning* and the *Today* show asked long, earnest, searching questions about the dangers of burnout of women police officers and I provided long, earnest, thoughtful answers saying that my decision was based more on the changing priorities of my life than fatigue, ennui, or fear. Being forty-five and all.

Plus, it was 1993. Time for a change. Or so we'd all been told and evidently many agreed. A new regime. A new life. Time for a change. What a load. I moved back to my hometown, Roundup.

Roundup lies along the base of Wyoming's Wind River Range—an island in the middle of nowhere out west where the air and water are as clear and sharp as diamonds and the sky big and blue.

Being born a Bennett in Roundup is a big deal. And if you are born a male Bennett you are provided with meaningful responsibility and accountability in one of the family companies. Meaning you automatically get a job for life. If you are born a female Bennett, as I was, you are provided with luxury and an indulgent attitude about how you intend to occupy yourself until you attain and fulfill your own true self as wife and mother.

I'm not complaining because that's just the way it was when I was a young woman. Things were only in the very beginning of change. But the specter of children and the Junior League drove me from Roundup. And just to be contrary and because you got to wear a uniform and work around men all the time, I decided to be a cop. So while my older brother Elias learned to run the family's cattle ranch, the Circle B, and my younger brother Christian followed my father around and learned to run the railroad and the newspaper and the banks, I, Lilly, slogged around at the Police Academy in California getting kicked and spit on and yelled at.

Two decades later almost to the day, on the first of June, I left Santa Bianca a heroine without anyone discovering the truth as far as I knew, and came home to the ranch and incorporated myself as Bennett Security International, Inc.

The international part was easy to set up—I just installed phone and fax lines in the Roundup National Bank's offices in London and Paris and in a friend's villa in Tuscany, a nice touch for a Wyoming-headquartered firm. Face it, most people think we westerners still communicate with the outside world by telegraph via Cimarron, and here I was, if you were to judge by the impressiveness of my engraved letterhead, running Interpol from the Circle B.

Even though I had phones and faxes in all those fancy locales and hoped I'd be called in to solve a major jewel theft in Monte Carlo, it was more likely I'd spend long, hot, dusty weekends in Puerto Vallarta investigating condo time-share scams. I knew I'd never be called to go to Canada, the only other foreign country within shouting distance. I don't believe they allow crime up there.

Here I am back home. I miss Santa Bianca. But when I was in Santa Bianca, I missed the ranch. There you go.

Chapter Two

*R*oundup seems more beautiful. Even the neighborhoods shine with what looks like fresh paint and uncharacteristically clean streets. Maybe it's just me looking at the city with new eyes, but things seem to hum.

Outsiders call Roundup a hick town and a cow town but we call our town a city and call outsiders suckers or dudes unless the outsider's interests are of a financial nature. In those instances, a Roundup banker, city councilman or Junior League belle can be as charming and earnest as the next big-city slick politician. Unfortunately, though, our superior attitude about outsiders' inferior abilities makes us in Roundup prey to more than our share of hucksters. We're a little bit gullible that way. Scoundrels with lofty ideas about amusement parks or tax shelters or irresistible oil deals fleece the people of Roundup on a regular basis before heading off to one of two places: Arizona, to toss up a retirement village or, as is more seldom the case, federal prison for tax evasion.

We take as a compliment an easterner's observation that the skills of Henry Clay, the Great Pacificator, would go for naught in this town where steely-eyed stare-downs and contention and downright contrariness are the name of the game. Consequently, over the years the city has taken on a curious appearance that earns it the distinction of being used in the world's leading schools of architecture and city planning as the prime U.S. example of how a city should *not* look or be planned. We like that. The Neo-Greco-Gothic-Bauhaus Art Museum in Roundup and the Royal Palace in Lima, Peru, are the only two edifices in the Western Hemisphere that I know of where a visitor can see virtually every stage of architecture on and in one building. Besides, after a while it becomes endearing to round a corner and stumble upon a Venetian campanile atop a Gothic fortress, and when you're in Roundup, you never think you're anywhere else.

The Roundup Symphony Orchestra, the Roundup Opera Company—which took on a world-class je ne sais quoi when Caruso chose to spend his summers performing with it in the 1910s even though we still call it the "opry"—the Roundup Civic Ballet, and all touring theatrical and evangelical productions do time in Bennett Auditorium which, built to serve many masters and seat three thousand revved-up Rounduppers, serves all poorly. But the audiences, grateful for any break from the prairie wind and the failing football team, applaud with indiscriminate enthusiasm all who venture out onto the large stage, whether the act was any good or not. The fact that the audiences for the cultural events at Bennett Auditorium have to pay an extra add-on tax that goes to pay for the stadium where the failing football team embarrasses itself every Sunday fuels the cultural contention. One time, on the fourth tee of the Roundup Country Club, the symphony president complained to the mayor that the orchestra was going broke and could use a little of that tax money its customers paid into the athletic fund.

"The football team's only got twenty players," the mayor said. "Your orchestra's got more than twenty fiddle players alone. There must be fifty of 'em. I think you outta look at getting rid of a few of those fiddles. That outta save you thousands." Roundup will never be accused of being hoity-toity.

Roundup has three private clubs—Oil, or Energy, as it's called today (Energy is a flashy and capricious staple of Roundup's economy), WASP, and Jewish. Originally, the clubs' only common element was their membership restriction to White Men Only. But as years passed and people ceased to discriminate, or at least be discriminating, the clubs' rosters became almost indistinguishable. Whenever the oil business takes a dip, newcomers to town are courted fervently by all three nominating committees. My father, Elias Caulfield Bennett III, says all the problems at the private clubs stem from women.

"We started letting women into these clubs and everything went to hell," Father says. "They bitch and moan about the Men's Grill and now they're raising hell about tee times. Women are wrecking everything." No one will ever accuse Roundup of being enlightened, either.

Only a handful of Blacks live in Roundup. A dozen handfuls of Mexicans form the backbone of the domestic work force, Roundup being closer to Mexico than Mississippi. The blue-collar laborers are Slavic immigrants who keep their section of town looking as if they expect a Prussian general to arrive for inspection at any moment.

Our ranch, the Circle B, which now lies about forty-five minutes outside of town, was there before Roundup itself. In the 1860s my great-great-grandfather laid claim to 200,000 acres of hill country southeast, south, and southwest of town and became one of the West's first cattlemen. Small creeks and streams tumble down through the forests to wide, endless grassy valleys where our sleek, gentle herds of Black Angus graze. They drink from the Wind River alongside elk and deer and moose and antelope and coyotes and bear and mountain lions. And all this goes on under our big, big sky. The big sky that lets us breathe.

When people come to the mountain west, they say, "Oh, I miss the water." And when we're off visiting them, they ask, "Don't you miss the mountains?" No. What we miss is the sky. The space itself is the source of a westerner's strength, not the earthly backdrop. Even all those years living right on the Pacific in Santa Bianca, looking as far out to sea as was humanly possible, the sky never seemed quite big enough. A lot of it has to do with the humidity. We don't have any. Everyone else does and it limits one's vision.

Houses on the ranch are typically western: rough log chinked with white cement to keep out the wind that Wyoming is known for. The wind that blows without interruption east to west from the Alleghenies to the Rockies. And straight down the front range of the Rockies from the North Pole to the south. Wyoming gets it from every direction. All the houses have green shutters, black shingle roofs, window boxes, and stone chimneys. The barns are painted red with black roofs. The cattle pens are lodgepole pine.

The Circle B also has a few oil and gas wells pumping away here and there, and that never hurts.

To get to the Circle B, take the four-lane freeway east from Roundup, then turn south onto the blacktop country road that winds along Little Squaw Creek through a pale yellow, dusty sandstone canyon whose rock walls turn dark red in stormy weather, and finally go right onto a poorly maintained dirt road that passes through a small western-style tourist-trap village, Bennett's Fort, that languishes at the ranch entrance.

My cousin, Bucky Bennett, has been mayor of Bennett's Fort since I can remember and makes his living robbing Rust Belt and midwestern tourists all summer long and charging movie companies an arm and a leg to film his hokey western storefronts. Tourists flock to the Fort to see daily High-Noon shoot-outs between the Deputy U.S. Marshall (played by Cousin Bucky) and the Outlaw or the Bank Robber (played by Cousin Buck's son, Bucky, Jr., mayor-elect). Most of the time, Buck is standing behind the bar serving up watered-down "sasparilly" in the saloon for five bucks a shot; and they come in droves to ooh and aah over the deep gouges made in the earth by the covered wagons which rolled past on the Oregon Trail. Cousin Bucky refreshes the gouges each spring by driving his Belgian team back and forth in his restored Conestoga wagon, drinking Stolichnaya and listening to the Beach Boys, the Beatles, and the Rolling Stones on his Walkman. There's no such thing as repeat business in Bennett's Fort.

It does, however, have a U.S. Post Office that provides postal service for the ranches and country homes and lends the town an air of authority and authenticity.

I moved into what had always been my summer house on the Circle B. It's a nice big old ranch house with a veranda on three sides, the kind of place that encourages you to put your boots on the table and throw down a shot and a beer. My favorite pieces of city furniture mixed perfectly with favorite summer ones, which actually resulted in a very elegant country home with antique Persian rugs on the oiled cedar floor and Georgian silver candlesticks on the pine refectory table in the dining room. Above the living room fireplace a pair of Texas longhorns topped an antique English oil painting of my great-great-great-grandfather's prize steeplechaser. A proper interior decorator would have found the house too mixed up. I found it cozy and charming and I brimmed with the promise of happiness and harmony.

I swore off men for the time being. Wink called a few times from Santa Bianca, wanting to come and visit at the ranch.

"Forget it," I told him. "We both had to give up things. I gave up my job and you gave up me." I guess I was angrier than I thought. But isn't that just like a man? Especially a married man? To see that mess as just a minor interruption in a long-term illicit romance? He wasn't special anymore. Only special lovers came to the Circle B and there weren't any of those around at the moment, so I kept mostly to myself and my dog Baby and my horse Ariel. We lived an arcadian existence and I concentrated on trying not to drink too much and trying not to smoke at all. I did fine on the smoking but my brothers and I liked to have a few hundred glasses of whiskey every now and then.

I slept. With no emergencies to jar me awake in the middle of the night, ten years fell off my face and I became less abrupt, more likely to have a conversation than throw an order.

The work for my new clients had to do with security safeguards and systems, and while the dodging of imagined rather than real bullets kept me busy enough, it did not intrigue me. I longed for the fellowship and the hours and the Santa Bianca P.D. I missed the exhilaration of backstage where the elements of danger and mystery and adventure are shared together over cups of strong coffee and cigarettes at three-thirty in the morning and you're either in it or you're not. I missed my friends.

Labor Day had come and gone and it was mid-September, my favorite time of the year, and Friday, my favorite day, and although autumn's first snowfall was predicted for that night, I sat in a large pool of sunshine at the kitchen table, finishing nut-bread toast with real butter and marmalade and a cup of coffee with caffeine and reading an article in the morning paper about whether or not to build the new airport which was already under construction, when the phone rang. It was an old school girlfriend, Ellen Butterfield, managing editor of the *Roundup Morning News,* which her family owned.

Because her family owned the morning paper and mine owned the evening and, most agreed, better edition, our lifetime friendship was founded on athletic and scholastic competition and intellectual rivalry. As the years passed and Ellen saw that I had no intention of going into the newspaper business, that I'd taken myself out of the game, we accepted each other as old friends, life friends, but not best friends.

"Welcome back," she said.

"Thank you," I said. "I didn't think I would be nearly as happy to be home as I am. Everyone's being so friendly, I'm afraid I'll get spoiled."

"You're probably already spoiled," Ellen laughed. "I'm glad you're coming to my party tonight."

"Me, too. My first major social function in Bennett's Fort in twenty years. I can't believe your father is seventy-five."

"I know."

"What's up?" Neither of us had ever been a chatterer and I could tell we'd just exhausted our capacity for small talk.

"I'm not sure exactly," Ellen said. "It's just a feeling I have and I'd like to come out and meet with you privately for a few minutes."

"My day is completely open," I said. "You name the time."

"One-thirty?"

"I'll see you then."

We hung up and I looked out the window into the bright morning where the golden aspen leaves rustled like taffeta, and smiled. A private case. I was as excited as a hunting dog waiting for the command to race into the corn husks and bring back the dead pheasant. And I didn't even know the problem yet.

Chapter Three

Friday afternoon

When I opened the door, Ellen and I tried, and failed, to check each other out surreptitiously to see which one of us was holding up better. I'd say it was definitely me.

Ellen had let time have its way with her face and body. She still could have looked pretty with a major face-lift and a complete makeover—but obviously that was not on her list of priorities. She had joined the genre of no-nonsense, no-imagination, no-flair, no-fun female executives. I wondered if she had become a man-hater, a lesbian, a sexual-discrimination watchdog, and a whistle-blower.

Something, maybe the disillusioning discovery of Life's Big Tricks, had petrified Ellen's lips into a straight angry clench and permanently flared her nostrils as though she were ready to let someone have it; and once-healthy pink skin drooped in payment for sunburns gotten at the Roundup Country Club. Blemishes flowed under her skin like grains of sand and her lips bore only remnants of pale pink lipstick.

Actually, now that I think of it, I'd say Ellen looked a great deal older than I. Substantially. Deeply lined and pugnacious. For the first time, I saw some of her father in her. The meanest man I ever knew.

She hadn't bothered to keep her hair its natural warm brown. Cut short, back from her face except for a few bangs, drab gray streaks painted the difficult canvas. She was New-York skinny. What a switch from our school days when her curves left mine in the dust. I wasn't exactly fat but I had no sharp edges and it didn't look like I was going to get any anytime soon. It was all I could do to keep what I had under control.

My skin, on the other hand, was still smooth from no sun, thousands of dollars' worth of creams and hours a week of care, and all the sleep I'd been getting lately. My hair was copper-chestnut colored, short and mostly naturally curly, and I always wore makeup because I never knew what the day would bring.

In spite of Ellen's general unkempt mess, her dark brown eyes blazed with intelligence and humor. So did mine. I had Bennett eyes: the color of Bisbee turquoise.

Ellen followed me through the house to the library. She stopped to admire the brightly painted windowpanes in the double doors.

"I'm glad you left these intact," she said. "Didn't your grandmother or great-grandmother or someone paint them?"

"Yes," I said. "During World War Two, Grandmother occupied herself by commemorating momentous family milestones by painting these pictures on the panes. There are thirty-six of them in all."

"Who's that?" Ellen pointed to a girl jumping a horse over a log.

"My aunt."

"And that?"

"My father." The small figure, dressed in tall waders, held up a large trout, the date "8-14-37" painted in red block numerals beneath. "And that's my grandfather having a stare-down with that moose." I turned and pointed to the moose head hanging above the library fireplace. A half-smoked cigar was stuck between the moose's lips, something my older brother, Elias, had added as a child when he got bored with shooting pool balls at his pet garter snake, Elmer, on the pool table. Another glass square was filled with the Navy Cross and the dates of my uncle's short heroic life.

"Come on in." I pulled the doors to, closing them with a soft old click, and indicated the chair in front of my walnut desk. "Would you like a cup of coffee? Tea?"

"Nothing, thanks. I don't have much time." Ellen sat forward on her chair and laid her forearms on the desktop, as if to make it her own. An executive unaccustomed to being on the asking side. A watch with a black suede strap and a gold ring with a single row of diamonds and sapphires were her only jewelry. She folded her hands together and her eyes scanned the bookshelves behind me.

"You can say anything you like," I reassured her. "I sent Celestina to the market, so no one even knows you're here."

Ellen's face reddened. "You read my mind." She laughed nervously.

"How're things going at the paper?"

"Remember when we were little? And you were going to take over the *Evening Star* and I was going to take over the *Morning News* and we would both be Dagny Taggart?" Ellen and I grinned at each other, wondering which one of us most personified Ayn Rand's heroine. "Tough. Beautiful. Invincible. Cold-blooded. Right."

"Sure," I said.

"Well, as I get older, I'm beginning to accept some things. And unfortunately, one of them is that I will never be publisher of the *News.*" She laughed. "It's okay. I mean, there's nothing I can do about it, so why aggravate myself? Four years ago, I got passed over as next-in-line for publisher. Father brought in a crony, Roland Tewkesbury, to stand in if he dies or retires before Wally can take over."

"Who's Wally?"

"My half-brother. You have been gone a long time. He's seventeen. A chip off the old block. My father is completely unable to grasp that a woman could possibly be capable of being competitive and successful anywhere but in bed."

"Mine, too."

"Sad, isn't it?"

"So what *are* you doing at the paper?"

"Associate publisher. Could be a lot worse, I guess. It's okay." Dissatisfied with the conversation's direction, Ellen twisted the ring on her finger.

"Just start," I said.

"Yes. That's always the best way, isn't it?" She took out a cigarette.

I nodded and thought how nice it was to be back in familiar territory waiting for a witness or victim or suspect to spit it out. To concentrate more on their gestures than their words, which went onto tape anyway, and try to figure out by how much they were customizing their tales to fit their needs and mine. I drew circles on my notepad and watched the Wind River roll along through the meadow outside the window while Ellen fiddled around with her lighter.

"I'm sure there is nothing going on," she finally said, embarrassed, "but I'd like it if you could keep an eye on Pamela tonight at Father's birthday party."

"Pamela, your stepmother?" I said.

"Yes."

"How long have they been married?"

"Thirty-two years. Mother's been gone for thirty-two and a half." Her expression was wry. The bitterness and the sadness were gone. "It's funny. Pamela's been more of a mother to me than my own mother ever was. We all made such terrible fun of Pam when she and Father got married. But I'll tell you, she's a wonderful person."

"What's the problem?"

"I think she's being blackmailed."

"Oh?"

"She's been asking me a lot of questions lately about stock disbursement and control of the Butterfield Foundation. I'm one of the Foundation trustees. My father is chairman."

"Can't she get the information from your father?" I remembered Walter Butterfield as being a brute and a bully but maybe he'd changed.

"You know what he's like." So he hadn't changed. "I imagine Pam's a little afraid of him, although she doesn't act like it. She's definitely earned her stripes staying married to him all this time." Ellen shifted in her seat. "No, her questions are more in the nature of under what circumstances could an individual that was not a family member become a stockholder."

"So?" I said. Ellen was quickly losing my interest.

"So why should she care? I'm curious."

"Ellen, let's quit pussy-footing around. What's the problem?"

She thought about it and then said, "You're right. Look, when the handwriting's on the wall, I'm willing to be a graceful loser up to a point, but now that I've lost my slot as publisher, I won't let anything get in my way over the Foundation. Something's going on and I want to know exactly what it is. Who. What. When. Where and How." Ellen ground out her cigarette and lit another. "I won't sit still for Pam or anyone else fucking around in my territory."

"Have you asked her what the problem is?" I said.

"Only to the degree of asking her if everything is all right and she says, 'Of course.' "

"Who would blackmail her? And for what reason? Does she have a family?"

"Not as far as I know." Ellen snorted a laugh. "You know, I don't even know where she's from. She's never mentioned parents or brothers or sisters. But wouldn't you think that, after more than thirty years, someone would turn up?"

"Maybe they just did."

"Certainly seems a reasonable possibility," Ellen said. "Will you do it?" She looked at the clock on my desk and then at her wristwatch. "I've got to go. I've got a three-o'clock meeting, but I'll see you tonight."

"What time's the party?" I asked.

"Seven o'clock at el Rancho del Sol."

She left before bothering to find out if I'd help out or not, but of course I would. I longed to work, and even though blackmail wasn't murder, my favorite, it certainly wasn't nearly as low as filming an illicit love affair with a hand-held video camera with an automatic zoom. That one still rankled. I wouldn't have minded so much being filmed making love if I'd been thinner.

Chapter Four

Friday evening

The Butterfields' country home, so grandly called Rancho del Sol—Ranch of the Sun—was actually a small spread of sixty enviably lush and hilly acres, forty-five minutes from downtown Roundup and about the same distance over rocky and rutted dirt roads from the Circle B.

The hill country outside of Roundup is deceptive because you can see so, so far and because the Wind River Range is always there in the distance to provide bearings and keep things in proportion, so that, when you're driving, you lose all sense of gaining or losing altitude, of driving through gullies and over hills, of getting anywhere at all. After a while, it seems that everything everywhere is straight and flat, an illusion enhanced by the fact that no one pays attention to the speed limits, so you're constantly getting nowhere at seventy-five or eighty miles an hour, and then all of a sudden you round a corner or crest a hill and there lies a gas station or, as was the case on this particular evening, there lay the adobe walls of the Butterfields' Rancho del Sol. The big two-story hacienda with its fifteen-inch-thick walls and rough beamed ceilings, obviously more New Mexico than Wyoming, obviously more Roundup than anywhere, glowed warmly down a cottonwood-lined drive that sparkled with *candlearias*. A maze of bougainvillea-filled patios and balconies dominated the adobe compound, which included a stable, a swimming pool, and a tennis court. Down around the bend, beneath towering cottonwood trees, a small adobe caretaker's cottage squatted by a wide arroyo, its creek bed dry and cracked in the late autumn. Usually, the view of Roundup and the Wind River Valley was spectacular but, as predicted, the temperature had plunged. Snow fell steadily.

An unbreathable blanket of Pamela Butterfield's perfume and smoke from Walter's cheap cigar greeted guests at the front door. Walter, who now had hearing aids in both ears, liked to say, "I smoke these cheap cigars 'cause then no one ever tries to borrow one from me." I'm quite sure he was right.

Pamela still looked like a big-boned, big-toothed gypsy. "LILLY," she said, the volume of her voice and the blackness of her hair undimmed by the passage of time. Some people sound like other people. Not Pam. Her voice was uniquely her own: always just short of a yell, full of enthusiasm, and way too fast. So fast that unless you concentrated, all you could hear was a kind of shrieking blur of sound, like a jet engine played in a low pitch. She kissed my cheek. "I'M SO GLAD YOU'RE HERE. WALTER, LOOK WHO'S HERE. IT'S LILLY BENNETT."

Walter still looked mean. Little piggy eyes buried in a fleshy red face. Nicotine had turned what was left of his small teeth dark brown. The bottom ones were worn down to little black nubs. White stubble covered his cheeks and neck. He hadn't even shaved for his own party.

My mind quickly flashed back to the time when, as a thirteen-year-old, I was changing into my swimming suit in Ellen's bathroom and he opened the door and stood there for the longest time admiring what he referred to as my "pretty little nips" and I thought I would die of embarrassment. He said things like that to me all the time. Horrible, disgusting, lewd things, and my parents never believed that Walter Butterfield would stoop so low as to talk dirty to a thirteen-year-old girl. In retrospect, I don't see how it could have surprised them at all—he talks that way to every woman—and he would have stooped a lot lower if I'd let him. I think they just didn't want to make a scene. They probably would have if things had gotten truly out of hand, but instead the information was filed among the family's collective arsenal as future ammo in the Bennett vs. Butterfield dynastic war chest.

Walter opened his arms. I stepped back.

"Happy birthday." I smiled.

"What! No kiss for Uncle Walter?"

"Happy birthday," I said again and passed on into the house. I wouldn't kiss that son of a bitch if someone gave me a million dollars.

The first person I spotted in the mob in the foyer standing behind the two stuffed polar bears raised up permanently on their haunches, mouths open, claws extended, was Christine Butterfield, Ellen's twin sister, who had run off to England about twenty-five years ago. I think my mouth was even hanging open a little, I stared at her so intently. I swear to God, it was like looking at *The Picture of Dorian Gray* come to life. I had the idea that Christine's four hard-living, dissipated decades had ground themselves into Ellen, all the way from London, leaving Christine relatively unscathed and internationally sophisticated.

Plus, Christine and I were wearing the same, very expensive, short black wool cocktail dress, and since she looked as if she might be anorexic, she looked much better in the dress than I did, except that my pearls looked better with it than her diamonds and her face had been poorly lifted, which surprised me, with all her money.

She was having a distracted conversation with a short, ruddy-faced fellow in white tie and tails. The watered blue moiré ribbon of the Order of the British Empire crossed his starched piqué vest and a tiny French légion d'honneur rosette dotted his lapel. I supposed it was Christine's husband, since I'd heard he was a big cheese. He was supposed to be so handsome. I accepted a glass of champagne from a nearby waiter and headed in their direction, but before I got there, he did a quick Japanese bow to Christine, turned and gave me a small smile and left. He had watery bug eyes, the same color as his ribbon, and chapped red lips.

"Christine," I greeted her, remembering that Ellen and I used to joke that Christine, like Otis Sistrunk, who attended the University of

Mars, came from a different planet, "Ellen didn't tell me you were going to be here."

Her kinky hair poufed along the top of her head like a curly platinum Mohawk. Up close she looked tough. The face-lift was worse than I thought. "I just decided to pop over at the last moment. A surprise for Daddy." She spoke with a slight British accent and reached up to touch her hair. Her brown eyes skidded around like a school of fish. Cocaine.

"Was that your husband?"

"Good Gawd," Christine moaned in such an upper-crust, affected way I wanted to punch her in the nose. "Me and Roland Tewkesbury? Married? That's a good one. He *works* for us."

"Sorry," I said. "I've never met your husband."

"Who? Rory? Actually, he decided to stay home. This is his busiest time of the year, you know." She ruffled her hand over the very top of her curls and then dug in with her fingers and tugged a few locks up into more prominent positions. She tossed down her champagne and held up her glass for a refill.

I studied her busy-ness. There was such a frantic quality to it I wondered what she was on besides cocaine and champagne. "No," I said, "I didn't know this was his busiest time of the year. What does he do?"

"Oh, he's involved with horses, and all the tracks are in full swing at the moment." Christine put her glass down on the sideboard, studied a silver cup of cigarettes for a moment before selecting one, picked up a heavy silver table lighter, clicked it unsuccessfully a couple of times, and set it down. "You wouldn't happen to have a light, would you?"

"Sorry," I said.

"Besides, I had some family business to discuss with Daddy and it's just easier when your husband's not around. You know what I mean?"

I began to say, "No, I don't know what you mean," when Ellen appeared at my side.

"Beat it," she said and Christine skedaddled like a wide-eyed chipmunk back into a woodpile. I don't think she'd even noticed we were wearing the same dress.

I couldn't help laughing. "Nice to see that you girls are just as close as ever. I didn't know she was going to be here."

"It's a game she plays with my father," Ellen said, disgusted. "She 'Pops' in and 'Daddy' gives her a few thousand pounds. She has to cry quite a bit to get it, though, and then, what her husband, Rory, doesn't gamble away at the track, she ingests one way or another, usually up her nose or through her veins. Then she comes back and begins again."

"Too bad," I said.

"Please." Ellen looked at me derisively. "We're years beyond that. I think things got off to a rough start for her today because she and Father were really going at it when I got here. Her tears almost sounded legitimate."

"Ah," I said, my cocktail conversation depleted.

Ellen bit her lip and looked at her father and closed the subject of Christine. "Come upstairs while I fix my makeup. There's something I want to tell you."

She didn't need just to *fix* her makeup, she needed to put some on. As far as I could tell, she hadn't taken the time to touch her hair or even replace the lipstick that had already been mostly missing that afternoon. I guessed she'd pretty much given up on men.

"Okay." I waited while my glass was refilled and then followed her up the wide sweep of polished terra-cotta steps—Pamela had painted the cast-iron banister gold—to the bedroom where we'd shared so many giggles as girls, the only room spared from Pamela's "If a little gilt's good, a lot's better" school of decorating.

Snowflakes whirled outside the doors that opened onto the small balcony where Ellen and I had taught ourselves how to smoke cigarettes when we were twelve. The same crisp white organdy spread, its hem embroidered with tiny pink buds, covered her four-poster bed. The same doll in a faded red taffeta dress with a plaid sash and a straw hat beckoned to us with outstretched arms from between the pillows. Dark green Venetian-glass swan lamps with rose ribbon-trimmed shades still swam across gleaming Queen Anne bed tables. Gold-framed botanical prints hanging above the bed and two plump chintz-covered armchairs on either side of a small fireplace completed the room. It was the room of girlhood. Small, tidy, secure.

I thought about all the highway we'd covered since those days when the most important thing we did was sit in front of the fire and talk alternately about boys and about how we'd put each other out of business when we took over the papers.

Ellen didn't pay any attention to anything in the room. No time for nostalgia tonight. She marched through quickly to the dressing room, set her drink down on the glass top of the big-mirrored dressing table where the apron matched the bedspread—pink buds on a field of white organza—laid her cigarette in an ashtray, and removed a compact and lipstick from her purse.

I leaned on the doorjamb. "What's up?"

"My father made a little announcement this afternoon in our regular Friday meeting." Ellen scrubbed a powder puff over her face.

"Oh?"

"He replaced me on the Foundation board with Roland Tewkesbury, claiming the Foundation needed newer vision. Have you met Roland yet?" She crossed her eyes and made a face.

"Sort of," I laughed. "Actually, I just saw him."

"I'm sure 'vision' wasn't the first word that popped into your mind. He is so stodgy and conservative and such a snob you want to dust off his shoulders. Anyhow, by making this move, Father broke his own rule that only *Butterfields* can sit on the governing boards of both organizations: the paper and the Foundation. Now Roland's on both as well, abrogating the Foundation's family legacy."

"Does this answer any questions about Pam?" I said. "Do you think the two incidents are related?"

"I don't think so. It makes me sick. The Foundation was the only area where I exerted any influence, where my father listened to me at all. At least I thought he did." Her eyes reddened a little but I could tell she was mad, not about to cry. She took a big swallow of her drink, which was a lot of straight, very dark something. "He's planning to make some big announcement tonight—I'm sure it's about retiring and making Roland publisher until Wally's of age, little asshole—and I know I'm going to have to be gracious about it. I am so mad I could kill him."

It interested me that she could speak such passionate words so lethargically, almost as if she were rehearsing them for a play, trying to memorize them or something.

"Plus," she recited, "I had a fight with Greg, my boyfriend, so he's not here tonight." She took another hefty gulp.

I caught my breath. Whoa. Hold it. Ellen? Boyfriend? Only two choices: older and broke and drunk, or younger and broke and drunk. I had a guy explain to me once that only a true patriot could date a lousy-looking poor woman because he had to wrap her in the flag and do it for Old Glory. But a rich woman was another story altogether. I know that's crude and probably not fair but, face it, Ellen was a physical and aesthetic wreck and her love affairs, at least the ones I kept up with before I lost interest, were inevitably Wagnerian at best, rife with Sturm und Drang and Bullshit. I bit my tongue.

"Plus, The Slut shows up and makes off with a few double-digit grand, which pisses me off royally because she does nothing but shove it up her nose."

"I understand," I said, assuming "The Slut" was her sister Christine. "I don't blame you."

Ellen took a deep breath. "Do you have any blusher?"

"Yes." I handed her my compact and she brushed some color onto her gray cheeks and then drew on her lipstick with such a heavy hand I was surprised the tube didn't squash onto her lips. She could have used some makeup classes but I supposed we were past that point in our lives.

"Thanks." Ellen handed back the blush. Her hand was steady. "Let's go back down and get this over with."

Chapter Five

The orchestra was playing "Michelle Ma Belle"—boy, am I sick of that song—when we got back downstairs and my first invitation to dance came from an old friend named Ken Wilbanks, who had married Shelley James right out of college and had lately moved from residential real estate into commercial.

"Roundup is booming again," he said enthusiastically. "We had a bunch of Canadians in last week and we're going to refurbish the Bannister block on Park Street with them."

"Congratulations." Kenny and I had stumbled all the way through dancing school together at the Roundup Country Club, but he'd forgotten that Miss Carlson told him he could move around a little bit with the box step.

Walter and Pamela Butterfield stepped onto the floor just behind us and after a minute I could tell that Walter had forgotten how to dance, too. Two couples united in Box-Step Hell.

"I'm glad the Bannister block is going to be salvaged," I said to Kenny.

He cracked a smile. "There are some pretty wild-looking buildings on it. The Canadians wanted to tear them down but my partner and I said, 'Heck, no!' Where else could you find a Mayan temple smack-dab next to a Moorish palace?"

There's no place like Roundup. "What's the overall plan?"

A quiet little quarrel had erupted between Walter and Pamela. He sneered while she dished it out under her breath. Why would some-one blackmail Pam Butterfield? Well, I thought, she no doubt had a lot of miles on her by the time she and Walter were married, and God knew what all she'd been up to since, so maybe the question was more a case of who of many possibilities. Or even of, why not? I smiled at Kenny and the Bannister block and tuned my ears into Pam and Walter's skirmish. Pam sounded close to tears.

Spies go to a special government school to learn special listening skills, but I had learned mine at dinner parties with partners like Kenny Wilbanks. My method worked just as well and you didn't have to spend a summertime in Virginia to get it.

"I can't believe you think that, Walter. It's unbelievable," Pam said.

"You used to have a sense of humor. Now you can't even take a little joke."

I maneuvered Ken around so I could get a partial look at Walter's balloon of a face which looked like a road map, booze had exploded so many blood vessels on it. Cigar ash covered the front of his tuxedo. I tried not to think about his breath.

"I don't know what you're talking about. I haven't done anything wrong." Pam worked to keep her voice down.

"Come on, baby. You can tell me." Walter's voice thickened.

"There's nothing to tell. This isn't funny, Walter. You're scaring me."

"Come on. You can tell me," he leered and I watched his hand crush hers, compressing the fine bones until she winced and jerked her hand free.

"Walter." Pam's eyes flared. She reminded me of a reared-up wild horse about to smack someone on the top of his head with its hooves. "Let go of me, you sick bastard. I could kill you."

"Eh," Walter said, "you're nothing but a goddamn pussy." Then he reached down and pinched her hard just there to make his point and walked off the dance floor.

Pam gasped, then spotted me dancing with Kenny and her mouth instantly smiled hugely. Her fast recovery from Walter's grab led me to believe that either he pinched her there all the time and she liked it or that fighting was maybe one of a dozen little sex games they played with each other.

"Lilly! I'm so glad you're here." Maybe Pam was more Cherokee than gypsy. The color of her skin looked almost as if a thin covering of bronze had been laid over hatchet-like features chiseled out of granite. "My God. It's been years."

Kenny and I stopped mid-box. Thank God. "Many years," I said. "This is a beautiful party, Pam."

"Isn't it *fun?*" She smiled. "Walter didn't want to do it, of course, but I said, 'My God, honey, seventy-five is a big number. Let's have a little fun for a change before we die of old age. Spend a little of that M-O-N-E-Y!' " She howled. "God, Lilly, you look *spectacular*. I always love that dress. So becoming. And Kenny! You look just as handsome as ever. How's Shelley?"

"She's terrific, thanks, Pam." Kenny smiled. "She's around here somewhere."

"I saw her. She looks more gorgeous than ever."

I wondered if we were talking about the same Shelley and also what Pam meant by "I *always* love that dress." How many more of them were there in Roundup? And I wondered what had happened in Pamela's past worth blackmail, and finally, I wondered how long it would be before Walter Butterfield got his.

The music started again, a cha-cha, and Kenny asked Pam to dance and I wandered over to the bar looking for my brothers, greeting old friends along the way. You could usually be pretty safe in finding me, or at least one of my brothers, at a bar. Elias and Christian were hanging around talking to a tall fellow who looked like a cowboy. My kind of cowboy. His black dress boots were polished and I could tell his evening clothes had been made for him, and not in Roundup, they hung on him so elegantly. His face was beaten up and rugged. He smoked a Havana and had said something to make my brothers laugh. A miracle.

Elias was my older brother. Elias Caulfield Bennett IV. By his name, he should have been running the railroad and the paper, but he ran the ranch instead and was perfectly suited to it. Whenever he went to town he drank too much and talked too loud.

"You look especially handsome tonight, Eli," I said and patted his stomach which usually drooped over Levi's but tonight was contained by a black silk cummerbund. He was overweight by about a hundred pounds of pure muscle. The little bit of hair he had left and his mustache were sandy, and his eyes, like mine, were turquoise with black flecks. Most people thought Elias was a grouch. I thought he was a sweetie, a grumpy Care Bear.

"Lil." He put his ham-sized arm around my shoulders. "Meet Richard Jerome."

Richard Jerome and I shook hands. He had bright, sky-blue eyes and craggy teeth.

"Hi," I said. "It's nice to meet you."

"Nice to meet you, too." His voice fit him perfectly. Rough.

"Richard here runs the opry." Elias handed me a tumbler of Jameson's Irish whiskey on the rocks.

"Ah," I said. "I love opera."

"He's also my roping partner," my tall, skinny, blue-eyed, black-haired younger brother Christian said and bumped Richard Jerome's shoulder with his own. Christian was only thirty-seven and was already publisher and chief executive of the paper. Our paper. The better one. The *Evening Star.* Not that morning rag of the Butterfields. "We're teamed together in the Roundup Rodeo."

"A gentlemen's pastime if there ever was one." I smiled and sipped my whiskey.

Richard Jerome just grinned.

"Do you specialize in heads or tails?" I grinned back.

"He's my heeler," Christian said. "Best there is, and from what I understand he's pretty good at tails, too. At least that's what the ladies say."

I kept smiling. "Where are you from? Valhalla?"

"Manhattan."

"A New Yorker in Roundup? Too bad. You'll leave or die of boredom before long."

"Would you like to dance?" he said.

"Yes, thanks. I'd love to."

Richard Jerome danced like a dream and I forgot completely about the Butterfield Affair until I saw Christine coming down the hall from her father's library—red-eyed and splotchy. She skirted the room and skittered up the stairs in search, no doubt, of chemical consolation.

Moments later, an inebriated Walter strolled into the ballroom in especially high spirits. He grabbed, pinched, and fondled his way across the dance floor to the orchestra.

"It's amazing what people are permitted to get away with when they're rich," I said to Richard. "Just watch him. The women are laughing and letting him do it because they're afraid if they don't they won't get a favorable write-up in tomorrow morning's society column. And their husbands don't want to make a ruckus because business is business."

"Yup," Richard Jerome said.

Honest to God. He had the most gorgeous eyes.

The music stopped and Walter fumbled around with the microphone which thudded hollowly over the loudspeaker system until the orchestra leader stepped forward and helped him detach it from the stand. Walter seized the microphone out of the man's hand with his swollen red fingers, and then his expression changed quickly to that of a naughty, indulged child. The room quieted. A happy, stupid smirk on his face, Walter swayed before his guests like a man with his shoes nailed to the deck of a ship in a storm.

"I'm glad you're all here tonight, and since it's my birthday, I can do anything I want. Right?" He leaned forward, with his chin jutted out like a bully, fists clenched, his red face shoved into the crowd.

The guests smiled back politely.

"You're all nervous 'cause you don't know what I'm gonna do. Right?"

A few laughs.

"You think I'm gonna moon ya or something. Don'cha?"

Fewer laughs.

"Well, I'm not."

A couple of boos.

"Take it off, Walter," a man called out.

"Nope." He puffed his cigar, realized it was dead, dropped the microphone on the floor with a loud *thunk,* relit the cigar, and then rethreaded the mike up to his hands with the cord. "Nope. I've got an important announcement to make, but first I'm gonna sing you a song."

The man behind us booed but Walter ignored him.

"Most important song of my life. Song was from a play back in the sixties and whenever I begin to doubt myself, I sing it." Tears brimmed in Walter's eyes. Most of us had never seen Walter Butterfield's maudlin side before. Not an attractive sight. His nose began to run. "Maybe it'll help you be successful, too." He drew his sleeve across his dripping nose and sniffled loudly before turning to the bewildered band leader. "Okay?"

In the dark as to what song Walter had in mind, but eager to oblige, the man beamed, "Ready when you are, Mr. Butterfield."

Walter launched headlong into "The Impossible Dream." After the second line, "To fight the unbeatable foe," he swung back to face the band leader like a giant menacing bear. "You're playing too goddamn loud. I want 'em to hear ME. They don't give a shit about you. Start over."

When they began again, all you could hear was Walter Butterfield panting and blubbering off-key out of dozens of speakers and by the time he finished, he was sobbing. I guess he'd sacrificed the Big Announcement of his retirement to The Quest because the microphone dropped to the floor and Walter kicked it with his foot as he stumbled out. The slam of his library door could be heard all the way down the hall. The only other sound was the *whoosh* of the spinning mike.

From the corner of my eye, I saw a flash of blue moiré as Roland Tewkesbury and his OBE and Ld'H and tailcoat disappeared in pursuit of Walter. A good lieutenant. A good consigliere. Off to console his boss. I didn't see Ellen racing down the hall to see if her dad was okay. You want to succeed? You pay the price. Ellen had taken her eye off the target.

"What the hell," Pamela said to the man next to her. "He'll get over it." She took the man's hand and led him to the dance floor. "LET'S POLKA," she ordered the band leader and her guests.

⌁ Chapter Six

Walter's serenade brought a natural sort of conclusion to the evening for many of the guests. It was past midnight and a long drive through the snow back to Roundup, and perhaps they could see that there was nothing but trouble ahead.

"God!" Pam hugged Paul and Jeannie Steadman. He was one of Roundup's society surgeons, specializing in plastics, nips and tucks of faces, eyelids, necks, and breasts. "I'm so sorry you're leaving. And so *glad* it's not me you're working on in the morning! You know," she whispered sotto voce, "I always call Jeannie the day before I come in to see you to find out what you're doing the night before."

"I didn't know you'd ever been to see me," Dr. Steadman said, always a gentleman.

"OH! You two, too? Do you have someone to drive you?" she asked the Higleys as they staggered out the door, both completely smashed, as usual. Mrs. Higley's matchstick legs shuffled forward, straight and stiff. A cigarette dangled from her mouth, its long ash threatening her sable. His toupee was skewed just enough to make him impossible to look at without bursting into hysterics.

"All set," Mrs. Higley said as Pam handed her off to the chauffeur. Cynics claim that Mothers Against Drunk Driving is actually just a front for the American Limousine Association, and I don't mean the cattle.

What Ellen had said earlier was true: People could say what they wanted about Pamela Butterfield. Make fun of her lavish theatricality, screeching fishwife voice, garish showgirl taste and blatant ambition—her enthusiasm seemed to me to be authentic, it definitely was infectious, and I liked her and was sorry that she was married to Walter but, hey, no free lunch, right? Pamela had made it her business to get a great set of manners from somewhere. She never got drunk at her own parties and she stood at the front door until all who were leaving and their taillights had disappeared into the dark, snowy whirl.

Those of us who chose to stay got drunk.

"LET'S LIMBO!"

I had a ball. Richard Jerome was one of the most charming men I had ever met in my life and he twirled and whirled and dipped me all over the place. Not a box step in sight.

"Are you married?" I said.

"No. Divorced." Richard led us through several fast spins.

"For how long?"

"Long time." He tossed me away and turned me back close in to his chest.

Perfect.

"Any children?" I asked over my shoulder while his arms encircled me from behind.

"Two boys. Both in college." Out Richard Jerome cast me again and then reeled me in and led me in a Texas two-step, side by side, step for step, all the way around the floor.

"Where?"

"Princeton."

"Both of them?"

"Yup." A series of fast-stepping high-speed spins ensued.

"Opera must pay better than it used to." I pirouetted beneath his arm, kicked back, and spun home to his embrace.

Richard smiled.

"Where did you learn to team-rope?"

"Wyoming." Out I went like a frisky heifer. Back in he wrangled me. The song ended. Big dip.

"Do you always ask so many questions?" Richard took my arm and guided me toward the bar.

"Just comes naturally, I guess. I'm used to quizzing suspects. Sorry."

"Do you suspect me of some crime?" He stopped and looked at me, delivering the question slowly. To my mind, an erotic invitation.

Yes. Fatal charm. "Not yet." I looked at his lips and I almost kissed them. "I just like to know who my partners are."

Lord, but he was sexy. And I could tell he thought I was, too.

Ellen and my brother Eli were making complete fools of themselves on the dance floor but having too much fun to care.

"She should have married him when she had the chance," I said to Richard.

"Who? Your brother?"

"Yes. They went together all through college."

"Why didn't they?" Richard said.

I shrugged. "Just didn't work out." I didn't tell him it was because Ellen had quit taking care of herself. Glamour attracted Eli, who apparently had never considered his bulk unappetizing, in a carnal sense. "I like my girls swank. The swanker the better," he liked to brag. But when it really got down to it, Elias was as shy as a kid around women.

"Come on." Richard grabbed a bottle of champagne and two glasses off the bar and we went over and sat down on the living room steps.

"Unlike her sister, Christine, Ellen's never had very good luck with men." I held my glass out for him to fill. "Their mother committed suicide when they were fourteen. On their fourteenth birthday, actually, and Ellen's spent her whole life trying to make it up to her father. We used to be pretty close friends but we've sort of fallen out of touch over the last few years."

"That's too bad," Richard said. "I went out with her a couple of times when I first moved here."

I almost said, "I'll bet that was a high point of her life," but demurred and asked instead, "Is she going to be upset if I'm talking to you?"

"No, no," Richard said quickly. "We're just friends. She's an outstanding woman with a lot to give but she's looking for a serious relationship or at least some serious intentions." He looked me in the eye. "I have no intention of getting serious about anything but business for a long, long time."

"Don't look at me," I said. "I have everything exactly where I want it at the moment."

We smiled and clinked glasses. Perfect mutual understanding.

I watched Ellen and suddenly felt sad for her and for us and for all the time gone. I wondered if she was still so vulnerable. Gave away all of herself at the first kindness? Probably not.

"Sometimes you can get to know a person too well," I said. "Do you know what I mean?"

Richard nodded.

"I just came to know her too well and realized that what she does with her life isn't my problem or my business, and rather than make a lot of judgmental remarks that I would later regret, I fell out of touch." I vaguely wondered why I was being so comfortably open with Richard but kept going anyhow. "We all make time for the things we want, don't we?"

"Yes." Richard put his elbows on the step behind him and stretched out his legs. They were so long. Gorgeous legs. "What about her sister? What's her name? Christine?"

Christine had reappeared, dry-eyed but a deathly pasty color, and had Rodney Williams's gape-mouthed attention while she gave him an expert demonstration of the Dirty Monkey.

"She's married to a broken-down English nobleman—a gambling addict, I hear," I told him. "She's only minutes younger than Ellen but I don't think they could be more different."

"Yes," Richard said. "I see what you mean."

Christine's concentration on peeling the banana or climbing the rope or whatever it was that that dance was supposed to accomplish was impressive. She licked her lips and jerked harder. Rodney's mouth fell open a littler farther.

"Wow," I said.

Elias and Ellen came over and sat down with us on the steps, both of them sweating and panting, Eli because he was fat and Ellen because she smoked so much. Her low spirits from earlier had vanished.

How Byzantine and unfathomable family relationships are, I thought. I was fascinated by the complexity of Ellen's relationship to her sister and her father and stepmother, and what she probably undoubtedly felt was a breach of loyalty by coming to me with her concern. Maybe opened the family box a little too far. She never would have done it if we'd remained close, regular friends. I had witnessed her and Pamela's closeness during the evening, laughing and talking together. I could tell they genuinely liked each other and I admired how well-concealed Ellen kept her personal agenda. Ellen had even danced with her father and they appeared happy and relaxed. She had refined her skills of manipulation as meticulously as Pamela had worked on her manners. Christine seemed the only one out of the loop. Shunned from this jolly family tableau. But who knew?

The four of us—Eli, Ellen, Richard, and I—sat along the stairs, unable to talk because of the noise; Pamela and Roland Tewkesbury danced nearby.

"LET'S TWIST AGAIN," Pamela sang along with the band. She was a pretty good twister. Tewkesbury was hopeless. Completely uncoordinated. But like her stepdaughter Christine, it didn't make much difference to Pamela whom she danced with. She did what she wanted regardless of what her partner had in mind.

Tewkesbury's arms flailed back and forth and his protruding, bloodshot eyes moved intently with Pamela's large bosom, which went in the opposite direction she did. By the time it caught up, she was moving the other way. It looked to me like it would hurt, but that's one of those things I'll never know.

We all got laughing watching them.

"One last dance." Eli tugged Ellen's arm and pulled her onto her feet. "Then I've gotta get out of here."

"Have you ever been married?" Richard asked me.

"No. I have such a ridiculously romantic notion of marriage and the man I'm searching for that I don't expect I'll ever find him. Which is okay."

I was getting sleepy sitting there on the steps, leaning against the wall. The band was playing a slow song and I closed my eyes. Richard took my hand.

"Come on," he said.

We drifted along in a heavenly sort of way. One dance blended seamlessly into another. My cheek lay dreamily against his shoulder. "Let's stay like this forever," I said.

"Okay."

The chanteuse sang a smoky, sultry "Two Sleepy People" and I snuggled closer. But then, in the middle of a big, slow, delicious dip at the end of the song, a gunshot ba-boomed from the direction of Walter's library. The sound of a big gun.

Adrenaline surged through me so fast I almost knocked Richard to the floor as I took off, running across the room and down the hall. I checked my watch as I went. One-thirty on the nose. I reached for my weapon. Shit.

The library door was open and inside in the smoke clearing from the blast stood Ellen holding a Browning over-and-under twelve-gauge shotgun. Across from her, behind his desk, was Walter Butterfield from the neck down. Neck up was mostly missing.

Chapter Seven

Early Saturday morning

Give me the gun, Ellen," I said.

"I didn't do it."

"I know." I looped my index finger through the back side of the trigger casing and balanced the barrel on the fingernails of my left hand. "It's okay," I said. "You can let go of it now."

She was easily disarmed, her grasp on the gun was so cockeyed—the fingers of her right hand clawed across the top of the stock while her left held the top of the barrel in a backhand death clutch. I laid the weapon carefully on the floor beside her.

Over my shoulder, Richard Jerome blocked the library's double-wide doorway against the few guests who remained. He looked as if he knew what he was doing, and for a second the realization that the opera business must be more complicated than I imagined flashed through my mind. Images of seething opera zealots, screaming irrationally because Iago Kabuki would stand in as Rodolfo for Pavarotti, who had developed a last-minute case of the flu. So what else was new? Why should they be surprised? As far as I could tell, Pavarotti hadn't been seen in person since 1981. I suspect there are as many people trying to prove Luciano is alive as there are trying to prove Elvis is dead.

Oh, well, this was just a small crowd, not even a crowd really, just a handful of dressed-up drunks jarred into sobriety by glimpses of Walter's gooey remains.

Off to the right was a gun rack built into the mahogany bookcases. Both of its glass-fronted doors stood wide open. At a glance, it looked as if there were about a dozen rifles and shotguns with one near the center missing, presumably the one Ellen had been holding. All the guns gleamed with good care—the burnished wooden stocks smooth and well-used, the barrels lustrous with hand-rubbed oil. Sterling-silver decoration shone from a couple of them. Seeing a gun rack in Walter Butterfield's office, especially a rack of working guns, surprised me. I never would have picked Walter Butterfield as a regular bird or game hunter. Behind the desk, the French doors out to the patio were slightly ajar, enough to let the snow and cold wind blow into the room, and I crossed over to them.

"What happened?" I said.

Ellen was starting to shake. "I was coming down the stairs when I heard the shot, so I ran in and there wasn't anybody here."

"What do you mean?"

"Dad was like that." Her finger pointed vaguely in Walter's direction. "And the gun was lying across the arms of that chair." She indicated one of a pair of red leather armchairs in front of the desk. "And whoever shot him was gone. Through there, I guess." Ellen pointed to the patio doors behind the partially closed draperies.

"Did you hear anything?" I said. "Footsteps?"

Ellen thought for a second. "No. The noise of the gun was so loud off the floors and up the stairs, I don't think I heard anything else." She looked at her father's body. "This is terrible."

A remarkable understatement from someone whose father's mutilated body and head were splattered all over, and starting to run down his green satin damask draperies.

"Yes," I agreed. "Terrible."

Through the storm I saw the quickest flash of a car's taillights—four small red dots, two on either side—as though the driver was surprised by something in the road and tapped the brakes inadvertently. No headlights led the way.

I turned back to Ellen to find that Roland Tewkesbury had elbowed his way through the crowd at the door.

"Somebody's murdered my father," Ellen told him. She didn't sound at all surprised, but then, neither was I.

"Don't say anything, dear." He lay his hand on her arm. He had a funny accent—maybe British, maybe southern. "Let me do the talking."

Ellen looked at him incredulously and then slowly removed his hand. "What do you mean, 'Let me do the talking'? You think I did it? What are you? Crazy?"

He turned his bulgy blue eyes to me for help. "I'm Roland Tewkesbury," he said. "Walter's attorney. The family attorney, actually. I saw Ellen holding the gun, so naturally, I assumed."

"I understand," I said. I swear, the man had on enough pancake makeup to go on stage at Radio City Music Hall and the possibility zipped through my mind that he and Walter had been lovers. "I'm going to call the police. Why don't we let them decide if Ellen needs your counsel or not?"

"Naturally." He turned to Ellen. "I'm sorry, dear. I didn't mean to leap to any conclusions."

"Ellen," I said, "you just stay where you are, okay?"

She nodded and frowned at Roland and looked very mad.

The operator picked up on the first ring. "Roundup Emergency."

"This is Chief Detective Bennett of the Santa Bianca, California, Police Department." The words snapped out smartly. "There's been a shooting at the Butterfield Ranch, east of Bennett's Fort. Mr. Butterfield is down. Send the police and an ambulance." Although the ambulance crew would have to notify the coroner and medical examiner to come on over and declare Walter dead, I reached down and checked him for signs of life. No pulse in his wrist or the half of his neck that was still attached.

I could see the emergency operator setting the wheels in motion, pulling a top-priority red card to take down the information. I hadn't been this happy for three months.

"Are there suspects on the scene?"

"One possible," I answered. "Disarmed."

"What kind of weapon?"

"Twelve-gauge shotgun."

"When did the shooting occur?"

"Within the last five minutes."

"What is your assessment of the situation?"

I told her I'd checked and the victim displayed no vitals, then I hung up and envisioned the call going to the police and to Roundup General for the helicopter ambulance and to Homicide, which would be in from the get-go on a deal like this. The television and radio and newspaper people would already have it and they'd be piling into their news cruisers and choppers. No policeman, detective, or news hound worth two cents would miss being in close to the demise of Walter Butterfield.

I put my face close to the windows in the patio door and tried to see out, but the snow was coming down too hard and I couldn't tell if there were footprints or not. But there was one print inside, the size of a large boot, headed into the room. Longer than two of my hand lengths. Thirteen or fourteen inches. It darkened the carpet and was slightly damp to the touch. I stayed there for a moment, letting the melted snow from the print dry on my fingers and when I got up, Ellen was gone. Richard Jerome still blocked the doorway and Roland Tewkesbury remained standing where I'd left him, gawking at Walter, who grew showier with each passing second.

"Where's Ellen?"

He closed his mouth and licked his lips and forced his eyes in my direction. "She had to go to the bathroom. I told her it was all right as long as she came right back."

"Oh, no," I said.

" 'Oh, no,' what?" Ellen stepped back into the room at that moment.

"You didn't wash your hands, did you?" I said.

"Yes. Why?"

"Well, if you had fired the gun, there would be silver nitrate on your hands. A residue from the blast. But it washes off very easily."

"But I didn't fire it," Ellen said.

"I know. But now you can't prove it."

"I see." Ellen looked madder than ever. Completely disgusted. "This is ridiculous," she said.

ᗕ Chapter Eight

When the doorbell rang a short time later, Pamela's voice chimed from upstairs. "WHO IS IT?"

We'd all forgotten about the widow.

"Los federales, señora," her maid called back.

"What do they want? Are we making too much noise?" Pamela laughed. Her high heels clicked down the steps. "God! I go up to put on a little lipstick and someone calls the cops. Hey! What's everybody doing in the hallway?"

"There's been an accident, Pamela." Roland moved quickly to the bottom of the staircase to try and keep her from descending farther.

"What do you mean, 'an accident'? What kind of accident?" Pamela tossed him aside like a balloon and strode toward the library. "Something's happened to Walter, hasn't it? What? Did he have a heart attack? He's probably just passed out."

"Please don't go in there, Pamela," Roland said. "You don't want to see. Mr. Jerome, please stop her."

Pamela Butterfield shoved her way past Richard into the murder scene.

"AHHHHHHHHHHHHHHHHHHHHHHHHHHHHHH," she screamed. It was a real horror-movie scream. "AHHHHHHHHHHHHHHHHHHHHHHHHHH." The kind you can develop only with lots of practice. Then she collapsed into Richard's arms. I indicated with a jerk of my head that he should take her upstairs and lay her down and, for a second, as I watched him carrying her up the steps like Clark Gable as Rhett, I was wildly jealous. How dare she? She was way too old to be Scarlett.

Shock had set in on Ellen. She sat on a small, uncomfortable-looking Moorish chair in the hallway, her face chalky white.

"Mr. Tewkesbury," I said. "Is there a family doctor?"

"Certainly."

"Why don't you call him?"

"Certainly." He didn't look much steadier than Ellen but the assignment cracked him out of his muddled state.

"From a phone other than that one," I added.

"Certainly," he said.

By then two patrolmen were wandering around the library, drumming their fingers on their holsters. A third stood at the front door pointing the way for two blue-uniformed, satchel-carrying paramedics who rushed to pronounce the victim.

I watched one of the patrolmen extend a hand toward the presumed murder weapon.

"Don't touch that!" I barked.

It's incredible in this day and age, with all the television police shows, that a policeman would actually reach out and touch a piece of unlogged evidence, but it happens all the time.

He regarded me truculently. "And who might you be?"

"Chief Detective Bennett," I said. "Former Chief Detective."

"Oh, yeah?" His expression became sarcastic but he didn't say anything. If he had, it would have been along the lines that women couldn't take police work. Not said, perhaps, in those exact words but that's what the message would have been.

The entrance of Jack Lewis, Roundup's black-eyed, balding-eagle chief detective, saved me from further indignity. Nothing about Jack was wasted. No words. No motions. His body was sparse, like a featherweight boxer's, and he always dressed in suits that were well-cut and clean and he always wore a pressed white shirt.

"You didn't touch that, did you?" he snapped at the patrolman.

"No, sir." The flatfoot straightened up fast.

"Both of you," he said to the two policemen. "In the hall."

"Yes, sir."

He and I shook hands. "Lilly, it's good to see you." He didn't mean it. When I was in Santa Bianca, he and I had a pretty good working relationship. Jack always had a bad attitude about my being rich and being from his hometown, but at least I wasn't on his doorstep. Now I was. "Sorry to hear you're burned out."

Rub it in, you defensive son of a bitch. You're in. I'm out. "Good to see you, too, Jack. How do you look so put together at two o'clock in the morning?"

"You know me, Lilly. I'm a busy man." His eyes moved openly up and down the length of my body once and then settled on my face. "I try to get it the right way the first time because I'm too damn busy to do whatever it was again. You're lookin' pretty good yourself." He put his hands in his pants pockets and rocked on his toes. "So what happened here? That used to be Walter Butterfield?"

"I was in the ballroom when I heard the shot and by the time I got in here, most of the smoke had cleared and Ellen Butterfield, Walter's daughter, was standing in the middle of the room holding that gun."

"She do it?" Jack said.

"No."

Jack walked over and stood in front of Walter's desk and stared at the corpse for a moment. One of the paramedics was speaking into his walkie-talkie, calling the coroner. Jack motioned to his assistant, a young detective who looked about ten. He crossed the room to his boss. Obedient. Quick. "Thanks, Lilly," Jack said. "Stick around, all right?"

"Right," I answered. There was nothing for me to do but leave before Jack had to ask me to straight out, and leaving was the last thing on earth that I wanted to do. I wanted to be in there, helping. Not my case. Not my team. No longer my problem. I felt like begging.

"Ask Miss Butterfield to come in," Jack said to the boy.

I forgot to tell him about the taillights.

⤳ Chapter Nine

Once they had provided Homicide with their names and addresses, the last guests departed. Richard Jerome was nowhere in sight and there was certainly no reason for me to hang around and humiliate myself, so I went back to the ballroom to retrieve my purse.

The orchestra was gone. All the lights were turned on high and over in the corner the bartender loaded glasses into racks while he listened to a hyped-up rush of conversation from Christine, who had changed from "our" dress into shiny black leggings, boots, and a turtleneck with a leather vest. She straddled a gilt chair. She was really thin.

I went up to her. "I'm sorry about your father, Christine," I said. "I know how close you were to him. Let me know if there's anything I can do to help."

"Oh, sure, right, thanks." She laughed giddily, having forgotten that anything had happened to her father. Her eyes reminded me of high-voltage wires.

"Bye," I said.

"Bye. Thanks for coming. Lovely to see you," she said in a cockney accent modeled to suit the bartender, I suppose.

I went to find my coat and found Richard Jerome holding it in the entry hall.

"Thanks," I said. He held the fur open and helped me into it and we left the house, arm in arm.

A line of squad cars kept the media blockaded at the far end of the driveway, but nevertheless, the minute the front door opened, television lights turned night to day. The glare made me ache with the desire to march down there and make a statement. They saw who we were or, more accurately, who we weren't. "Cut!" I heard and the lights went dark. We weren't anybody anymore.

The snow had stopped and the sky cleared, so the air was freezing. Like breathing ice knives. I snuggled into my coat.

"Can I buy you a brandy?" Richard said. "It'll fortify you against the snow."

"No, thanks. I really need to get home." My Jeep had already been brought around and a dark-colored Mercedes convertible idled behind it, presumably Richard's.

"Why?"

"Walk my dog."

"Oh? I love dogs."

"You're welcome to come to my place," I said, not really wanting to be surly and unsociable just because I'd quit my job. It wasn't his fault. "It's a long drive but the brandy is excellent."

"I'll see you there."

"You know where it is?"

"Sure."

"I'll follow you," I said, "in case that fancy car slides into a ditch and you need to be rescued."

"Never happen." He smiled and slammed my door.

God. But he was attractive.

Vivaldi's *Four Seasons* on the radio dispersed the hot, quick burn of embarrassment of being on the outside looking in, and I reran the afternoon's and evening's events. The coincidences of Ellen's visit, my overhearing Pamela and Walter's fight, and Walter's murder made me wonder if these pieces had all been handed to me on purpose, if someone wanted me in the mix from the start. But why would Ellen and

Pamela and Christine want to draw me into their conspiracy? If the coincidences were manipulated steps, I would have little insight, but if they were pure fluke, I had the possible benefit of perspective. I couldn't wait to see what happened next, and as we drove through the night, I blindly scrawled these thoughts onto a notepad on the seat next to me.

Suddenly, we were there. The long drive to the Circle B was over. Windblown snow drifted and crusted the roads and my flatland cowboy hadn't even skidded a little bit.

"Who do you think did it?" Richard said.

We sat at opposite ends of the living room couch, shoes off, our stretched-out legs covered by a Hudson Bay blanket, my little wire fox terrier Baby curled up asleep between us. The smoke from Richard's cigar smelled delicious.

I rolled the cognac around in my snifter. "There are a number of interesting possibilities and even more interesting potential alibis. I can see a scenario where the three of them—Pamela, Ellen, and Christine—planned it together."

The fire spewed out a burst of hot coals. I jumped up and shoveled them back and moved the screen into place.

"Tell me," Richard said.

I gave him a brief synopsis of my thoughts in the car and then said, "Ellen went to the bathroom and washed her hands, eliminating possibly incriminating evidence. Pamela was upstairs when the shooting occurred, fixing her makeup and presumably adding perfume and washing her hands. She was up there a long time, though. I wonder what else she was doing. And Christine changed clothes completely."

"Wait a minute," Richard said and rolled the ash off his cigar. "Pam was upstairs and Christine was changing and Ellen was holding the gun. I don't see how you can put Pam and Christine into the picture at all. If it's a conspiracy, Ellen sure got the short end of the stick. Maybe she's not as smart as we thought."

"I honestly don't think that Ellen did the shooting and they all certainly have motive." I climbed back beneath the blanket. "What do you think?"

"I've seen this opera before," Richard said.

"Oh?"

"*Tosca*. She murders Scarpia."

"Why?"

"Because he's a bastard and deserves it."

"How does it end?"

"Look it up."

"Thanks," I said.

"Keep going." He dragged Baby onto his lap. She stretched out and went back to sleep.

I told him everything in detail. Right down to the taillights. And the wet footprint on the rug. How unprofessional. How churlish. I did it out of some warped attempt to get even with Chief Detective Jack Lewis. As if to say, 'Hey Jack, the head of the opry knows more about this murder than you do, you sorry bastard.' I did it also because I knew instinctively that I could trust Richard Jerome.

"This has been made to look like a 'Crime of Passion.' " I made quotes with my fingers. "Walter Butterfield, son of a bitch, shot by his wife or his daughter. Important family, big money, motives that any number of people would be happy to substantiate. With good lawyers, any of them could get off with self-defense."

"So? What's the problem?" Richard tossed the blanket back, got up and threw another log on the fire.

"First of all, Ellen. Comes to see me out of the blue and delivers two messages: One, she's been passed over as publisher but can handle it, and two, there's something fishy going on at the Foundation and her stepmother might be being blackmailed, which isn't the point of the message. The point is that she will do whatever it takes to keep control of the Foundation. That's the bottom line, as far as Ellen is concerned. Whether or not Pamela is being blackmailed is mox nix. Next, when I get to the party, she tells me that her father's retiring and not only naming Tewkesbury as regent publisher but also removing her from the Foundation board and that he's going to announce his retirement tonight."

"I'd think she'd want to kill Tewkesbury," Richard said.

"You're right," I laughed. "But, for some reason, Walter didn't make the announcement. I know he didn't forget. He had the perfect opportunity when he got up and started singing. Walter Butterfield would never forget anything that would serve his interests. Something or someone stopped him from doing it and I believe the announcement is directly related to the murder. Next, Pamela." I told Richard the details of her fight on the dance floor with Walter. "Frankly, I don't see how she's stood him as long as she has. If it was me, I'd have murdered him years ago. And then, Christine. Well, anything's possible in her state of mind and level of addiction. I don't know what to say about Christine."

"What about the logistics?"

The way he pushed me along was so companionable. Not obnoxious. Not the devil's advocate. Just reasonable, interested questions.

"Well," I said, "there was no box of shells visible, which would lead me to believe that whoever did the shooting knew that Walter kept the guns unloaded. Anyone experienced with firearms doesn't keep loaded guns around the house, especially a rack of sporting guns. Maybe a revolver in your bed table but not a dozen shotguns on display in your library. So that makes this premeditated: The gun had to be loaded sometime before the encounter.

"Also, I grew up on a ranch. We always had guns around, so I grew up knowing how to use them, but I don't see Ellen or Christine or Pamela Butterfield as being experienced gun handlers, and judging quickly by the side of Walter's head that was missing and the angle from the gun rack, it looked like the shooting happened quickly by someone who was an experienced shot. Those guns pack a big punch and whoever did it must have thrown open the case, grabbed the pre-loaded gun, turned, shot, and escaped so quickly there wasn't time to recover from an unexpected recoil."

"Who do you think did it?" Richard said.

"I don't know," I said. "It'll be interesting to see how this develops."

Richard tossed his cigar into the roaring flames before replacing the fire screen. He came over and sat down next to me on the couch.

"That is exactly what I was thinking," he said. "Do you want some more brandy?" He took the glass out of my hand.

"No, thanks."

"Good."

∽Chapter Ten

Saturday morning

*T*hat opera singer better not be in bed with my sister, or I'll shoot the son of a bitch," my older brother yelled from the front hall. "Or maybe I'll give him a thank-you note. I don't know which."

I looked at my watch. Eight o'clock.

Elias crashed into the living room, chunks of snow sliding off his boots. Baby barked and jumped and bounced her front paws off his grand stomach several times in quick succession in her excitement to see him. Finally he caught her and stuck her, wiggling, under his arm.

Richard and I had fallen asleep on the couch. The fire was out, replaced by sunlight which reflected off the snow through the windows. The room was dazzlingly bright and warm.

I'll tell you one thing, I know Richard looked a lot better than I did in the bright light of day. I didn't care, though, I was so warm in his arms.

"Morning, Celestina," Elias called into the kitchen. "There'll be three for breakfast." He tossed the morning paper onto our laps. "Look."

WALTER BUTTERFIELD MURDERED.
DAUGHTER CONFESSES.

I stared at the headlines. "This is incredible," I said. "I was so sure Ellen didn't kill her father."

"Who says she did?" Elias said. "It's Christine they arrested."

"Christine!"

"She confessed."

"Christine Butterfield confessed?"

"What?" Elias said. "Is there an echo in here?"

"I don't believe it." I pulled my reading glasses out of my evening purse.

"So what?" Elias shrugged. "That's what it says." He left for the kitchen and returned with two cups of coffee.

"Christine's too drugged up and disorganized to shoot anything, even herself," I said. "When I left, she didn't remember there had been a shooting, much less that it had been her father."

"Maybe she was faking it." Eli handed one of the cups to Richard, who reached from beneath the blanket to accept it.

"No. It was authentic. I've seen too much of the real thing. Jack Lewis must be nuts." I put on my glasses and scanned the article.

"She's right," Richard said. "Someone who knew what he or she was doing did the shooting."

"Contract?" Eli said.

"Possibly," Richard said, sipping the coffee, one arm bent behind his head to prop it up.

"What are you guys?" I said. "Experts? And incidently, Elias, thanks for the coffee."

The phone rang and Celestina picked up in the kitchen. "Señorita Ellen Butterfield para tú, Lee-lee," she yelled.

"Gracias. I'll take it in my bedroom." I stood up and wrapped one of the blankets around me. "The guest room's back there," I said to Richard. "Make yourself comfortable."

He kissed the palm of my hand. "I already have. Thanks."

His eyes were so blue.

Elias blushed. But to me, and I think to Richard, too, it felt like we'd been waking up together every morning of our lives on the couch in the living room.

"Ellen," I said into the phone. "Elias just told me."

"It's insane." Ellen sounded weary. "We need your help."

"Well, I think you need a lawyer and a psychiatrist more than you need me," I said, "although I'm happy to do whatever I can."

Celestina came in and put a tray with coffee and toast on the edge of my dressing table.

"Do you mind coming to town?" Ellen said.

"Not at all. I'll leave in about ten minutes."

"Thanks."

I washed off last night's makeup and slapped on a fresh coat, pulled on jeans and boots, a yellow-plaid flannel shirt and red pullover, watch, earrings. It took twenty-five minutes. It used to take ten. Every year since I turned thirty, getting dressed took a minute longer.

When I got back downstairs, Richard and Elias were already digging into Celestina's Saturday-morning breakfast of huevos rancheros, hot chorizo sausage, and buckwheat-pecan pancakes. "Oh, sí," she was saying to them as she held the loaded platter next to Richard's arm, "Lee-lee loves murder. Mor'n eenythin'."

Celestina liked to lay on her Mexican thick for visitors. Her family had worked for mine on the Circle B for three generations. The closest any of them got to Mexico was when they took their children to Acapulco for spring vacation every year, but at home they steadfastly clung to the old Mexican ways. I liked that. We're all getting too homogenized.

"Bye," I yelled. Her breakfasts were so good, they didn't even know I was gone.

I jumped into the Jeep. Baby sailed over me and landed in the passenger seat. She loved a messy case as much as I did.

All the way into Roundup, driving fast through the slush on our dirt road, turning left onto the two-lane county blacktop and finally merging into the light Saturday-morning flow on the Interstate, I watched and studied taillights. But I never saw four small circles, two and two.

The traffic generally consisted of small four-wheel-drive Toyota and Isuzu and Mitsubishi trucks and wagons and small four-wheel-drive Suzuki Samurais. There were also an occasional Chrysler van and lots of GMC pickups. The only thing all the vehicles, Japanese and U.S. alike, had in common were they all displayed one version or another of "Desert Storm" and "Proud to be an American" stickers.

By the time I got to Ellen's, the warm September earth had melted the snow off the streets and sidewalks. The sun glared and reflected so splendidly through the thin dry air that it made me glad I'd decided to come back. There is no place on earth where the sky is bluer than Roundup. Tell that to an easterner, or a southerner, and they go, "Yeah, yeah, yeah." It's sad. They don't even know what you're talking about. Which is okay with me. They can stay where they are, believing their sky is as blue as mine.

⌒ Chapter Eleven

Detective Lewis questioned me for what seemed like hours," Ellen said. We were in her living room, which was more like a little French jewel box. "We never left the library at all. I thought we would have. They were taking pictures of my father and brushing fingerprint powder all over everything. Actually, I'm a little surprised. It was gruesome being around the body all that time."

Basic police tactics. Hoping to induce remorse.

"And Roland." Ellen shook her head and laughed in spite of the grim situation. "He was so puffed up I thought he was going to pop and he had absolutely no idea what he was doing. He kept taking these ridiculous poses that I'm sure he's copied from *Punch* cartoons, and he had on that stupid ribbon, and he was saying things like, 'Now see here. If you intend to arrest my client, kindly do so, or excuse her.'" Ellen's counterfeit British accent was better than her sister's. "Jesus Christ. Roland means well, but he should never be allowed to talk outside a boardroom. He's such an effete. It was all pretty grisly."

She stopped to light a cigarette and take a sip of coffee. She looked old and tired. Her hair hung in strings and she kept tucking one side behind an ear where it wouldn't stay. "Are you writing down all of this?"

"Yes," I said. "I always write down everything. I have to. I can't remember anything anymore."

"I know what you mean," Ellen said. "Anyway, into the midst of this dreary group in the library comes Christine. Out of her skull on pills or whatever. Gone. She walks over and stands in front of the desk and shouts at Father, 'Got you squarely this time!'

" 'What do you mean by that?' says Detective Lewis.

" 'What do I mean?' says Christine. 'I mean, I got him quite fair and square, didn't I? I certainly didn't miss.'

" 'You shot your father?' the detective said.

" 'I would shoot him again, if I had the opportunity.' "

Ellen shook her head with contempt. "Now is when Roland should have been speaking, right? He just stood there with his mouth hanging open. Like this." She paused to imitate his pink lips making a perfect "O" and then continued. " 'Roland,' I said. 'Aren't you going to do anything?'

" 'DON'T say another word!' he finally says to Christine."

"What did Christine do?" I asked.

"She shrugged," Ellen answered. "So, Lewis says, 'Miss Butterfield, I'm going to have to arrest you for the murder of your father, Walter Butterfield.'

" 'Fine,' says Christine. So, I'll be goddamned if he didn't read her her rights and take her away. The whole time I felt like I was taking part in some sort of Victorian drawing-room comedy."

"What did you do?"

"The minute I saw what was happening, I called an actual lawyer, Paul Decker, and he met us at the jail and at least got her moved to Saint Mary's for observation, where I imagine they'll be observing her for a very long time."

"Calling Decker was a good move," I said. Paul Decker was Roundup's version of what a big-time, flashy lawyer should be—a flamboyant, well-connected criminal attorney who had more connections in the police department than the mayor. "So you don't believe that Christine actually shot him?"

"No. I know her well enough to know that she wouldn't kill her only source of income, her own personal golden goose. No matter how low she has to go to get the money, I don't think she'd kill him. She doesn't have the guts, and besides, I don't think it even fazes her anymore."

"You don't think 'what' fazes her?" I said, knowing we were about to get somewhere.

Red patches flared in Ellen's cheeks. "I wasn't going to tell you this, but why not. I'm too tired to protect her, and besides, what's the point?" She looked at her cigarette and then at me. "From a very early age, certainly at least from a couple of years before Mother died, he forced her to have sex with him. It's never stopped."

"I'm sorry," I said. "Did it happen to you, too?"

"No. Only because I was never as pretty as Christine. We've both paid with what's dear to us, though. He used her body and her shame to control her and my mind and career to control me and we both lost."

"Did you kill him?" I said.

Ellen's demeanor was forthright and reasonable. "No. Why would I bother?" she said. "He took the last of it away from me publicly yesterday afternoon. Informing me was simply a formality, since the legal structure was already in place. Killing him wouldn't get any of it back."

"Who do you think did do it?"

"I don't know," Ellen said. "You and I both know that almost everyone at the party would like to have done it, and I include myself in that group. But there's a wide line between desire and capability, between wishing someone dead and actually doing the killing. I don't know who was there that has the capability. You could get a guest list from Pam, though."

"Go through with me again everything that happened," I told her. "Everything you remember. You said you were upstairs. Why?"

"I had gone up to use the bathroom and check my makeup and was just starting down the stairs when the gun went off. The noise was unbelievable. I thought we were being bombed!" Ellen laughed at the absurdity. "I stopped for a second and then ran down the stairs and saw Father's library doors standing open, so I ran that way because it seemed that the noise had come from there. You came in just after I did."

Not quite, I thought. She still had had time to pick up the gun. "Tell me everything you did and saw and heard before I got there. Describe the room to me exactly the way it was when you walked in."

"Smoky. There was a lot of smoke in the air from the blast and little bits of stuff floating around. The smell of gunpowder was very strong. Everything seemed warm. I knew my father had been dead just for seconds. He almost still seemed alive. Do you know what I mean?"

I nodded. I knew exactly what she meant. Alive. Dead. Snap your fingers. That fast. But a residue of life lingers for a time, like radio waves. Even if the transmitter is shut down, the waves keep going. Nothing can call them back. One time, when I was just starting out, I had to accompany another officer to a home and inform a wife that her husband had been killed in a car accident. She said, 'He can't be, I just got home and there's a message from him saying that he's on his way and will be here in time for dinner. I'll play it for you.' It's never left me. She played the tape but he was dead anyway. She played the tape over and over and believed he'd be home soon. Ever since then, I pick up my messages and then erase them instantly.

"I looked around for who did it because it was so quick," Ellen said. "But the room was empty. Like there was a presence, but there wasn't."

"Psychic imprint," I said.

"Exactly." Ellen nodded. "The gun was lying across the arms of the chair and I automatically picked it up. It was warm, like someone had just let go of it. Which obviously someone had."

"Did you hear anything at all?"

"First roaring and then complete silence. As though everything was holding its breath."

"Close your eyes and look around the room for me," I said. "Start on your left and go all the way around."

I don't know where Ellen had learned her recall technique, maybe from meditation, but she laid her arms on the armrests of her chair, crossed her ankles, put her head back on the headrest and closed her eyes, like a person in a movie who had just been hypnotized. She rubbed her thumbs and fingertips together, sensitizing them, bringing her mind into focus.

"Behind the door there are bookcases to the ceiling, with cabinets below that go around the corner to the fireplace. There wasn't a fire. That big nutty portrait of Pam over the mantel." Ellen started to laugh and opened her eyes. "She's posed in English riding clothes with a horse that's wearing a western saddle and lariat. She is such a ditz sometimes."

"Keep going, please," I said.

"Okay." She closed her eyes again, straightened her back and folded her hands in her lap. "Let's see. Go around the corner, more bookcases, doors to the patio, I think the drapes were drawn across them most of the way, side table with a computer next to the desk. God. Father in his chair. Blood was still pumping out of the side of his neck." Ellen's eyes flew open and she stood up quickly and took a breath. "I didn't remember that until just now. Jesus." She shook herself, picked up a cigarette and lit it. "God." She shuddered and wrapped her arms around her. "Do you want me to keep going?"

"Please."

"Give me a moment."

"No problem. Take your time."

Ellen went to the window and looked out at the park and the city and the Wind River Range beyond.

"All right," she said shortly, "I think I can keep going now." She sat back down. Smoke drifted up quietly from the cigarette between her fingers. "Bookcases and cabinets begin again to the right of the desk, go around the corner. The little light was on above the Rembrandt, bathroom door, bookcases, gun case standing open. Gun across the arms of the chair on the right." She opened her eyes. "That's it."

"Was the bathroom door open or closed?" I said.

Ellen looked at the floor and concentrated on the question. "I don't know," she said finally. "Closed, I guess. I'm sorry, I don't remember."

"Did your father keep the guns loaded or unloaded?"

"I have no idea. But I'd say loaded, I guess. I mean, why else have them?"

I found that a reasonable question. It reminded me of a bank robbery, a real bloodbath with four guards murdered in cold blood on a Sunday morning because the bank had a policy against arming its guards. Can you believe it? Why were they there? To show the robber where the money was? Give me a break. That's like people who say, "Don't keep a loaded gun in your bed table because if a burglar comes in and you pull your gun you've just changed the rules." Damn right, I say. Shoot him.

"Do you know anything about guns?"

Ellen shook her head. "No. I've never even fired one. Oh, wait. That's not entirely true. Elias tried to teach me to shoot skeet one time up at the Circle B. He gave up pretty quickly."

"What about Pam or Christine? Do they shoot?"

"I'm quite sure that Christine doesn't and I have no idea about Pamela."

"Did your father do a lot of hunting?"

"I think he went duck hunting occasionally and always on the One-Shot Antelope Hunt, but I don't think he ever hit anything."

The annual One-Shot attracts all the top business leaders and politicians from Colorado, Wyoming, and Montana for a twenty-four-hour hunt during which time each hunter may fire one bullet. They all gather in Lander the night before, arriving by private jets and helicopters, making the small airport look more like Sardi Field in Aspen. Then they go camp out and get drunk and the next morning, after a big open-range cowboy breakfast and some major hits of Bloody Marys which are usually about four parts vodka to one part tomato juice, they climb into these big flatbed trucks with slatted sides so they look like a bunch of Mexican farm laborers and drive around the prairie trying to shoot fast-running, surefooted Wyoming antelope who run in herds and change direction, all together, faster than a blink. And when the trucks change direction to continue the chase, all the drunks with all their loaded, round-in-the-chamber, bolt home, safety-off, ready-to-fire rifles fall down on top of each other and usually, by the time they're back on their feet, sighting in, the antelope change again. This goes on for four hours in the morning and is followed by a chuck-wagon lunch. Participants are invited to go out again in the afternoon, but most of them take off. A fifty-year-old liver can take just so much.

I think the antelope view the One-Shot as their annual version of the Boston Marathon. Hard work but minimal fatalities.

Ellen's description of Walter Butterfield's hunting activities didn't jibe with his gun collection. They didn't look like props.

"Did your father have any friends?"

"I don't think so. He and Roland had breakfast a couple of times a week but I wouldn't say they were friends. And other than that, he had cronies he drank and played cards with at the country club, but I don't think he had any actual friends."

That news didn't surprise me.

I swung by McDonald's and picked up a double cheeseburger and a carton of milk on my way to the Butterfields' and thought that everything Ellen had said could be true except the part about her going upstairs to fix her makeup. She didn't fix it earlier, why start at midnight?

Chapter Twelve

Late Saturday morning

A tiny dog, a horrible little black-and-white thing with a smashed-in nose and a pink bow around its topknot, jumped off Pam's lap and started running in circles and yapping when I was shown into her upstairs sitting room. Pamela, dressed in a smart black suit with a chrome-yellow blouse, was on the phone.

"What! Are you kidding, honey?" she was saying. "Walter's favorite flowers? Walter could give a crap about flowers but he always gave me white roses, so let's make the whole thing white roses." She beamed at me and did a little wave with her fingertips and said nothing to the dog. "Hi, Lilly darling. Please sit down. Don't you look fabulous? So 'ranchy.' I'm almost done. Walter's secretary and I are planning the funeral. God, it's going to be fabulous." She turned back to the receiver. "Yes, honey. Lilly Bennett just got here. Okay. Okay. Three o'clock Monday afternoon. That way it'll make all the evening TV and the front page of the *Roundup Morning News*. Okay. Okay. Good. Okay. Bye-bye. Bye."

She plunked down the phone and spun her lime-green Naugahyde recliner around to face me. I was happily ensconced in a hot-pink velvet, plump bergère chair, admiring a life-sized golden statue of Eros pinching Aphrodite on the nipples next to the fireplace, and wondering how far I could kick the yipping cur across the swimming pool and garden through the French doors.

"Lord. What a lot to do, I had no idea." Pam pushed a loose strand of her hair back. "Let me get you a drink. What do you want? MITZI! You stop that racket."

Mitzi whimpered and whined, jumped onto Pamela's lap and started barking again.

"Nothing, thanks," I called over the commotion, understanding why Pamela yelled all the time. I would have loved a Bloody Mary. "I just wanted to ask you a few questions and see if you'd give me a copy of last night's guest list."

"No problem. Mitzi, you're being a naughty girl." Pam held the dog up in the air and wiggled it close to her face. I used to put people down for talking baby talk to their dogs, but I do it all the time with mine, and besides, it works. The awful little thing stopped.

"I think it's silly that Ellen got ahold of you," Pam said. "It's pretty darned obvious to me that Christine did it. I mean, she confessed and everything. She and Walter had a terrible fight. Are you sure you don't want a Bloody Mary or something?"

"No, really." No Bloody Mary. No cigarettes. Life was barely worth living.

"Well, I'm going to have one."

Pam walked behind her personal bar, a large pink-padded, silver-buttoned tufted thing between the windows, and mixed herself a stiff drink. She dropped a cheddar-cheese Goldfish on the floor for the dog.

"Ellen is convinced that Christine didn't kill their father," I said. "That she physically isn't capable of it, and I'm inclined to agree. For the time being, I'm going on that supposition. Do you mind answering a few questions for me?"

"Heavens, no! I mean, if you really think someone else did it, we ought to find out who. My God, I don't want some murderer running around loose." She took a big swig and then carefully blotted the small drops of tomato juice off her lips without affecting her lip-stick—a skill I've never been able to achieve.

"Let's say Christine didn't murder your husband. Who else do you think could have?" I said.

"What! Are you kidding? Take your pick."

"I'm sure some people are already saying that you did it?"

Pam had a great laugh. HA-HA-HA. She laughed. "I came close many, many times, but, my God, Lilly, we just celebrated our anniversary, and after thirty-two years, you know what you've got. It was bad, but it never got worse. We accommodated one another. I won't miss him but I didn't kill him."

"Pam," I said, "last night on the dance floor, I overheard you and Walter fighting. He was accusing you of something."

Pam looked embarrassed and then acted offended. "He was just pretending."

"No." I shook my head. "I don't believe that. I got the feeling he had a reason for saying what he did. Ellen thinks you're being black-mailed. Are you?"

"Blackmailed!" Pam hooted. "Don't be ridiculous. Why would anyone blackmail me?"

"Everyone's vulnerable," I said. "Everyone has secrets. Everyone."

Pam's voice became hard-edged and businesslike, and all the PR rah-rah fell away like a gauze curtain in a high wind. "Why do you think any of this is your business?"

I chose not to answer.

"It was nothing, Lilly, and it's none of your business. I mean it. It was just a game we play. Walter and I played lots of games like that." She blushed. Her bronze skin turned coppery. She ran her hand across her glossy, bouffant black hair. Her large fingernails were polished in dark burgundy. "You know. Harmless games. They just made him look forward to the party-after-the-party. Do you know what I mean? I really don't want to talk about it."

I knew what she meant, but I didn't especially believe her.

"Pam, I'm not meaning to be antagonistic or to embarrass you, but we need to explore every possible angle."

She took a deep breath and squeezed the dog. "Mitzi, Mitzi," she said, "Lilly's being mean to Mommy."

"Pam, please tell me. Is someone blackmailing you?"

She went to the bar and mixed another drink. "It was a *joke*. Christine said she did it and she did. She's nuts. Jesus Christ! Why don't you drop it? I'd think Ellen'd be grateful for her sister's confession. Ellen was holding the gun, for Chrissakes. Most of the time she's as nuts as Christine."

Mitzi started barking.

"I know you were upstairs when the shooting occurred, but you didn't hear the shot?"

"Mitzi, you hush now. Mommy can't hear the questions. I did hear a crash but it sounded like one of the terrace doors slamming shut. The terrace is right below here and that's what the doors sound like. The library's downstairs at the other end of the house. It's a long way away."

"Do you know if Walter kept his guns loaded?"

She shook her head. "No. I only know the one in the bed table is. I don't even know what he did with those guns. I think they were just to show off how macho he was."

"Do you know anything about an announcement Walter was planning to make last night?"

She shook her head. "No. But he and I weren't exactly confidants. He didn't normally offer information and I didn't normally ask."

"Did Walter have any friends?"

Pamela thought about it. "I don't think so. Not that I know of, anyway. Walter's life was business. All he cared about was screwing people. Literally and figuratively. You might want to check with Miami."

"Miami?" I said.

"Miami McCloud. Walter's mistress."

"Miami McCloud?" I repeated.

"I don't think it's her real name but you can find her out at the rodeo. I imagine she lives in a trailer out there, I think that's the way those people live. She's the star trick rider." Pam burst out laughing.

"Don't you love it? But frankly, Lilly, I think you're wasting your time."

I stood up and Mitzi instantly started. Yap. Yap. Yap. Yap. Yap. Yap.

"Thanks, Pam. I'll keep you posted."

"God, yes. Please do. And please be sure to come to the funeral. It's going to be beautiful. All white roses. Everything white. Fabulous."

Before I left the house, I went into the library and over to where the wet boot print had been on the carpet next to the patio door the night before. The carpet was dry and the image was gone, but in my mind I could still see the size of the print. Fourteen inches. Maybe Big Foot murdered Walter.

The room had been cleaned, as had Walter's swivel armchair, which remained behind the desk. The draperies were gone.

I sat down in his chair and adjusted it as it had been when I'd first seen him. From the angle the blast had hit, it seemed he had been looking in the direction of the gun case, confirming the likelihood that the killer had removed the gun from the rack, turned, and fired. Fast. I thought back about how long it had taken me to get to the library after the gun had gone off. Not more than fifteen or twenty seconds. So I went over to where I imagined the killer must have stood and tested the process. Ba-Boom. I gave myself half a second to lean into the recoil, placed the gun across the arms of the chair in front of the desk and ran for the patio door, using the assumption it had already been ajar, stepped outside and pulled the door to behind me. Six or seven seconds at the most. That meant that in the period between the killer's departure and my arrival, Ellen had entered the room and picked up the gun. Easily possible. What bothered me about the boot print was that usually people with feet that big can't move that fast. Maybe there were two people and the one with the big feet stayed by the door.

I thanked the maid and climbed into my Jeep, and on my way down the drive I passed a man on a horse I took to be the person to whom the Butterfields referred as their "foreman," although I doubt he did more than pose since they had a full-time gardener, no crops and no livestock save the horse he rode and a couple of others. He was young and good-looking in a soft Tom Cruise sort of way. I waved and he tipped his hat and gave me a slow, appraising smile. In my rearview mirror, I watched him dismount and go in the front door. His feet looked semi-big.

Why didn't Ellen tell me about Miami? And if someone named Miami was keeping Walter happy, who was keeping Pamela company?

I drove back to town.

Chapter Thirteen

Saturday noon

*I*t was quiet at the *Evening Star*. Saturday noon. Everything written except Sunday morning's front page. The guard handed me a visitor's pass and offered to teach Baby some tricks while I was down in the morgue.

"Good luck," I told him. "Start with 'Sit.' "

I thought about going up to my brother Christian's office and calling Ellen and asking her to get whatever information she could out of the *Morning News* personnel files about Pamela and any old news clips about her and Walter, but decided not to. I was pretty sure that Walter would have had those files stripped and destroyed and I didn't think Ellen needed to know everything I was doing.

Walter Butterfield's paper, the *Roundup Morning News,* had recently moved into a new home, a pale gray granite-faced, boxy high-rise constructed vaguely in the shape of a personal computer console and screen, but our *Evening Star* remained in its old digs, an elegant pre-World War One Beaux-Arts Federalist office building with oversized windows and a wide staircase leading up to the front doors over which were engraved the words "Unto Thine Own Self Be True," probably a worthy newspaperman's credo in the old days. I thought Christian should replace it with "Screw Your Mother If It'll Sell Newspapers." He did not agree.

Although the building was old, the interior was regularly restored and updated to accommodate new technology, and the sub-basement that housed the newspaper's morgue, now known as the library, was as clean as the real thing. Morgue, that is. Brightly lit. Long rows of white Lucite tables with computer screens and microfiche viewers.

The library research assistant, a bloody-eyed young lady whose hair, eyes, sweater, corduroy pants, and scuffed boots were all the same dirty rust color, sat at a white desk that she'd wrecked with cigarette burns. Her skin was white by birth but her face and hands had turned that yellow-gray color smokers get. I think she needed glasses because she squinted hard at her screen.

"Yes?" she complained up at me. Her teeth were rusty, too.

"I'd like to see the Walter Butterfield file, please," I said.

"Sorry, can't release files to visitors without written authorization." She grabbed a smoldering cigarette off the desk and threw it into one of the four heaping ashtrays that surrounded her.

"I'm Lilly Bennett," I said. "Elias Bennett's daughter and Christian Bennett's sister." The last twenty years never happened. That would change soon enough, but it sent a creepy shot of déjà vu through my bones. If I hadn't left Roundup, in addition to being a daughter and sister I would have been someone's wife and I never would have been Lilly Bennett, cop or anything else. I congratulated myself.

"Oh, okay." She gave me a halfhearted smile. "But the file's checked out anyway for his obituary."

Pamela had said they "just" celebrated their thirty-second anniversary. "Would you pull the June through September 1961 society columns and legal notices?"

She gave me a contemptuous look and shook her head. "Now that's a first," she said sarcastically.

"What do you mean?"

"I never had anyone come in here on a Saturday afternoon to read society columns."

"Now you have." My noblesse oblige was exhausted. "Just get 'em, all right?"

The girl flipped through her computer file, found the right location. "Wait over there." She waved her arm toward the center tables and stomped into the sea of file cabinets and returned shortly with a stack of folders from which old newsprint dangled and flapped.

"I thought they'd be on microfilm," I said.

"Not yet. The society page isn't what any of the real people who work here would call a priority." She placed the folders on the table. "Try not to get them out of order."

"What's your name?" I said.

"Kristin Black."

"Miss Black, I suggest that if you intend to advance or even stay in the same career opportunity with this organization, you undertake to adjust your attitude, and I further suggest that when you're dealing with a member of the Bennett family that you stand up straight, tuck in your blouse, and use 'sir' or 'ma'am' and put a little respect in your demeanor; otherwise you're going to be running out of cigarette money very soon. Have you got that, Miss Black?"

"Yes, ma'am."

"That is all."

Part of the problem with our country is that there is no leadership and no one has any damn guts. We're raising a nation of slothful, surly sissies and I'm sick to death of them.

I opened the file and began to scan the columns. Summertime parties. All the women wore white gloves and hats like Jackie Kennedy. Pillboxes. They looked great.

July tenth. "In a private ceremony in a suite at the Waldorf Astoria Hotel in New York City, *Roundup Morning News* Publisher Walter Butterfield married Miss Ramona P. Gryczkowski, a native of Roundup. Federal Judge Stanley Barbour officiated."

Now there was a name—Ramona P. Gryczkowski. She wouldn't make that one up.

There was no picture.

"Do you have a Roundup phone book?" I called down the room to Miss Black.

"Yes, Miss Bennett." She pulled the fat book out from under her desk, carried it down and set it on the table without looking at me.

"Thank you, Miss Black," I said. This girl must have a very sad life.

There were five Gryczkowskis listed: Jacob; Paul; Paul, Jr.; Michael; and Michael, Jr., all living in a three-block area of one another in the section of North Roundup known as Little Budapest. I could picture the neighborhood perfectly. The kind of place where you wouldn't mind eating off the sidewalk, it would be so clean. The houses were like their residents: secure, hard-working, thrifty. The kind of neighborhood cops came from, not murderers and blackmailers.

I photocopied the article and the phone-book page and laid my file folders carefully in a wire basket beneath a sign that said RETURNS and put the phone book on Miss Black's desk. She was gone. Perhaps brushing her teeth.

When I got back upstairs, Baby was standing on the guard's desk barking right at his face.

"How are those tricks coming along?" I picked her up and stuck her under my arm.

"We both learned a lot," he said.

I don't think he was sorry to see her go.

On Monday, I'd go to Billy the Kid High School and check around. Meantime, I'd go back to the ranch and see what the boys were up to and have a drink. After all, it was Saturday night.

❧ Chapter Fourteen

Saturday evening

*I*t was almost six-thirty when I got home and the sun was just setting. An unremarkable sunset in a cloudless sky. The sun just sort of went down, no particular pyrotechnics. Last night's snowstorm had knocked almost all of the aspen leaves off the trees, leaving only a few golden-orange flashes here and there among the large black swaths of spruce massed on the hillsides. Most of the snow had already melted and the temperature had started dropping fast and would freeze the muddy ground into crunchy little hills. The corral was empty. All in all, a cold and dreary sight.

Richard Jerome's car was gone.

Of course it's gone, you jerk. What did you expect? That he'd spend the day waiting? No. Well. No. Well. I really kind of hoped he'd be here. No note. Nothing.

I fed Baby, poured myself some whiskey on the rocks, and then went upstairs and drew a hot bath with lots of pink bubbles. I keep a television set on the dressing table in my bathroom because that's where I seem to spend most of my life, either putting on my makeup or taking it off, so once I'd climbed into the tub, I punched on the evening news with the remote.

Like a giant boa constrictor, the press was squeezing the guts out of the Walter Butterfield murder. They'd reached the tabloid level quickly because that's the best that murder deserves. The ultimate disgusting insult. The TV screen behind the announcer had a red silhouette of a dead body with the word MURDER stenciled in black across it.

"Christine Butterfield remains under close observation tonight at Saint Mary's Psychiatric Institute, Tom," Marsha Maloney, *Evening News* anchor, told her coanchor Tom O'Neil, who frowned and concentrated.

"YO! MARSHA!" I called. "OVER HERE. Tell us. Tom already knows what happened." She didn't hear me.

"According to friends we spoke with today, relations between Mr. Butterfield and his daughter became strained in 1961, shortly after the suicide death of the first Mrs. Butterfield and his quick remarriage to model Pamela Butterfield."

"MODEL!" I said. "Oh, Jesus."

"Sources close to the family said that Christine ran away to England when she was eighteen and married playboy Lord Howard Gordon-Asprey." A photo of two people sitting at an outdoor table in what looked like Capri drinking what looked like Americanos flashed onto the screen. They both had on dark glasses and could have been anybody. "She and her father have been estranged ever since. Lord Asprey," Marsha giggled, "I wonder if I should be saying Lord Gordon-Asprey?"

Tom shook his head, lost. Where do TV news people come from? If they were really as moronic as they act, they wouldn't know how to read and they wouldn't be able to learn. I just don't understand.

" . . . was unavailable for comment but I was able to track down Christine Butterfield's best friend in London, who agreed to speak with us on the condition that she remain anonymous. She had this to say in an interview earlier today."

A map of England came on the screen with a bull's-eye that emanated radio waves from London and a woman's voice, garbled by the long-distance satellite and the station's electronic garbling "to protect her identity," warbled out.

"Lady Asprey has been under a psychiatrist's care for a number of years," the voice said.

"Was she getting better?" Marsha's voice asked.

"Oh my, yes. She told me a number of times that she felt truly ready to face her father again after so long a separation."

"Was she looking forward to the reunion?" Marsha said live into the camera to the pretaped interview. Television producers think everyone who watches TV is stupid.

"Oh heavens, yes. She was terribly, terribly excited that she would have the occasion of his seventy-fifth birthday to fly in and surprise him."

"I guess she did surprise him," Tom said and shook his head and tried to look compassionate.

"This is the biggest bunch of bullshit I've ever heard in my life," I said and switched around until I found *Jeopardy!* which I played until my drink was empty and the bathwater cold.

I called information for Richard's home number. Unlisted. That really made me mad. I pulled on my terry-cloth robe and went to the kitchen to make another drink. There on a yellow Post-it on the kitchen phone was the note. "Call me," it said. And gave a phone number.

⸺ Chapter Fifteen

Monday morning

About nine-thirty Monday morning, I dropped in on my brother Elias at the breeding barn where he kept his office. Cattleman of the Year and Horseman of the Year awards decked the walls and a life-sized bronze statue of Circle B Wind River Ranger, Eli's grand champion Black Angus bull, stared happily and placidly out from the corner. Eli had looped his prep-school tie around the old bull's neck.

We shot the you-know-what, as one does on a ranch, about various espionage tools for eavesdropping and the like. My brother should have been head of the CIA. He knew more about spying on people than James Bond. He probably would have become CIA director if his knees hadn't been shot out from under him somewhere in Cambodia where no one ever was.

He'd stayed with the Agency for a few years, desk-testing new surveillance equipment and futuristic electronic listening devices, but it just wasn't like the old days. He couldn't go out in the field anymore, so, like me, he came home to the ranch. I think they still called him up from time to time. He denied it. He did some specialized work for big defense corporations and I'd retained him as a surveillance consultant to my own firm, Bennett Security. For a big fat guy who ran a cattle ranch in Wyoming, he was as technologically au courant as one can be. At least as far as I could tell.

He poured me a cup of coffee and after about an hour we'd developed a pretty good shopping list to keep an eye on the Butterfields. As we were wrapping up, he said, "I had an idea and it turned out to be pretty good."

"Oh?"

"Saturday morning after you left for Ellen's, I called Cousin Bucky, you know—Mayor for Life of Bennett's Fort—and asked him about the Marshal's Office there. And just as I had suspected, it turns out it's an actual, authentic, authorized, federal district but there hasn't been anyone there since four years ago, when Marshal Dan died. Just a part-time secretary. Anyhow, Bucky made a few quick phone calls over the weekend and he dropped in early this morning and said he'd secured your appointment as U.S. Marshal of Bennett's Fort."

"What!?" I laughed. "You're making this up."

"No. It's true. Now you've got a badge, papers, access, jurisdiction, the works. All you have to do is stop in and see Bucky and set up the swearing in when you've got time. But he gave me this to give to you in the meantime, since swearing in's just a formality." Elias stood up and hitched his Levi's up over his stomach and handed me the beautiful gold star badge which was clipped inside a navy leather wallet. "Congratulations," he said and shook my hand as if he were president of the United States.

I was speechless. It never in all my life occurred to me that Marshal Dan had been the real thing. "Elias, you are wonderful" was all I could think to say.

"This means you can run your own investigation." Elias beamed. He seemed more excited than I was.

"Jurisdiction," I said. "I'm quite sure I don't have jurisdiction in Roundup, but Jack Lewis does out here, regardless?"

"Yup."

I thought about that for a minute. "I can work around that," I said and fingered the star, which I'd stuck in my pocket.

"There's one hitch," Eli said.

"Oh?"

"Bucky will know more about this than I do, but the Department of Justice, which controls the Marshal Service, doesn't want people knowing that this office is legitimate, so even though it enables you to run an investigation, you still have to run it, publicly, as a private investigator. But you can get federal judicial orders to simplify things."

"I see."

"Oh," Eli grinned. "I just remembered, there's one other hitch."

"I'm about to quit being grateful to you, Eli," I said. "What is it?"

"Every Saturday during the summer, for the benefit of Bucky's tourist industry, you have to have at least one High-Noon Shoot-Out with the Outlaw on the Main Street of Bennett's Fort."

I headed into town, laughing.

The day was sunny and beautiful and I was happier than I'd been in ages.

Richard and I had agreed on Sunday night that all we'd been having was "fun." None of it was serious and there were no long-term implications. That we could both shake hands and walk away and just leave the weekend for what it was: great fun. But, with a jolt I realized that that morning, for the first time in twenty-five years, I had put on my makeup without giving a special smile to Jamie Flaherty. My dead fiancé caught in a silver frame. Dead twenty-five years now. Always twenty-five years old. Always a promising young Philadelphia lawyer. Always in his Marine uniform, shiny little gold bars on his shoulders, last seen in Con Thein. So far I hadn't met anyone who made me feel as good as he had. If a man was great in bed, he usually didn't have more than two good conversations in him, and vice versa.

"Life is full of compromises," Mother stressed on a regular basis. She had started riding me hard about getting married now that I had quit smoking, and her habit was to emphasize imperfections. "I hate to see you going into the last half of your life alone."

The only thing that bothered me about my life alone was that I liked it so much. But the last forty-eight hours sure had been fun. Being appointed a U.S. marshal was icing on the cake.

ᗒ Chapter Sixteen

Walter Butterfield's mistress, Miami McCloud, the trick rider, lived not in a trailer at the stockyards, as Pamela wanted to believe, but in an expensive glass-fronted high-rise on a park in downtown Roundup with a view practically from Montana to Colorado. The doorman announced me and sent me up to the twentieth floor. The penthouse. Even if he had not told me to turn right, I would have known. A mural covered her entry doors: a girl sitting on a rearing horse with the words "Miami McCloud" arched above in a multicolored rainbow.

I was completely unprepared for Miss McCloud when she opened the door. She was a giant. A linebacker. Her huge hands and their long red fingernails held a tall frosty glass of iced tea. Her bosoms were as big as basketballs and she had thousands of white, white teeth and her enormous bouffant hair was as white and sugar-spun as cotton candy. She was a jumbo-sized Dolly Parton. I liked her immediately.

"Yes?" she asked. Her voice was deep and friendly.

"Miss McCloud?"

"Yes. Did we have an engagement?"

It was hard to pick out her eyes behind their triple row of false eyelashes.

"No. I just dropped by on the chance you'd be in." I smiled up at her and showed my badge. "I'm Lilly Bennett, U.S. Marshal of Bennett's Fort."

"Bennett's Fort! I thought that's what the doorman said, but you can never tell what the hell these people are talking about half the time. Well, come on in!" She held open the door and I dragged through the long fringe on the sleeve of her turquoise-and-white cowgirl shirt as if I were walking through a beaded curtain into a bar. "I just *love* that little town. Cutest little thing I ever saw. I hope you came by to issue me an invitation for a Saturday shoot-out. I haven't been there since Marshal Dan died. Oh, my, where're my manners? How about a cup of hot java or a nice cool glass of iced tea or lemonade, or even a beer if you can drink it on duty? Marshal of Bennett's Fort. Get it? *On duty!* You are the *cutest* little thing."

I was afraid she'd slap me on the back in a display of sisterly horseplay and shoot me through the glass wall of her living room. Thank God she didn't.

"Now you just sit on down and make yourself comfortable while I get you something. What'll it be?"

"Black coffee would be great, thanks," I said.

"Coming right up. That's right. You just sit down on that divan right there." She pointed. I sat.

Walter sure did like enthusiasm and size in his women. Between Pamela and Miami, I'm surprised any cloud ever dared to cross his path.

The apartment was as comfortable and plump and soft as she. I admit, like Pam, I had a stereotypical vision of how rodeo people lived and I suppose I had been expecting her to be a faded slattern in a chenille robe covered in cigarette ash and Naugahyde and Formica and Mel-Mac and stacks of dishes in the sink and cartons of microwave dinners overflowing the wastebasket, a blaring TV. But the living room was infinitely feminine, tastefully done in two or three expensive chintzes of pink and yellow roses and blue ribbons. Glass-fronted shelves with recessed lighting that illuminated a collection of antique English and French and German porcelain creamers covered one wall. The table lamps at either end of the sofa were Dresden statues. An oversized, well-brushed, white Persian cat stretched along the top of an armchair.

"You must hate to leave here when you go on tour. It's so pretty and peaceful," I said. "Don't you go away for months at a time?"

"Oh, heavens. I just hop in and out and besides, I'm always staying in the best hotels. Sweetie, that's my horse, even flies most of the time now. He likes it. In the show his name is Rex, but I call him Sweetie." She carried my coffee cup and a café-filtre glass pot with a silver plunger from the kitchen, which I only glimpsed through the door but it looked like my favorite kind of kitchen. Big and sunny and pure white. She put the tray down on the table next to me. "You thought we all went on the road like a bunch of gypsies in a caravan? Like an old-time circus? No, we're a modern rodeo troop. Haven't you seen our plane at the airport? We've got our own 747! Painted up like a stampede." She pushed the filter down through the coffee, trapping the grounds on the bottom. Her motions were extremely delicate, lady-like. "I got so darned fond of this filtered French coffee on our trips over there, it's all I have. I hope you don't mind." Miami McCloud did not breathe or punctuate. She poured me a cup. "Did you say cream or sugar?"

"No. Neither, thanks."

"She's a beauty. They bought it almost new from some broke airline or other. Carry all the animals in front, upstairs and down, don't you just love those upstairs-downstairs planes? I do. And us rodeo crew in the rear. I'll tell you, it's the only way to go. But to answer your question, yes, I'm a real homebody and I miss it terribly but I just don't give it much thought because there's nothing I can do about it if I want to keep living the way I want. I like nice things and they don't come cheap."

Finally she sat down in the armchair, beneath the cat, and crossed her legs. She had on white fringed Spandex pants and white-and-turquoise cowboy boots with tasseled silver disks down the sides.

"Now, I've been using up all the air in here and you've come to talk about our shoot-out. When did you have in mind?"

"Actually, Miss McCloud, I came to talk about Walter Butterfield."

Her mouth opened and closed quickly, like a guppy's.

"How well did you know each other?"

Miami's brow furrowed like an angry child's and her eyes blurred with tears. "Pretty well."

"I understand you were his mistress. Is that true?"

She nodded miserably. A flood of tears brimmed over and poured down her face. "I'm sorry," she said, dabbing at them with a lace-edged linen handkerchief. "I miss him so much and there's nothing I can do. No one knows how much we loved each other except his wife who couldn't stand him, but she'll be getting all the sympathy notes and I'm just so, so sad." Miami broke down into sobs.

I felt sorry for her. Being the other woman stinks, especially when disaster strikes.

"Where were you on Friday night?"

"Why? What difference does it make?"

"Because it's possible, likely even, that Christine Butterfield didn't shoot her father."

"So you think I did?" Miami looked so insulted I was afraid she'd leap across the tea table at me and rip my face off.

"Not necessarily," I said.

She twisted her hankie and took a deep breath. "You may as well know, I was out there."

"At Rancho del Sol?"

Miami nodded. "I snuck into his library from the patio to give him his birthday present. He was there alone and awful, awful unhappy. He'd been crying." Miami's eyes flooded again and she blotted them and blew her nose. I wondered what kind of eyelash glue she used, since they hadn't moved.

"Do you know why he was crying?"

"Walter was very emotional, he used to cry all the time. He was so sensitive. And he was also pretty drunk Friday night. He was saying something about he couldn't make the announcement because then it would all come out."

"What would all come out?" I said.

"I don't know, Miss Bennett." Miami blushed. "I wasn't really listening. I was busy giving him his birthday present."

I could not even begin to imagine doing that to Walter Butterfield. This girl must have a cast-iron stomach, I thought.

"Everyone thought Walter was a mean, drunken son of a bitch, but he was just a very unhappy little boy who needed love and understanding. Just like the rest of us." She patted the hankie across her cheeks and dabbed her nose. "So we spent a while together and then he told me I'd better get going. That he was having enough trouble with Pamela and if she caught me there she'd kill him. He was feeling much better when I left. And then that crazy daughter of his killed him. That selfish little whore," she said vehemently. "I'd like just a few minutes alone with her."

I could tell that if Miami McCloud ever got close to Christine she'd rip her limb from limb.

"How long were you and Walter lovers?"

"About ten years."

"Do you have any idea who else might have killed him?"

Her shrug was childlike. "I don't know. I know he had lots of enemies but we never talked about his family or his business. When we were together, we lived in our own little world. We'd sit out here on my terrace and laugh and laugh and I'd cook us lunch or dinner or whatever; his wife never, never cooked for him. I cooked all the time and it made Walter so happy. He was so easy to please. We went everywhere together. When I was on the road, he'd come and meet me, all over the world. That's how I got all the porcelain creamers. We collected them everywhere we went. We had so much fun. You know, when we were together Walter didn't drink hardly at all, and besides I think I'm the only person who didn't care about his money. I make plenty of my own. I just cared about him. I loved him." The sobs came back and she buried her face in her hands.

I went and got a box of tissues off the kitchen counter. She accepted it gratefully and once she'd gathered herself back together I asked her what time she'd left the ranch.

"Just about one-twenty. Maybe a couple of minutes sooner."

"Why are you so sure of the time?"

"Because Walter said that if the party wasn't over by two o'clock he was going to bed anyhow, and that it was almost already one-fifteen."

"What kind of a car do you drive?"

Miami looked surprised. "That's a kind of funny question to ask," she said.

I shrugged my shoulders. "I don't know what to tell you, I just need to know. Why is it a funny question?"

"Well, I guess just because I've been all over the TV and papers and everything because I have a new white Lamborghini. One of those hundred-and-fifty-thousand-dollar jobs. Only one in Roundup. Would you like to see it?"

"I might stop and look on my way out," I said. "Tell me. Are the taillights two and two? Like this?" I demonstrated.

"Yep. Pretty much. Why?"

"I saw taillights flash a minute or two after Walter was shot and I suspect when we find the person driving that car, we'll have found Walter's murderer."

"Well, my car's like that, Miss Bennett, but so are some others like Corvettes and Ferraris. I was there but I swear to you that I didn't kill Walter."

Either Miami was lying about the time or there was another car with a taillight configuration similar to her Italian sports car. Intuitively, I believed her.

"Were you wearing cowboy boots?"

"I always wear my boots."

"What size?"

"Fourteens. Tony Lama makes 'em specially for me."

The boot print must have been hers. I couldn't imagine that Walter Butterfield would have two friends who wore size-fourteen cowboy boots and came to call on him via the patio the snowy night he was murdered.

I stood to go. "Thank you for the coffee, Miss McCloud. I'll probably be back in touch with you. I'm very sorry about Walter."

"Thank you. That's nice of you to say so, Miss Bennett." She stood, too, and hoisted the cat into the crook of her arm where it nestled into the fringe. "Tell me, why haven't the Roundup Police come to see me?"

"They've accepted Christine Butterfield's confession, so they aren't conducting an investigation."

"Oh, I see," she said. She thought for a moment and then asked, "How many people know you're talking to me?"

"None. Why?"

"I'm a family entertainer, not a home wrecker. I can't afford any bad publicity."

"I know."

When we got to the door, I stopped before stepping out. "May I ask you a personal question, Miss McCloud?"

"I imagine."

"How long have you been a woman?"

If my question surprised her, she didn't show it. "All my life," she said smoothly.

"I meant physically? Legally?"

"Just twelve glorious years."

"Did you know Walter Butterfield before?"

"No. I lived in west Texas then." For a second, a furtive look eclipsed her bright features and I knew that there was probably a Miami-sized problem in her hometown. "I moved here after the operation and made a fresh start. New name. New town. New me. I met Walter at a cocktail party."

"Thank you again for meeting with me," I said.

"Bye-bye," Miami smiled. Her teeth, her hair, her clothes, and the cat were all the same color.

I stopped in the underground garage on my way out after telling the doorman I wanted to see Miss McCloud's car. "Oh, sure," he said. "Everyone's been wanting to see that one."

Its flat, shiny white spoon nose shimmered around a cement pillar like a shark sleeping in sea grass. A sexy machine built for speed and grandeur. The taillights were just as she'd said but I couldn't say for sure if they were the ones I'd seen Friday night.

As I drove off, I thought about how much Roundup had changed in twenty years. I'll bet back then we didn't have a single transsexual in the vicinity and now we had one who had been the lover of the owner of the morning newspaper. What a story that'd make. I started laughing. Mr. Mean. Mr. Womanizer. Mr. Ultimate Chauvinist Pig had a mistress who used to be a man! I loved it. I didn't think she shot him, though. She seemed legitimately bereaved to me but then again, an individual who's lived a lifetime of sexual concealment must be extremely accomplished at masking every honest emotion just to survive. Who had been concealing the most? Miami or Walter?

Chapter Seventeen

Monday noon

*F*our-wheel-drive Subaru wagons filled the parking lot at Billy the Kid High School, where I was pretty sure Pamela Butterfield, aka Ramona P. Gryczkowski, had been educated, and I wondered what had happened to the old broken-down jalopies that used to lie like piles of rusted-out junk in Billy the Kid's lot.

During the sixties and seventies, the then fifty-year-old school building fell into disrepair and the school itself developed a reputation for knifings of "Anglos" by "Chicanos," of "Blacks" by "Anglos," of "Chicanos" by "Blacks," and so forth. We never had many Asians in Roundup. At some point during the eighties, the school principal, along with the Black, Anglo, and Chicano parents and various community leaders, said "That's all," and became the first high school in the country to install metal detectors at all entrances, require that students wear uniforms, and institute mandatory drug testing. The ACLU went nuts. "Fuck the ACLU," the parents and school board said. "These are our children, and they don't have rights until we say they have rights and at the moment they don't."

I'd never been inside Billy the Kid High School before. As a matter of fact, other than Pamela Butterfield, I didn't think I knew anyone who had attended Billy the Kid. It had been a trade school on the wrong side of the Wind River when I was growing up. Things surely do change.

"Which way is the library?" I asked the receptionist.

"Right down the hall, ma'am," she said. "Would you like for me to show you?"

"No, thanks. I can find it."

"Okay." She smiled.

A cardboard sign stood on the reception counter: Roundup's Subaru Dealers Salute Billy the Kid Straights: Straight from Drugs—Straight-A Grades.

"What does that sign mean?" I asked.

"Oh," she said casually, "all the Subaru dealers have this incentive program where they loan a free wagon to every student who stays drug-free and gets straight As for a year. If they maintain the record all the way through high school, they get to keep the cars."

How wonderful. My only incentive in high school had been to get out.

Class was in session. The halls were remarkably quiet and my high heels sounded like pebbles dropping on the marble-patterned floor. I tried to tiptoe, but every now and then, a heel hit.

Like the rest of the building, the small Edwardian library had been splendidly restored. Mrs. Petty, the librarian, sat at an elevated oak desk at the far end of a long, narrow row of tall bookcases and small oak study desks, each with its own light. Most of the carrels were full and only a couple of students looked up when I came in. It was like being at Oxford.

"May I help you?" Now this was a librarian, not some broken-down twenty-two-year-old with an attitude problem like Miss Black at the newspaper. She looked about my age. I could tell she knew her business and didn't take any crap from anyone.

"I'm Cathy Miller," I said, "I graduated in the Class of 1954."

She believed me. I was six in 1954. My disguise of bright blue eye shadow behind silver-framed Sophia Loren glasses with stems that swirled up off the bottom of the frame, a way-way-too-tight size 6 lime-green nubbly wool suit and run-down bone-colored pumps had turned me into a fifty-seven-year old Billy the Kid graduate who put in eight hard hours a day for survival, not career satisfaction. I guess I was glad.

She smiled at me patiently.

"And I wanted to look at the yearbooks from 1952, '53, '54, and '55," I said in a rush. It was crazy, this authority figure was actually making me nervous. "I've got a bet with a friend."

"The yearbooks are over in section eight." She wrote some numbers on a slip of paper which she handed to me. The smile had turned sympathetic.

Ramona P. Gryczkowski graduated in 1955. Her inky-black hair dipped low over one eye and her lips smiled alluringly from the tiny picture. She looked like trouble.

I flipped through the book searching for other pictures of her and her friends—dances, athletic teams, dramatic productions, choral groups, that kind of thing, and Bingo! Ramona P. Gryczkowski had been homecoming queen. Quarterback Carl Rosak was king. I wrote down the names of their six attendants.

The lunch bell rang and I waited until the room had cleared before putting away my materials and shoving the heavy books back into their slots on the shelves. The librarian was still at her station.

"I won the bet!" I said. I don't know why I wanted her to like me. Pathetic.

She gave me an even more compassionate gaze. "That's nice," she said sadly.

"Bye," I said.

The corridors swarmed with girls in uniforms of white blouses, dark green V-neck sweaters, and green plaid skirts, and boys in khaki pants, white shirts, ties, and green blazers. I'd never been in a public high school at lunchtime before. It was loud. My school had been small, and lunchtime was usually as quiet as the rest of the day because no one was happy to be there. We all just got through the best we could.

I pushed back past the main entrance, past doors with waffle-glass

windows: the Principal's Office—Please Knock; the Faculty Room—
Do Not Enter; the Nurse's Office—Come In. In the girls' rest room I
closed myself in a stall and, to the nostalgic background music of gig-
gling girls smoking cigarettes, I took off the glasses, put on large gold
earrings, a gold charm bracelet and a huge rhinestone ring, unbuttoned the tight jacket by three buttons so I was voluptuous instead of
just plain bulging, changed into shiny black patent high heels,
sprayed on some Giorgio perfume, spiked my hair with glosser gel,
put on large dark glasses, and crossed the hall to the Records Office—
Come In.

A small bell with a sign, "Please Ring," sat on the counter. There
were four desks beyond the counter but only one was occupied. Just
what I'd hoped for. I rang the bell. The young clerk with bouffant
platinum hair, blue frosted eye shadow, and pink frosted lipstick—a
look that has never gone out of style in Wyoming—wove around the
desks toward me.

"Hi," I said. "I'm Cathy Miller and I'm with 'Dream Date' in Los
Angeles."

"Oh, sure." Her expression was skeptically hopeful.

"No, really, I am." I handed her a business card that identified me
as a Dream Date Research Assistant, Dream Date Productions, 5555
Sunset Boulevard, Hollywood, California. My charm bracelet clanked
on the counter.

"Gee," she said. "That's neat. What're you doing in Roundup?"

I could tell she thought I'd come for her, come to take her back to
meet her Dream Date, and I felt like a crumb. "We're going to do
some oldies shows in February, you know, around Valentine's Day,
with old people, like in their fifties?"

"Oh? Uh-huh." She realized I wasn't interested in her and tried to
hide her disappointment and her embarrassment that she had let herself think so in the first place.

"And I need your help."

"Oh, yeah?"

God, I felt terrible doing this. "One of the old couples we'll be re-
uniting are Ramona Gryczkowski and Carl Rosak. They were the

homecoming queen and king here at Billy the Kid in the fall of 1954."

"Oh, yeah? Cool."

I smiled conspiratorially. "Have you seen our show?"

"Oh, sure," she said.

"Well, you know all the Dream Dates are surprises. Just like you in your job, we're used to dealing with extremely confidential information."

"Absolutely," she agreed importantly.

"I'm hoping you can help me," I said. "I need to get Ramona's and Carl's parents' names and addresses from you. Mrs. Petty, the librarian, was pretty sure you'd still have them in the files. You've seen the show, right?"

"Oh, yeah, I watch it all the time."

"Well, you know we always invite the parents and the brothers and sisters, and starting with the parents is usually the easiest way to start finding everyone. People get married and change their names and move away and get divorced and remarried and . . . well, you know, it's wild."

"Tell me about it," she said. "My family's all over the place."

"Oh, really?"

"Yeah. My aunt and uncle moved out to Kansas and my brother's in San Diego."

"Wow," I said. "Then you really know that usually if anyone's going to know where everyone is, it's the parents." I took a clean sheet of paper out of my briefcase and copied "Ramona P. Gryczkowski" and "Carl Rosak" off the piece of Dream Date Productions letterhead where I'd neatly printed their names as well as those of their attendants.

"What are those other names?" she asked.

"Oh, those are just some of Carl and Ramona's friends. I don't know if they went to school here or not."

"I can check, if you want me to."

"That would be great," I said and added their names to the list. "If it's no trouble."

"No problem," she said. "Class of '55. Right?"

"Right."

"I'll be right back."

I stood at the counter and contemplated my lack of integrity for the few minutes she was gone. I had to lie to her and the librarian. I had no jurisdiction in Roundup. I couldn't get a court order. It wasn't hurting anyone. As a matter of fact, I told myself, I think I even made the records clerk feel better.

"Thank you so much." I laid the filled-out sheet carefully in a manila folder which I returned to my briefcase. "Now listen, this is very, very secret. But the show will be on February twelfth, and we'd like for you to be our guest in the audience."

"You would?"

"Sure, what's your name?"

"Terri Waters."

I wrote it down. "Okay. Done. If you're in L.A. on Tuesday, February eighth, that's when we'll tape the show, there'll be a ticket waiting for you."

"Gee," Terri Waters said. "That's great. Thanks."

"Thanks, honey," I said. "You're going to help make romance happen."

She smiled. "Bye."

There was no such TV show as Dream Date. I took no pride in that. I drove to the Roundup Country Club, went downstairs to the ladies' locker room and took a shower to get rid of the Giorgio, washed my face, fixed my makeup, and changed into a navy suit with gold braid that was not a size 6 but fit and went to the ladies' sitting room and made a few calls.

I grew up in a home ruled by an occasionally benevolent dictator: my mother. A regime of edicts, directives, and direct orders. Sort of the rich man's version of Tough Love. Do that again and you can't go to the country club for a week. Or, no Margaux for you at dinner. The minute a standard was attained, it was raised.

My mother had suffered incomprehensible, at least to me, deprivation during the Great Depression, and all my life I never could really understand her fully, never reassure her enough, never put her completely into a context I could relate to. Until the day I went to pick up my little wire fox terrier, Baby.

The breeder, Shirley, was in the business of raising international grand champions and had kept two puppies out of the litter of five until they were ten weeks old before she decided which would get the nod as the contender for Best in Show, Top Dog, at the Westminster Kennel Club. She didn't keep Baby because she was just too sweet.

So, I go out in the country to meet Baby, expecting a sweet maternal scene, a touching good-bye between my puppy and her mother. And Shirley and I stand around her big country kitchen and she takes Baby and her mother out of their pen where they've been snuggling and puts them on the kitchen floor and, all of a sudden, the mother starts chasing Baby around like she wants to kill her. Every time she caught her, she'd whop her a good one with her paw, making Baby cry. Just mauling her, like a wild animal. At one point, Baby was hiding under an Early American hutch and her mother, too big to get under there with her, kept batting her and trying to bite her.

After a minute or so, I said to Shirley, who seemed completely oblivious to the brawl going on under our feet, "Don't you think I should try to rescue her? I mean, it really looks like she's trying to hurt her. Badly."

"Oh, no." Shirley waved her hand. "This is how the mother teaches the baby to be tough. These little dogs are quicker and braver than other small breeds. They're very independent and resilient. Her mother's just teaching her to protect herself. She wouldn't really hurt her."

Well, Eureka. There it was. My mother's a wirehaired fox terrier and so, I guess, am I.

All this is a long way of saying that all my life my mother, in addition to the edicts and direct orders, has also issued succinct proclamations which I was free to believe or not. My choice. But which, more often than not, have proved to be right. For instance:

There are two places where a woman can always go to reach safety if she is lost or in danger, or just to make a few phone calls in a nice private setting: a good hotel or the ladies' locker room of a good country club.

It's true.

Chapter Eighteen

The phone book indicated that former homecoming king Carl Rosak was now an insurance man with Aetna Life and Casualty with an office in Little Budapest, the same neighborhood where he and Ramona and all their friends had ruled the roost as teenagers. As a child, I remember going to Little Budapest with Mother when she was president of the Roundup Ladies' Auxiliary. The self-contained Hungarian, Germanic, Prussian, Polish village of four dozen square blocks within the city looked pretty much the same as it had when I was little. The streets were still narrow and enormous elm trees still towered over the small one-story frame houses which sat well back from the street and all looked freshly painted in white with either green or yellow trim. Iron bars had been added to the windows of a few homes and two of them even had floor-to-ceiling bars completely surrounding their front porches, turning them into cages. I suppose it was so that the residents could sleep with their doors and windows open in the summertime but it gave the impression that dangerous, crazy people who'd used up their health-insurance benefits so they'd been turned out on the street, lived there; the ones from whom the community needed protection; that those houses were where the neighbors went in the evening with their cocktails to watch the show from a safe distance. Here and there, chain link replaced the old wrought-iron fences around the large grassy yards where roses and yellow chrysanthemums and red geraniums basked in the sunny, warm autumn afternoon. No sign remained of the early snowstorm three days earlier.

Teenagers, in Billy the Kid High School uniforms, stood in the street, gathered around a Subaru wagon. Two boys with their ties now off and two girls whose long dark hair flowed in masses of curls across their shoulders looked under the hood and poked each other in the ribs and laughed while another boy revved the engine loudly. As they politely stepped out of the way so my car could pass, they studied me openly, probably memorizing my face and license number so that, in case a stranger should be reported to have made trouble, they could say that it was a dark-curly-haired woman in a red Jeep with California plates. Baby barked at them. So easy to be brave when all the doors are locked.

Carl Rosak's storefront office sat on the town square. The Church of the Holy Rosary, the Holy Rosary Rectory, and Holy Rosary School ascended on one side of his office building and Saint Joseph's Church of Poland, Saint Joseph's Rectory, and Saint Joseph's School, where I assumed he and Ramona had studied as children, ascended on the other. The Orthodox Church of the Transfiguration with two chunky towers and stained-glass windows hunkered stolidly across the square.

As I pulled up to park, a woman in a clear plastic overcoat and scarf with a white barking miniature poodle crossed in front of me and entered the square. The high-strung little dog, so like Pamela's Mitzi, made me wonder if perhaps, like paprika, small yappy dogs—too little for a proper goulash, too big for a sandwich—were an Eastern European idiom left to the middle-aged women to raise and simply make the best of it.

Mr. Rosak had told me over the phone to come at five when I called him from the country club. Even though I gave him my real name, I lied and told him I was doing an insurance investigation.

"I usually take off between five and seven for Little League practice and dinner before I get to my evening appointments. Most of my clients work but there's no practice tonight, so you can come right at five."

"Thank you. I'll see you then," I'd said.

"If I'm not home for dinner at the stroke of six, my wife has a fit. You know how these old girls get," he joked. "So don't be late."

"No, sir. I understand perfectly."

He greeted me personally and I never would have recognized him in a million years from his high school yearbook picture. He'd not kept his matinee-idol looks. It even looked as if he'd taken up boxing, unsuccessfully, after football. His face was fleshy and pugnacious and his nose was pugged, as if smashed in so many times it was reluctant to pop out again. Carl Rosak had the edges of the erotic danger and violence that accompany hooliganism. His gray-black crew cut looked like he shouted it into attention, it stood so firmly on end, and his black eyes flicked with mischief and threat.

Twenty years' worth of pictures of Carl Rosak with Little League teams—baseball, football, hockey—adorned the wall. "I never should have been a businessman." He indicated the pictures. "I should have been a coach. Come on in and have a seat."

Mr. Rosak held open the door and as I passed him I picked up the scent of English Leather and a mild whiff of vodka. He was dressed in a tan business suit with a green-and-yellow argyle sweater vest, the kind Dan Rather wears, beneath his jacket.

"Thank you, Mr. Rosak." I sat down and pulled off my gloves and took my notepad and glasses out of my purse. He didn't ask to see any ID and I didn't offer.

Various sizes of gold-framed pictures of him and his wife and their children and what I supposed were their grandchildren decorated the credenza behind his desk. The pictures were all basically the same, with the straight-backed subjects sitting on fences in the Sears-Roebuck back lot, an Autumn in New England countryside draped behind them.

Mr. Rosak sat down and blocked their view.

"You're nice to see me," I began.

"My pleasure," he smiled. "I'm always happy to make time for a pretty girl."

I smiled widely. I seldom mind when men make such suggestions. Sometimes I even find it flattering. But what if I were to say, "I have some tickets in my purse to the French Riviera, will you come away with me right now?" I wonder if they would. Probably. And then I'd be stuck in some world-class locale with some third-rate jerk who sucks air through his teeth, leaves the bathroom door open, and orders the most expensive wine on the list regardless of color or kind.

"I hope you can help me," I said. "I'm looking for information about an old friend and classmate of yours at Billy the Kid High School. Ramona Gryczkowski."

Carl Rosak blew out his breath in a quick, soft whistle and smiled. "Whew. That's a blast from the past! I haven't heard her name in years."

"Really? This is such a small community, I'd think you'd see Gryczkowskis all the time." I could tell his heart had missed a click when I said her name.

"Yes, I do. But no one ever mentions Ramona."

"Why not?"

He shrugged and picked up a metal disk engraved with an insurance award. "She just sort of disappeared."

"When was the last time you saw her?"

"Years ago. Not since the summer we graduated from high school." He rolled the disk back and forth between his hands.

"You were very close to each other, weren't you?"

"Oh, yes. We were steadies," Carl Rosak laughed. "She had my class ring that she wore on a chain around her neck, my letter sweater. The whole deal. You know, engaged-to-be-engaged."

"Those were the days, weren't they?" I said, working to keep him loose. He kept his eyes moving between the disk and the door and I was sure he was afraid his wife was going to come busting in and accuse him of infidelity. "What happened? Why didn't you get married?"

"Oh, you know." He let the award circle and clatter itself back down onto the desktop and looked back up at me. He picked up a rubber band and began to stretch it between his fingers. "I'd gotten a full scholarship to college, football, but my father said, 'No way my son's going to make his living playing football.' So he made me go into the Army and when I came back from basic training—I only had three days home before I left for Germany—she was gone. Gotten a job and moved to California. She left me a note saying she'd met someone else and never wanted to see me again. My heart was broken." He put his hand over his heart and grinned.

"Jeez," I said. "Cruel woman."

Carl Rosak laughed. "Those are the worst, aren't they? Young love? I can still bring it back."

"I know. I just got over mine this weekend."

He laughed appreciatively.

"So you never saw her again?"

"No. I met Gisela, my wife, in Germany. We've been married for thirty-four years." He pivoted his chair and looked at the smiling fat woman in the picture who in another time or another country probably would have been missing most of her teeth by now. "Why are you interested in Ramona Gryczkowski? What'd she do?"

"Her husband was murdered last Friday night, maybe you've heard of him. Walter Butterfield?"

"Ramona was married to Walter Butterfield?" he said. I could tell he already knew. There was just a little too much gee-whiz in his expression.

"Yes."

Carl Rosak whistled. "Woo. Mrs. Fancy. That was quite a shooting. Didn't the daughter do it?"

"She's confessed, we're just wrapping up some loose ends and felt it was important to run a background check on Pamela, uh, Ramona."

"Sure," he agreed enthusiastically.

I closed my notebook and put it back into my purse. "You've been extremely helpful, Mr. Rosak. Funny how people's lives go, isn't it? Didn't you ever try to find out what had become of Ramona?"

Now that the notebook was gone and I was making moves as if to leave, he relaxed visibly. A simple tactic that said, "Now we're off the record, the official part's over. Let's be chums."

"Yes, well, I didn't get back to Roundup for some time. After I got out of the service, I went to college in Illinois, that's where all our children were born." Mr. Rosak waved his arm in the direction of the credenza, as if indicating a hoard of thousands cheering outside his window. "When we came back I asked a friend if she ever saw Ramona and she said she'd come back from California right after I'd gone overseas and gotten a job downtown, but then a year or two later, she just disappeared. Mrs. Gryczkowski's never been too anxious to talk about her. Even when we were little, Ramona's mother was always telling Ramona she was a bad girl. Which she wasn't at all. God, she was so beautiful. Like a wild animal. Exotic. Do you know what I mean?"

"Yes." I could see why he was feeling wistful with Big Old Gisela glaring out at him from her gold picture frame. She was balanced so precariously on the country fence I knew if I watched her long enough, she'd fall off. "What about the rest of the family? Her father? Her brother?"

Rosak looked at his watch and stood up. "Mr. Gryczkowski's been dead for a long time. He died just after I left for Germany. Ramona's brother Mike is a lot younger. Now there's a young man with his hands full. He's got six children. Mike and Donna's kids make up about forty percent of the Little Budapest Little League."

"Is Ramona's mother still alive?"

"Oh, sure. She lives in the same house a couple of blocks over. Mike and his family live next door to her. If you're going to see her, I'd call first. Now's probably not a very good time. She'll be fixing dinner. Mike and Donna and their kids eat with her every night. Funny." Mr. Rosak walked me to the door. "I haven't thought about Ramona for so long. It's almost as though she never existed."

"Thank you for your time, Mr. Rosak," I said.

"Always time for a pretty girl."

"One more thing. Where were you last Saturday morning at one o'clock?"

He looked like I'd slapped him. "I, uh, uh. I was home in bed. Why?"

"Routine."

Chapter Nineteen

Monday evening

Dusk had fallen by the time I'd driven the two blocks to the Gryczkowskis' and pulled up across the street from the two red brick houses. A decorative black wrought-iron fence encircled the yard, which was filled with tricycles and soccer balls. A couple of mixed-breed dogs were chained to a tree. Bright lights and loud television noise blazed from the big square windows of the larger of the two homes.

This was whence Pamela Butterfield, née Ramona P. Gryczkowski, came. Raised a devout Catholic, no doubt. Raised to believe that if you didn't work hard to get something, then it must be an ill-gotten gain. Well, Pamela had certainly earned everything she had. I wondered which window had been hers and in which tidy little room she'd dreamed her dreams and seen them come true.

A big-framed man whom I assumed to be Ramona's brother Michael had just finished sliding the noisy doors of a single-car garage shut. He crossed the garden and went up the side steps into the house. Children's happy shrieks carried through the windows.

I waited for a minute before going up and ringing the bell. He opened the door and just seeing his face took me completely off guard. Michael wasn't Pamela Butterfield's brother. He was her son. Michael Gryczkowski, Jr., was the son of Ramona Gryczkowski and Carl Rosak. I knew why Pam had gone away and I knew why her mother didn't want her back and I knew why her father had died. I knew what made her vulnerable to blackmail. What I didn't know was how much, if anything, Mike Gryczkowski knew.

"May I help you?" he asked pleasantly.

"I'm sorry," I said. "I think I'm at the wrong house." I turned and hurried down the walk before he had a chance to ask me which house I was looking for and drove quickly back to the town square in time to see Mr. Rosak striding around the corner toward dinner. I jumped out and caught up with him.

"Why didn't you tell me?" I said.

"Why didn't I tell you what?"

"That Mike Gryczkowski is your son."

"What? That's ridiculous. Mike's not my son."

"Mr. Rosak, you and Ramona had a baby, didn't you? And the Gryczkowskis adopted him as their son."

Carl Rosak reversed course and I followed him back to his office. "Please tell me what happened," I said.

"You tell me first why you want to know," he said angrily. "What possible difference does it make?"

"It's not that complicated. Walter Butterfield was murdered and it's possible that blackmail was involved. If Pamela has a son, that could cast a different light on the circumstances of her husband's death."

"Please, Miss Bennett. It's all such ancient history. All you'll do is hurt people by bringing all this up again."

"I don't want to hurt anybody, Mr. Rosak, but if Pamela or Walter Butterfield are being blackmailed, she also needs protection, and whoever's doing it needs to be caught."

"I can guarantee that no one from around here, not Michael, not me, not anyone, is blackmailing Ramona. I didn't even know where she was until you told me, and Michael only knows he had a sister who died when he was a baby." Carl Rosak was sweating. "You could ruin his family and my family if you start asking the Gryczkowskis a lot of questions."

The phone rang and he grabbed it. "Yes?" he shouted in a high voice. He listened. "I'm just leaving now." Rosak slammed the phone down and stared at it as if it were a snake about to bite him. "My wife. Dinner's ready."

"I already told you, I don't want to ruin anyone's family. Tell me what actually happened."

He struggled to keep his panic under control. "I wanted to marry Ramona but she refused. She said she'd rather die than end up like her mother, so she ran off somewhere and had Mike. I was in Germany by then. She left him at her mother's door when he was just a few days old and never came back."

"Tell me, do you see Ramona now?"

"No!" He shook his head adamantly. "All the rest is just the way I told you. I haven't seen her since I left for the Army thirty-five years ago. As far as her mother is concerned, Ramona's dead, and like I said, Mike thinks he had an older sister who got killed in a car accident."

"Thank you, Mr. Rosak," I said. "You have my word it'll remain strictly confidential unless I find some evidence that indicates it shouldn't."

He sat back in his chair, limp and pale. "God. It would be terrible if all this were made public." He wiped his face with a white handkerchief and took a deep, sighing breath. Then another. "My family. My business. Mike's family. God."

"Mr. Rosak," I said, "calm down. You're hyperventilating."

"Hell, yes," he yelled. "Who the hell wouldn't be? You just come waltzing in here looking like a nice girl, pretty long legs and nice clothes, wanting to talk insurance investigations and ruin my god-damn life." Judging by the deepening shades of Carl Rosak's face, hysteria was getting the upper hand. "You're like one of those damn television people."

How insulting! "That's it, Mr. Rosak. Get ahold of yourself. This is no exposé. I'm investigating a homicide and you're awfully excited about something that you claim doesn't even concern you. Now listen to me before you die of a heart attack. I have a date with a man I've waited my whole life to meet, I am already late and I'll be goddamned if I'm going to be later because of having an hysterical dead insurance man in Little Budapest on my hands."

Carl Rosak stared at me with his mouth hanging open. I guess Gisela Rosak wasn't as tough as she looked if my little tirade got his attention so easily. "Take in a deep breath," I ordered. "Let a little of it out. Now hold your breath while I count to ten. Okay, let a little more out. Hold it. Okay, let a little more out. Again. Again. Again. Slowly. Right."

His color leveled out and he grinned up at me sheepishly. "Thanks," said the old football star. "I wasn't hysterical, I have a little heart trouble."

Who cares? I thought. I just wanted to meet Richard. Rosak sat up in his chair and straightened his tie and slicked his hands across his bristly hair. He rustled his shoulders around a couple of times and cleared his throat. "Tell me, how does Ramona look?"

I thought about that for a second. "Pretty much of a mess," I answered. "You're better off with Gisela."

Carl Rosak smiled. "Good night, Miss Bennett." He closed the office door behind me and pulled the shades.

I doubled the speed limit downtown to meet Richard in the Rouge Royale Tavern, the red-flocked, gilded-to-death bar at the Roundup Grand, our town's finest hotel, upon which the Taj Mahal has nothing.

He wasn't there yet and for the first time in my life, I didn't get all riled up. I didn't mind. For the first time in my life I truly believed he'd get there just as soon as he could. I went into the ladies' room and fixed my makeup and by the time I got back he was standing at the 1860 Gold Rush, brass-studded, gargoyled mahogany bar with two full glasses of whiskey in front of him. He looked even better than I remembered.

"What was your wife like?" I asked after we'd caught up on my murder and his opera.

"Promiscuous and not terribly bright," he said without rancor.

"Ah. Well, that pretty much says it all, I'd say."

"Yup."

"Did you get divorced because she was especially one or the other or both?"

"We never should have gotten married in the first place. I knew it and I'm sure she did, too, although I never discussed it with her. I remember standing there during the wedding, saying those words, making those promises and knowing there was no way that I'd uphold a single one of them. Four years later, a year after I'd had a vasectomy, I discovered she was taking birth-control pills, which, of course, she lied about and denied." Richard paused to light his cigar. "Want me to keep going?"

"Yes."

"We were restoring an old summer house that had been in my family for a long time on Fishers Island; she and the boys were there for the summer and I was commuting from the city on the weekends. So, this was shortly after I'd found the pills, I arrived on Fishers in time for dinner and found she had moved the roofer into my bed. I turned around and went back to New York and filed for divorce. My only regret is that I didn't fight for custody of the boys. Gee, Lilly, I'm really glad you brought this up," Richard said angrily. He swallowed his drink and signaled the bartender for another round.

"What did you do then?"

"Quit my job at Morgan Guaranty and moved to my family's cattle ranch up north along the Big Horns, right outside of Buffalo. That's when I met Elias and Christian, down at Frontier Days in Cheyenne, and Christian got me started with team-roping." Richard smiled. "It was great. I spent the next three years drunk and screwing and rodeo-ing."

"I'd think there would be better places to pick than Wyoming to sow your wild oats," I said. "There just aren't that many girls here."

"Who said anything about girls?" Richard smiled. "Wyoming is like New Zealand, where men are men and sheep are nervous."

What a guy.

"Then I went back to work at the bank so I could spend more time with my sons, and once they were safely in boarding school I decided to make my avocation my vocation. So I resigned my seat on the Metropolitan Opera Board and went to work for them, and by the time the spot opened up here in Roundup, I was ready."

"Do you like it here?" I asked.

"Truthfully?" His blue, blue eyes drilled me.

"Of course truthfully."

"I've had more fun with you in the last seventy-two hours than I've had in the two years I've been in Roundup."

Oh, yes. "I know. I feel the same way. I'm sorry I brought up your ex-wife, I just wanted to know."

"No. It's okay. The whole thing pisses me off."

"How long ago was it?"

"Eighteen years."

"Gee," I said.

"Gee, what?" He was really getting mad.

"Well, I mean, it *was* eighteen years ago. I'd think you'd be getting over it by now."

"When children are involved, no one ever gets over it."

"Apparently not."

After cocktails we drove to the ranch and grilled a couple of steaks and drank a bottle of cabernet and then climbed into bed and watched a video of the afternoon's dress rehearsal of Donizetti's *Lucia di Lammermoor*. The Opera Ball, one of two crowning jewels of Roundup's social calendar (the other being the Debutante Ball at Christmastime), would open the opera season in three days. Looked perfect to me. Richard was asleep by the end of the second act.

I lay in bed next to him and while the Lammermoor family carried on I thought about Ellen and Christine Butterfield and Miami Mc-Cloud and Pamela Gryczkowski Butterfield and Carl Rosak and their son Michael Gryczkowski and wondered if Michael had anything to do with Pam's inquiries into non-family members' holding stock in the family interests. Probably so. The circle was getting wider and wider. The last thing I remembered before drifting off to sleep was Lucia staggering around on her wedding night in her blood-soaked nightie. Promiscuous and not terribly bright.

Chapter Twenty

Tuesday morning

*H*ot Spur, Richard's sorrel quarter-horse stallion which I learned he'd been keeping at the Circle B for two years, practically lapped my quarter-horse mare Ariel on our morning run the next day. Baby tried to spook him by leaping from a high rock outcropping but, like Wile E. Coyote, she missed completely.

I swear, that man rode like Apollo. I pulled up and watched his run across the valley, silhouetted by the rising sun, the river behind him. He urged Hot Spur like a cowboy in a movie, leaning forward in his saddle, flicking his reins across the huge stallion's withers, his hat pulled low on his head. By the time they returned to the barn, both he and his horse were red-cheeked and panting hard, their breath like shots of crystal mist in the frigid mountain air. Lordy. There's something about a man and his horse that gets me hot.

Richard almost missed his 7:30 A.M. ride into town in my brother Christian's Alouette helicopter, which he used for his daily commute.

"Told you he was a great tail man," Christian yelled at me over the whining turbine.

Richard laughed loudly and slapped him on the shoulder. I smiled and waved and once the chopper disappeared, Baby and I walked back to the house. I took my time doing my makeup and dressed with particular care in my best whipcord skirt, starched white stock shirt, lapis-lazuli earrings, doeskin jacket, and rough-out boots and headed in to assume my official duties as U.S. Marshal of Bennett's Fort.

The town had not changed from my childhood. Probably not from my father's childhood. Ticky-tacky souvenir and western-wear shops lined the main street. Cousin Buck's office sat atop the Silver Dollar Saloon where an Iowan could get a shot of truly rotgut whiskey and a watery beer for only five dollars. The Marshal's Office was across the street and down a few doors from the saloon.

Buck had said to meet him in the Golden Nugget Café.

The Golden Nugget hummed with customers, most of them retired couples now that school was back in session and all the families had returned to Des Moines and Dubuque and Denver. Buck was sitting at the counter eating breakfast and reading the morning paper. I cut through the crowd and greeted him warmly. Like Eli, he was big and burly and smelled like Castile soap.

"Why, hello there, Marshal." He put down his paper and gave me a hug. "Welcome to Bennett's Fort, Wind River Territory. Join me for a bite?"

Buck was eating all my favorite things for breakfast—blueberry pancakes, country sausage, fried eggs, lots of melted butter, and hot syrup.

"Just coffee, thanks." I regarded Buck's breakfast. "If I die before you do," I said, "I'm really going to be mad."

We were interrupted by the arrival of the sultry foreman of the Butterfield place. He slapped Cousin Buck on the back. "Mornin', Buck," he said.

"Dwight. Meet the new federal marshal. Marshal Bennett. Dwight Alexander. Walter Butterfield's factotum."

"Oh, yeah," Dwight said, smiling, not catching the insult. "I saw you the other day. You'd been meeting with Mrs. B."

Dwight Alexander was a young man with one thing on his mind. Sex. He had dusty blue eyes that looked semismart, just smart enough to find their way appreciatively and expertly around a female body, and full lips that curled shyly. He kept his thumbs hitched in the front pockets of his Levi's and drummed his fingers on his buttons which made my eyes refuse to stay above his belt line for very long. I knew I was looking at Lady Chatterley's Lover. Miami McCloud's counterpart. I didn't know where he'd been on Friday night but if he'd been upstairs with Pamela, I understood why she'd been putting on her lipstick for so long and why she might not have heard the shotgun blast. There'd been a whole lot of huffin' and puffin' going on at Rancho del Sol that night and not just on the dance floor.

"I'm glad we ran into each other, Mr. Alexander." It took all my self-control to keep my eyes on his face, not his drumming fingers. "I was going to call and see if I could come by and ask you a few questions, but now that you're here in town, maybe you wouldn't mind dropping by the office in a few minutes."

"I'd like that a lot, Sheriff Bennett," he said to my breasts.

"*Marshal* Bennett," I corrected him.

"Yeah. Marshal. I'd like that." He smiled as though we shared a secret. "I'll just have my breakfast and then I'll come down."

Cousin Buck settled up and we left. "I'd be willing to bet that boy has more illegitimate children in the West than Brigham Young," he said as we crossed the street. "I got Sarah off to boarding school just in time. She went out with him once when she'd just turned sixteen and he'd just got to town, before we knew anything much about him. Knocked her off her feet with his red Corvette and easy smile. Didn't bring her home until three o'clock in the morning and her whole neck was black with hickeys. Here we are." He held the door open to the U.S. Federal Marshal's Office and we stepped inside.

"Does the Justice Department know this office still exists?" I said.

"Of course," Buck said, offended. "They love this office. It's actually a district, and the U.S. Department of Justice considers it the Museum of the Western Branch of the U.S. Marshal Service. Just look at the walls—these are all authentic pictures of some of their most famous arrests of America's most notorious outlaws. There's the James Gang and the Hole-in-the-Wall Gang and the Elders and Billy the Kid."

"I don't think Billy the Kid was ever arrested, Buck," I said.

"Yep. He was. Just not for very long. This desk of yours, it's Wyatt Earp's actual desk from Dodge. His chair, too." Buck ran his hand lovingly across the smooth old wood. "You probably already know that you're joining a very exclusive fraternity, Lilly—there're only ninety-four marshals in the country. The Justice Department keeps the office looking fake, like a movie set, so it never occurs to anyone to think it's real, which is the way they want it. But every inch is as real as can be, including the bars on the cells. As a matter of fact, there've been a number of times, off season, when we've kept high-profile, high-risk federal prisoners here because this district is isolated and unknown. I've always been a deputy marshal and I hope you'll keep me on as one; of course you'll want to name a couple of your own."

All I could do was shake my head.

The door opened and a tall, slim man in his fifties entered. He wore a gray suit and a button-down shirt and a striped tie.

"Perfect timing," said Buck. "Lilly, meet Circuit Court Judge Bill Fullerton."

Judge Fullerton and I shook hands, and after exchanging a few pleasantries he swore me in, using Wyatt Earp's Bible, and then I, in turn, swore in Buck as my deputy. We did a little official business before they left and Dwight Alexander arrived.

"This place is pretty hokey," Dwight said. "You'd think they'd try to make it look a little realer."

Chapter Twenty-one

"Tell me, Dwight," I began once I'd settled into Marshal Earp's chair. "How did you happen to land in Bennett's Fort?"

Dwight Alexander, who had perched on the table across from me and circled one boot in the air in a relaxed manner, shrugged. He twisted and balled a gum wrapper in his fingers and I noticed he had a way of touching the corner of his lips with his tongue before he spoke. "Once I got out of college," he smiled over at me, "I went to Bennett College," he smiled again, "named after your great-grandfather, right?"

I nodded.

"And just in case you want to check up on me, you'll find I never did graduate but I went there for six years and my old man was getting on my case, so I dropped out and I didn't feel like going home and someone told me that Mr. Butterfield was looking for some help out at their place." He snorted derisively. "What a joke this job is. Foreman. All I have to look after is my vegetable garden and drive Mrs. B. to town. But don't get me wrong. I love it. Hard work and I don't agree. Anyhow, Mr. Butterfield and my old man knew each other in business or something, so I applied and got the job."

"How long ago was that?"

"About three years."

"How old are you, Dwight?"

"Twenty-six."

"Where were you last Friday night, Saturday morning, about one-thirty?"

He licked his lips again and twisted the paper. "I don't think I'd really better say."

"Why not?"

"I'd be compromising a young lady."

"Dwight, you might as well go ahead and tell me because I'm going to check up on you sooner or later."

"You going to arrest me? And keep me in your jailhouse?" His blue eyes held mine and one side of his mouth curled up. "I think I might like that."

"Where were you?"

"Well, actually I was just getting home about one-thirty. I got there just ahead of the cops. I'd been visiting Molly, the little blonde who works in the Golden Nugget Café. Maybe you saw her. She's a little young for me, though. I like older, more experienced women."

"Do you still drive a Corvette?"

"Yeah. How did you know that? Oh, sure, Old Buck told you. He's still sore about his daughter. Jeez, it was just an innocent little evening. You would have thought I'd—" Dwight stopped and closed his mouth. "Sorry, Sheriff. I meant to say he got awful heated up over our first date and she's a nice girl. She's been gone about since I got here and when she comes home for vacation Buck's got her scheduled up for things at the country club nonstop. She's all grown up now. She's a freshman at Stanford and a debutante and she didn't even ask me to be one of her escorts. And I'm a heck of a dancer."

"How was your relationship with Walter Butterfield?"

"Okay, I guess. I didn't see him much. Mostly he was loaded whenever he was home, so I cut him a wide berth. He reminded me too much of my dad. Fat, drunk, rich old fart with a mean streak as wide as the Rio Grande. We had a couple of run-ins over the way I'd dug an irrigation ditch, so I'd just 'Yassuh' him whenever I saw him. I didn't want to get into it with him. Besides he had a right to be mad.

What the hell does a boy from Grosse Pointe know about digging ditches anyway?"

"Did you shoot him?"

Dwight reddened and caught his breath. "Me? Hell no! I have a perfect setup, in case you hadn't noticed."

I stood up. "Thanks for stopping by, Dwight."

"You aren't going to arrest me?"

"Not today."

I didn't add that if I hadn't just met Richard, I might have jumped his bones.

✐ *Chapter Twenty-two*

Tuesday, early afternoon

*T*he lobby of Saint Mary's Psychiatric Institute was very quiet. I don't know why I always expect a psychiatric hospital to have muffled shrieks and screams coming from behind padlocked doors and wild-eyed psychos in straitjackets trying to escape, with starched-cap nurses and hypodermic needles in hot pursuit. These days mental hospitals are pretty much like everywhere else—undistinguished and indistinguishable. Ever since for profit got into the act and doctors started bending over for the insurance companies, Aetna and Cigna and their ilk decide whether you're nuts or not, sick or not; and, if you are, how long you have to get well. Medical care has little to do with anything. It all depends on what the numbers and the charts say, same as ancient times: cast the stones and read them.

"Good afternoon, is Dr. Cleveland in? I'm Lilly Bennett."

"Yes, Miss Bennett. I'll tell him you're here." She picked up her phone.

A hefty black woman swaggered by with a large ring of keys attached to her belt. The keys bounced menacingly on her huge hip. It made me feel better. I mean, I'm not saying it should all be like *A Nun's Story* or *Marat/Sade,* but I think mental fireworks can liven up a place. If a mental hospital is like anywhere else, why bother to go? I had a friend who, if he couldn't get his doctor to check him into Saint Mary's for the weekend, took a suite at the Grand. But he loved the hospital best.

"Much more interesting people," he said. "Food's as good and you are treated like a baby. Just check your problems at the door and then they give you a lot of great drugs and you can just hang out for a few days. No drugs at the hotel."

The doorway to Mack's sparse offices opened and he limped into sight, leaning on his cane, a slight surrender to the rheumatoid arthritis that was slowly wrecking his body. His hair was so light a shade of gray it was almost white. Deep smile lines creased his tanned face.

Mack Cleveland and I had known each other all our lives and usually when I saw him I wondered if I should have fought harder for him when I had the chance, before my red-haired friend Joanna bewitched him and he panted down the aisle after her twenty years ago. But today I thought about how glad I was that I hadn't. I thought about seeing Richard Jerome at Walter Butterfield's funeral at three and meeting up with him again later.

"Miss Bennett." Mack smiled and bowed slightly and waved the way with his arm. "Please do come in." An air of opulence accompanied him, as though he and his manners had been beamed in from turn-of-the-century England. "Would you like some herbal tea? Or perhaps a little cappuccino?"

"Cappuccino please, Mack." I kissed him on the cheek on my way into his office. "I never realized that King Edward's throne room had a linoleum floor and a metal desk and metal armchairs."

"Metal is very in this year. At least the seats are padded, along with some of the walls," he grinned. "I keep saying, 'Next year we'll fix up the offices,' and I'm sure one of these years we will." Mack sat down heavily and hooked his cane over the back of his swivel chair. His wheelchair, a racer with no arms and big canted wheels, sat over in the corner, empty and facing the wall.

We made small talk until the secretary brought in my cappuccino and his pot of tea and then closed the door behind her.

"You wouldn't by any chance be here in regard to Miss Butterfield?" Mack said.

"I need to see her."

"Do you have permission?" He poured a stream of green-gold tea into a yellow-and-blue Limoges cup.

"No," I said, "and I know I'm putting you in a difficult spot, but legally you're the one who ultimately controls her accessibility. You and I both know the minute she was moved to your care, she officially ceased to exist. No one will know I saw her but you and the unit's staff."

"Why do you need to talk to her? She's extremely unstable."

"She's always been unstable." I sipped my cappuccino and tried to blot the scalded milk and powdered cocoa off my lips as skillfully as Pamela had blotted the tomato juice off hers on Saturday morning. "The whole family's unstable. But, in spite of her confession, Mack, I don't believe she shot her father and I want to ask her a couple of questions that will confirm that fact."

"Legally, I can't let you see Christine without permission from the judge and her lawyer, Paul Decker, although I don't think he'd mind. It's her family who's insisted that she remain isolated," Mack said, "until the doctors finish evaluating her, which I estimate will take ten or fifteen years. I'd say Christine Butterfield's in the system to stay."

"How is she?" I said.

"Well, she was extremely agitated when she came in and we had to restrain her."

"Physically or chemically?" I asked, fighting the image of people climbing the walls, slathering like dogs, their eyes rolled back in their heads so only the whites showed, being dragged down and hog-tied with heavy leather straps by big burly attendants who are saying, "Now, now, Mr. So-and-so, you don't want to be a bad boy, do you? You don't want us to use the you-know-what?" While all the while huge hypodermics are being prepared.

"A little of both, actually. The substance-abuse team that took over when she arrived had to use some padded restraints and keep her in seclusion for a few hours until the Haldol got her calmed down and stabilized. Since then, we've kept her pretty even, just a few doses of a light antidepressant. She's on Trofanil, I think." Mack tamped tobacco into a pipe, struck a match, and puffed the pipe into existence.

"Her plea was filed yesterday morning," I said. "Not guilty by reason of insanity."

Mack nodded. "Naturally. And, I might add, they're quite right. The district attorney's psychiatrist has already seen her, so now that the observation period has begun, we have to demonstrate extreme diligence in keeping her as drug-free as possible. She's hurting. Badly."

"Why did she confess?" I said. "Do you think someone put her up to it or was it spontaneous?"

"How much do you know about Christine?" Mack asked.

I considered his question for a minute, sorting through what I knew and what Ellen had told me. "Well," I said, "she's been a heavy drug and alcohol abuser since she was sixteen. She's married to a man who is addicted to gambling and probably to drugs as well and who uses her for money, which has kept her in the position of depending on her father, not her husband, for her financial support. And I know that her father has been abusing her sexually since she was twelve or thirteen or so and she's always been completely lost. And that's about it."

Mack listened carefully, weighing what I had said. He fiddled a little with his pipe before speaking. "Christine wants to be punished. She confessed to killing her father as her way of confessing her sin that she participated in the incest. And probably also that she had thoughts of killing him. She is a borderline personality, sometimes psychotic, sometimes neurotic. Manic-depressive. Taken to an extreme, this is the type of disorder that leads to multiple personalities."

"Do you think Christine has multiple personalities?" It was hard for me to accept that I was having this conversation about a woman who was not only a peer but a childhood acquaintance. I kept thinking, But I knew her. I knew her family. When was all this going on? I was over at their house all the time. Incidents and instances flashed through my mind but I couldn't see in any of them behavior that would indicate that Christine's mind was dividing itself and separating from her body.

"We've seen no evidence so far but the heavy drug use can mask any number of latent conditions. It's quite likely that the condition exists, though."

I felt so sorry. So sad. It wasn't as though we were having a conversation that I hadn't ever had before. Maybe not identical circumstances but certainly similar. I guess because it was someone I knew it brought the tragedy more to life. Christine was not some drugged-out stranger who I could convince myself probably deserved it in the first place. "What's her frame of mind now? Is she lucid? Can she answer questions?"

"Well," Mack's voice expressed uncertainty. "She's been in detox for over seventy-two hours, so she's pretty mad and depressed and her antidepressants are at the minimum. I would describe her as erratic at best."

"Just five minutes," I said. "I'll be careful."

I followed him into an adjoining consultation room that was only slightly more comfortable than his office.

"Wait here," Mack said. "I'll bring her in. Let me remind you of one thing: Give her your understanding, but do not give her your sympathy."

"No problem."

Christine ambled in in a soft yellow running suit with yellow-and-white-checked trim. Her eyes were red and swollen from crying and her skin was mottled. The frizzy Mohawk was brushed out and she didn't have on any of that tough-looking makeup. She already looked a lot healthier than she had on Friday night, even though I knew she didn't feel it.

Mack escorted her by one arm and gently helped her get seated across the conference table from me and lit her cigarette with a gold lighter from his pocket.

A bull-necked, muscle-bound attendant stood directly behind her.

"Do you want a cup of tea, Christine?" Mack asked.

"No, thanks." She seemed lamblike. "Hi," she said to me. We made eye contact for a split second before she focused on her hands.

As soon as I saw Christine, I wasn't sorry for her anymore. I knew instantly that she'd been in detox before and knew the ropes. Knew the pathways to evoke sympathy. Could summon the dazzling powers of manipulation that experienced addicts keep honed to such unique perfection. Looking at her, I got mad. I know she was molested by her father and that's horrible. But believe me, everybody's got a story, and hers was nothing compared to many, and here she was devoting her life to complaining about the raw deal she got. She had lots of money, no responsibility, a good education, enough to eat, and good health before she began to wreck it, and look what she did with all of that. Right down the toilet. Plus, as far as she was concerned, it was everyone else's fault.

"Christine," I began, "I know you feel lousy and I appreciate your seeing me. This will just take a couple of minutes."

She shrugged like a four-year-old child being scolded. Come on, Christine, I thought, get ahold of yourself.

"Ellen doesn't believe that you murdered your father. Did you really do it?"

She reached one shaky hand up and tugged on her hair the way she had at the party, pulling the top curls higher, and then she inhaled deeply and let the air out as though she'd breathed her last. Her shoulders drooped and her eyes slid away in despair. Tears began pouring down her cheeks.

"Christine?" I said.

"I don't know. I'm pretty sure I did. I said I did. I don't understand why I'm here. Can you help me get out, Lilly? I'm not a drug addict."

"Christine, have you done a lot of hunting?"

"Hunting? What do you mean? Like on horses?"

"No. I mean bird hunting, ducks, geese, pheasant."

She shook her head. "I don't think so. Maybe. I don't remember."

"Well, you must be a pretty good shot. You got your father practically right between the eyes."

"Yeah." Christine smiled at the memory of her father's gruesome demise.

"Was the gun cabinet open when you got into your father's study?"

"Gun cabinet?"

"You know, the one over next to your father's desk," I said, purposely placing the case on the opposite side of the room from where it actually was located. "The one where you got the gun to shoot him."

"Oh, yeah. Yeah. It was open."

"So, you went over and took the gun out of it and shot him?"

"Yeah. That's pretty much the way it happened."

"What was he doing while you were getting the gun and loading it and aiming and all?"

Christine thought about that, and as the time passed seemed about to express a couple of possible scenarios and finally said, "He was just sitting there. Working."

I couldn't help laughing. "Working? In the middle of his birthday party he went to his desk and sat and watched you load a shotgun and worked?"

Christine nodded and chuckled. "Yeah. Yeah. Pretty much. Crazy, huh?"

"He didn't say anything like, 'What are you doing?' or 'Please don't shoot me?' "

Christine turned serious. She leaned across the table. "Lilly, will you help me get out of here? I'm not an addict. It's ridiculous that they're saying I am. Would you ask Ellen to get me out?" Her face twisted with agitation. "Call Rory and tell him to come get me."

"You're wrong, Christine," I said. "You are an addict. And you need to stay here until you're well."

"Fuck you," she said derisively. "You always were a Goody Two-shoes. You and that loser of a sister of mine."

"Come on, Christine," Mack took her arm. "Time to go."

"I did shoot my father!" she shouted from the door where Mack turned her over to a nurse. "I should have shot him the day I was born."

I thanked Mack and left Saint Mary's for Walter Butterfield's funeral. As I drove the short distance to the cemetery, I thought about multiple personality disorder. I'd had a number of run-ins with it and knew that Christine, some Christine or other, could have murdered Walter and been entirely justified in doing so.

Chapter Twenty-three

Tuesday afternoon

Just like our three country clubs, Roundup has three cemeteries: Mount Carmel, which is Catholic; Emanuel, Jewish; and Wind River, Protestant, which around here means either Episcopal or Lutheran. We don't have too many Presbyterians or Methodists. No particular reason. We just don't. There are maybe three or four dozen families that are Southern Baptists, mostly Black. None of the cemeteries is very pretty or located on what could even vaguely be interpreted as prime real estate, because since its founding, no one in Roundup has ever been willing to part with a piece of land that could support a couple of head of cattle or render a few barrels of oil or gas. So all three graveyards lie on lifeless, godless, wind-swept rocky outcroppings and give the impression that their deceased are trapped in a restless, bone-chilling, teeth-rattling sleep, wondering what the hell they did to deserve dying in Wyoming.

The Wind River Cemetery spreads across a barren mesa top. A tall wrought-iron fence incongruously surrounds the place, providing protection from neither snow nor wind nor support for any living thing such as climbing roses or hedgerows. The fence was originally put there in the early 1900s to keep coyotes from digging up the graves. I don't think that's an imminent danger anymore but around here, one never knows.

Also, the cemetery is equidistant between Saint Mary's Psychiatric Hospital and the Roundup Country Club, which makes it convenient for the club members, who usually drop dead either in the country club bar or at Saint Mary's while drying out.

When I got there for Walter's funeral, a pretty good-sized crowd had already assembled, maybe fifty or sixty people. Not a bad turnout but not too great either. From the looks of some of the attendees, the bartender at the country club had said to Walter's unshaven, drunken, drooling gin-rummy crones who passed their days staggering between the bar and the card tables, draping themselves over each other, that if they would go to the funeral, he'd give them two free rounds. It was clear none of them had been out in daylight for a long time. They all were pasty-white and wore dark glasses and kept putting up their arms and hands to block the sun from their faces. Cringing would really be a better description of what they were doing. The country club ought to buy a van for occasions like this. Keep the members off the roads.

The small parking lot was full, and cars had pulled along the edges of the curved drives around the wide grassy areas where families' plots huddled. I drove around for about five minutes vaguely looking for my two-and-two taillights. I was certain that the murderer would be on hand today, just as I was certain that the murderer hadn't necessarily been driving the car whose taillights I'd seen. Let me correct a myth: The murderer usually returns to the scene of a crime, but does not always attend the funeral of his victim. But today, I knew he or she would.

Large marble and granite mausoleums with names carved forever over bolted steel-door entrances had been erected throughout the cemetery. And there were some beautiful statues of angels, some with their enormous carved wings unfurled, taking off joyously for heaven, others with their wings draped in sorrow, a small huddled figure concealed within their protection. It's interesting how survivors memorialize those they've lost. I've always thought it took a lot more guts to put up a statue of a happy angel jumping up to heaven than one crying. I know. I know. We're all going to have a big, fine old time in Heaven and all those left on the ground should be happy that that person's suffering is over. Well, we all know it's simply not that easy. If you really loved someone, it is virtually impossible to be happy that you're never ever going to see him again. I've seen more death in my line of work than most people and believe me, it's not usually a great thing. Of course, there are exceptions. Walter Butterfield, for instance.

I waved at Chief Detective Jack Lewis. He and his little sand-crab assistant leaned against Jack's squad car. The little guy had a video camera that he was filming all the cars and people with. Jack barely acknowledged me. Could scarcely raise his hand even slightly. I knew he wanted to give me the finger. Well, the feeling was mutual. I pulled in and parked behind my father's Jaguar, put on my cowboy hat, and walked over to join my family.

I kissed Mother hello and Daddy, and Christian's elegant wife, my sister-in-law, Mimi. She was tall and sleek and utterly charming. I really liked her. We didn't grow people like Mimi in Roundup, they had to be imported. Christian had met her in Chicago, where she'd been the city's top debutante and a model, and if she ever thought Roundup was the end of the world, she never let on. She had on a sort of palomino-colored cashmere suit. I'm sure it was Armani, it was so luxurious and fit so perfectly.

"Can you believe your eyes?" my mother said, referring to the Butterfield family monument, which rose up before us like the Arc de Triomphe. It must have been fifty feet high with the name

BUTTERFIELD

carved in gigantic letters across the transom.

"The only thing missing is L'Étoile."

"How long has this been here?" I asked.

"He finished it about fifteen years ago," my father said.

"Who else is buried under it?"

"No one. He's the first."

"He certainly was consistent," my mother concluded the conversation. She smoothed the gray kid gloves that matched her suit. "Cousin Hank is doing the service. I saw him as we arrived."

Cousin Hank was in truth The Very Right Reverend Henry Caulfield Bennett, bishop of the Wind River Diocese for the Episcopal Church. He was tall and handsome and dignified, with lots of white hair, and he took his job very seriously until rodeo season. Cousin Hank had three Champ Bronc Buster belt buckles.

"Oh, good," I said. "I'll look forward to seeing him. I'm going up on that rise to watch the goings-on."

"Oh, why, Lilly?" my mother bitched. "Why can't you just stand here with your family for a change?"

"Because I'm working, Mother," I said patiently. "So don't spend your energy getting all riled up about it."

She shook her head. "I just wish you'd settle down."

Mimi and my father both laughed.

"I'll see you guys later," I said.

"Well, make sure you keep that hat on," Mother wrapped up. "We have simply no ozone left at all and this sun will absolutely wreck your skin." Tough love.

From the small rise off to the side, I could see the full Butterfield funeral layout. Walter's grave, a couple of feet forward of the center of the central arch, yawned deep and open under the cloudless sky. Wet burlap bags covered the heaps of dirt. On either side of the grave were six white wooden pedestals, a dozen all together, each with a gigantic bouquet of white roses. Four gold-painted Chinois chairs, the bamboo kind rented for gala fund-raising dinners, formed a semicircle around the foot end of the grave. This was where the family would sit. They had arrived while I'd been talking with my family and now marched in a slow procession from the road.

Two young acolytes in white surplices and red cassocks, one carrying a large gold cross and the other swinging incense, led Cousin Hank, who could only be described as spectacularly opulent in gloriously weighty cream-and-red satin vestments encrusted with wrist-thick gold braid. His red bishop's miter and solid-gold pectoral cross finished him off to perfection. Hank was Ultra High Church. He could afford to be. As Mother said, "If one is going to enter the priesthood, it is so helpful to have money of one's own." Right again.

Walter's casket followed Bishop Bennett, a large bronze rig heaped with white roses carried by funeral-home employees, since Walter didn't have any what could be called close friends. Not close enough to be pallbearers anyway.

The family followed: Pamela, Walter, Jr., Ellen, and Roland Tewkesbury. They took their seats around Walter's feet and Cousin Hank stood at what would have been Walter's head if he'd had one.

I spotted Richard hurrying across the lawn. He looked extra sharp in a navy pin-striped suit, white shirt, red-and-yellow tie, cowboy boots, dark glasses, and hat. He stopped and looked around and then looked over where I was and headed straight for me.

"Hi," he whispered and took off his hat and kissed my cheek.

"Hi," I whispered back. We held hands for a second.

A moment later Miami, whom it took me a second to recognize, because she had her hair pulled into a sedate ponytail and wore a black trench coat and dark glasses, appeared quietly at Richard's side. He squeezed her hand, too.

Bishop Hank surveyed the congregation and then said something to Pamela, who nodded. "SHALL WE BEGIN?" he shouted over the wind.

Silence fell.

"Lord, let me know mine end," he projected the beautiful ancient words in his prairie-trained voice.

I studied the family. The will had been read just before the funeral and I wondered if everyone was happy. From their looks and behavior, it didn't appear as though Walter's Last Will and Testament had held any nasty surprises. He didn't appear to have left the whole shebang to the Hare Krishnas or some other wacky gang.

Pamela and Ellen and Roland and the son, Wally, wearing his Connecticut prep school tie and blazer, dirty khaki pants, run-down shoes, and a Big Attitude, comported themselves in hushed, dignified, mournful quiet for about the first thirty seconds of the ceremony and then Pam began to bawl loudly. I'm sure it was because of the ridiculous getup she was wearing. It looked like one of Christian Lacroix's jokes. The black suit was made from suede, kid, taffeta, velvet, chiffon, and three different kinds of lace, with hot-pink touches: feathers, passementerie stitching, and the crinoline peplum lining of the tight jacket. The suit was enough to make anyone cry. She accidently blew her nose through her point d'esprit lace veil.

"Remember thy servant, Walter, O Lord." Bishop Hank spoke louder, reluctant to let Pam hog all the attention. But he was up against a pro. She turned up the volume. It was like listening to the American Gladiators of Noise. People began to titter.

Wally, possibly the only truly bereaved person in the place, looked ill at ease with his mother's antics and traded glances with Roland Tewkesbury, who made little frowns and moues of his lips and understanding nods of his head. He put his arm around the boy's shoulders and squeezed him and the boy shrugged him off.

"Unto Almighty God we commend the soul of our Brother Walter departed," Hank droned on and on. Thirty minutes had passed.

"God," I said to Richard. "What is Hank doing? This is the longest funeral I've ever been to. It's getting hot out here." The incense thickened the air.

"Maybe he's charging her by the word."

Not a single person looked sorry except Miami. Her grief had almost diminished her physically, almost made her small and vulnerable. Richard handed her his handkerchief and she slumped against him like a child. A six-foot-two child.

Ellen lifted her dark glasses to squint at her watch while Hank begged the Lord to take her father's soul. I'm quite sure He would not and all of us wished he'd quit trying.

Then, a miracle. Pamela glanced up in our direction and saw Miami. A storm cloud crossed her face and she turned and spoke angry words to Roland, who shook his head. She looked at her watch and then looked at Hank and snapped her fingers. "HEY," she said and when he reached the end of the phrase, paused, and graced her condescendingly with his eyes, she drew her fingers across her neck and said loudly, "The End. Wrap it up."

The Very Right Reverend Henry Bennett was speechless. He had met his match.

"I'm sorry," Miami said to us. "I can't stand this anymore. I have to leave."

"I'll take you to your car," I told her.

We crossed the dried-out lawn, through blinding spotlights caused by reflections off Dwight Alexander's mirrored sunglasses. He leaned on Pamela's black Mercedes-Benz limousine smoking a cigarette with one hand, and drumming his fingers on his fly with the other. He pointedly ignored Miami.

"I'm sorry to ask you about this right now, Miami, but I need to know. Did you go to the reading of the will?"

She nodded. Tears poured down her cheeks from behind her glasses and she wiped them away with a hankie that had a small picture of her and her horse Rex, rearing, embroidered on it. "It was very, very difficult, as you can imagine. Being in Roland Tewkesbury's office with Pamela and Ellen. They all hate me. I wasn't going to go, but my attorney said I had to. Walter was true to his word, he did what he said he was going to do. He left me four blocks of downtown Roundup and paid off my condo, which he didn't need to do." She broke down. "I didn't need or want anything from him. I just want him. I can't believe I'm never going to see him again."

I asked about the balance of the estate.

"Oh, the standard. He left half the estate to Pamela and a quarter each to the girls. He gave Ellen the ranch and Christine the house in town, but Pamela has life tenancy on both properties. No bequests or anything like that. Walter wasn't very philanthropically inclined."

No kidding.

"Bye."

Miami climbed into her car and closed the door.

I could see Pamela approaching her car at a quick clip; Roland and Wally rushed to keep up with her. "That goddamn circus tramp is wrecking everything," she yelled at them over her shoulder. "And what the hell was that damn priest doing? Running for president?"

"You said you wanted the same service as the Duke of Windsor had," Roland puffed. His face was bright red, a combination of sunburn, windburn, and exercise.

"You said Episcopalians were fast. That's why I chose him. I thought it'd be maybe fifteen, twenty minutes. Christ, I feel like I've spent my whole life at this stupid funeral. It's too goddamn hot. Get me outta here." Dwight closed the door behind her.

I started to call to Ellen but she had climbed into her own car, slammed the door, started the engine, and was peeling out before I could even get the words out of my mouth.

No reception following the service had been scheduled.

I wandered back over to where Richard had joined my family. He and Christian were laughing about something.

"I can't believe there wasn't even a brief eulogy for Walter," Christian said.

"I can," my father replied.

"They didn't even sing 'Happy Trails to You,' " I said.

"Why would they?" Richard asked.

"We always sing it at our funerals," my mother told him.

"You do?" he said.

"Lilly," my mother said, "do you know Richard Jerome? He is the most charming dinner partner in the Rocky Mountain West."

"I know."

"Richard," she said, "do you remember the Saunders girl I was telling you about?"

"Yes, I do."

"Well, she's back in town and I'll arrange for you to meet. Maybe one evening next week?"

"Forget the Saunders girl, Mother," I said. "Why didn't you introduce *me* to Richard?"

"Oh, he's far too nice for you," she said. I knew she didn't mean it. It was just her way of trying to bully me back into the Junior League. Into a life that had meaning to her.

"I'm sorry, Katharine," Richard said to my mother. "I'd love to have dinner next week, but I'm afraid the Saunders girl or any other new girl is out. I'm seeing someone."

Mother's face fell and she looked at me as if it was all my fault. For once she was right. "Oh, I'm so sorry," she said to Richard. "No, that's not what I mean."

"Kate means it's nice to see you, Richard, and please bring your lady friend to dinner sometime soon," my father said.

"Yes," Mother smiled. "Is she a Roundup girl?"

"As a matter of fact, she is."

"Really." I knew exactly what Mother was thinking: If it's not the Saunders girl, and not someone I've introduced you to, then she can't possibly be anyone at all.

I couldn't stand it anymore. "It's me, Mother."

"My God," she gasped. "It's a miracle."

Truly.

⤳ Chapter Twenty-four

"You're late," I said out of my car window to Eli, who climbed out of his dusty truck as I was leaving the cemetery. "And you really missed a show."

"I know. I've been busy. I just came by here so I could catch you." Eli was a little grumpy. "You ought to get a phone in your car, you know."

"I have a phone in my car, Eli. I just haven't been in it."

"Where're you going?"

"The office at Bennett's Fort," I said, "and then back to the ranch. Why?"

"On your way home, meet me out at the top of Wittier Gulch for a couple of minutes. There's something I want to show you."

The Wittier Gulch Mesa, out toward Bennett's Fort, was a desolate, hard spot despoiled by power and telephone wires strung in the days when their prominent display boasted a ranch's or town's modernity and affluence. It was also one of the highest points in the Wind River Valley. Dozens of mesas—large, multi-layered sandstone tabletops—surrounded by deep twisting arroyos, textured the high, arid plain. In the spring, the arroyos overflowed with water from the mountain-snow runoff, sweeping away more rock, but by this time of the year they were dry, ready for winter.

It was late afternoon, and the mesa gave off a quiet, mystical aura. The brown prairie grasses looked pink in the afternoon light as I bounced along the dirt road to the mesa top. Finally I crested the hill and there, sitting among some scrubby trees alongside a power pole, was a large white GMC Step-Van, with a Roundup Gas & Electric logo on its side and so many antennas on its roof that a tiny bird could not perch. The Butterfield's Rancho del Sol was visible in the valley.

When I turned off the motor of my car, the rear door of the van opened and Elias stepped out. Brick-red Roundup Gas & Electric overalls strained around his stomach. He had a huge grin on his face and bowed deeply. "Welcome to my labor-a-tory," he said.

"Jesus Christ, Eli. Where'd you get this stuff? NORAD?"

"Here and there. I told you I know some people who know some people."

"I guess you do. I'm sure glad they're on our side. What exactly was it you did for the government?"

He ignored my question. "As soon as I get the dishes up, Rancho del Sol and all its communications—telephone, fax, verbal conversation—will be under surveillance. Maybe another hour or two. I wanted to put in video room monitors but I didn't have time. Did you get the warrant?"

I nodded. "This is impressive wiretapping, Elias."

"Welcome to private enterprise."

No one would ever suspect Eli Bennett—Roundup's big friendly pacifist cowboy eccentric—of treachery. But there was a dark side to Elias I never wanted to delve into too deeply. Down the road from us in Colorado was the international headquarters of a mercenary army. They weren't bivouacked there or anything. They kept in touch through "Mercenary Diary," a newsletter filled with grotesque pictures of people, usually somewhere in Africa, hanging by wires that passed through their heads via their ears, and articles about how to blow up airliners. These soldiers of fortune who raced to the world's trouble spots and fought for the highest bidder were misfits, survivalists, and psychos. Those who stayed behind engaged in defense industry espionage to keep the most advanced technology and equipment available for the troops.

I knew Eli wasn't associated with this group's activities but I'd seen a stack of the newsletters in his office and I knew he kept himself abreast of the movements of that underworld of losers. And I knew he could deliver skulduggery's most complex apparatus at the drop of a hat.

Winters are long in Wyoming. Some people have too much time on their hands.

"Let me ask you a question, Eli," I said. "Is any of this equipment stolen?"

"No."

"Any of it illegal?"

"No. Not as long as you've got the warrant."

"You swear to God?"

"I do."

"Okay," I said. "Well, then raise your right hand."

I swore him in as my deputy and he was so happy and excited his eyes filled with tears.

"I've already been all through the house and hanging the radar dish won't be any problem," he explained enthusiastically. "Nobody'll notice. You could hang a B-52 up here and no one would notice. Besides"—he held up one of two small black screen dishes—"these are almost invisible."

"What do you mean, you've 'already been all through the house'?"

"That's why I didn't come to the funeral," Elias said. "After Pamela left, I went down and rang the bell and said I was with RG and E and that I was there for a gas inspection and had to take meter readings on the whole house. So the maid turned me loose and I put mikes all over the place." He waved his arms around for emphasis. "I'll be out here for a few more hours until I get everything working right. What do you have on for tomorrow?"

"My only scheduled appointment is with Roland Tewkesbury at the *Morning News* tomorrow afternoon," I said.

"You mean Miss Havisham's wedding cake?" Elias said. "Tewkesbury always reminds me of *Night of the Living Dead*. You want to wash your hands after you touch him."

"Oh? I'll keep that in mind. I met him at the party last Friday night but I don't think I touched him."

"If you had, you'd remember."

I walked back over to my Jeep and opened the door and leaned on the seat. It had been a long day. "I need for you to check backgrounds on four people: Miami McCloud, she's the trick rider at the rodeo."

"I know who she is," Elias said, taking a small notepad out of one of his jumpsuit's jillion pockets. "She's got the Lamborghini."

"Right," I said impatiently. I was anxious to get going and peeved that everyone seemed to know more about everybody than I did. "She was also Walter Butterfield's mistress."

"Oh, yeah. Everybody knows that."

"Well, I'll bet *everybody* doesn't know she's a transsexual."

"What's that?" Elias said.

"For God's sake, Eli, you're almost fifty years old. Don't you know anything? That means she used to be a man." I was really getting ticked.

"You don't have to yell at me because I don't know what a transsexual is, Lilly. Frankly, I find it rather refreshing that I don't know. And you're right, I didn't know Miami used to be a man. Wow." Elias was shocked. "That is something."

"I'm sorry," I said. "I didn't mean to hurt your feelings but I'm tired and I want to get this day wrapped up so I can go home and be with Richard. I know it sounds stupid, but I am totally obsessed with him."

"That's nice," Elias said. "He's a nice guy. So who else do you want me to check out?"

"An insurance agent in Little Budapest named Carl Rosak and a Roundup National Bank Junior VP Michael Gryczkowski. Little Budapest branch."

"Who're they?" Elias looked up from his pad.

"You're going to like this," I smiled. "Pamela Butterfield's maiden name is Ramona Gryczkowski. She went to Billy the Kid High School and she and Carl Rosak were sweethearts. She got pregnant and abandoned her baby, named Michael, with her parents and took off and eventually ended up as Mrs. Walter Butterfield. Rosak and Gryczkowski both seem pretty straight but their motive for blackmail is impeccable."

"God." Eli scribbled furiously on the little pad. "This is really cool." He looked up. "Who else?"

"Dwight Alexander."

"You mean the Butterfields' hand?"

"Yup."

"What'd he do?"

"Maybe nothing. But he and Pamela are lovers and I'd just like to know more about him."

"Pamela Butterfield and Dwight Alexander are lovers?" Elias said. "God! This is great."

I couldn't help but laugh. "That's it," I said and reached around and pulled on my jacket and gloves, as the air had begun to cool. "Can I bring you a sandwich or something?"

"Nah. I brought a pizza. I'll stick it in the microwave." He pointed through the truck's open double doors to a kitchenette toward the front where a full-sized microwave sat on top of a regular refrigerator. "I could live in here for months. If you want, I'll keep Baby for you. I got her her own chair."

Eli proudly indicated three director's chairs, each with a name stenciled on its back: "Captain Kirk," "Marshal Lilly" and "Baby," where the terrier now stood on her back feet while she pawed the computer keyboard.

"How much did all this cost you?" I asked.

"Not as much as operating my own helicopter, like some people in the family." Eli had always been defensive about the fact that he'd decided not to join the Establishment like Christian, so he was always taking pot shots at him.

I started my engine and whistled for Baby who, as usual, ignored me. Eli went in and picked her up and handed her through the car window. "Where did you get the truck?" I asked. "This looks like an actual RG and E truck and coveralls."

"They are. I called Bob Baldwin, you know, the president of RG and E, and told him we were making a movie on the ranch and needed one of his trucks to sit in the background to make this one particular scene authentic. The overalls were his idea in case the movie director wanted to have a couple of guys working on lines or something. He wanted to give me a truck with a cherry-picker rig which, believe me, would have been helpful in hanging the dishes, but you need two guys to run 'em."

Chapter Twenty-five

Tuesday night

I was glad to get home. I fed Baby and then went upstairs and lit the fire in my bedroom. The air had turned cool but, to tell the truth, I'll find any excuse to have a fire, especially in my bedroom, which is particularly cozy. A large pale-pink-and-white rag rug covers the wide plank floor which my great-grandmother had painted white and it has always been kept that way. A down comforter with a white damask cover adorns my king-sized bed and large soft pillows in pink-and-white antique linen cases, some decorated with bouquets of trailing satin ribbons and satin flower buds, lean against the painted headboard. The bed sits against one wall, and on the walls to the right and left of it, french doors with simple, white muslin curtains lead to small balconies. There are two wide armchairs with ottomans and a chaise, all covered in old-fashioned floral wool. The rough granite fireplace is opposite the bed.

The dog, her stomach full, lay down in front of the fire and let out a long, deep sigh. Her daily toil was done, her job complete. She was exhausted.

She slept soundly through the local news while I did my exercises and through CNN while I took my bath. By the time I saw the landing lights of Christian's chopper, with Richard Jerome aboard, I was in the kitchen, sipping whiskey and mixing chopped tomatoes, onions, cucumbers, and giant capers into a salad and thinking how fine life was.

Cooking brings me enormous happiness and occasional culinary satisfaction and success. I got spoiled in Santa Bianca where life's beauties, including superior food and wine, are everyone's priority and the fishes and fruits and vegetables are the freshest imaginable and the table settings are as pretty as the food. Why people buy, on purpose, food that is pre-prepared or has chemicals or preservatives or NutraSweet, escapes me. Well, maybe NutraSweet if you're a diabetic but, good Lord, frozen meals loaded with BHT and *wrapped in plastic?* Give me a break. The only carcinogens I ingest on purpose are in wine, bacon, and sausage. That's it. Well, occasionally a bologna-and-cheese sandwich. I do admit to having more fat in my diet than I should, but it's all natural.

Anyhow, this evening's dinner was simple—grilled salmon with Celestina's green chili pesto, salad, rice with cilantro and piñon nuts, warm buttered tortillas, and California chardonnay. Very healthy.

While the helicopter roared down and settled in the meadow, the phone rang. It was Richard.

"We've had a couple of things come up that need some attention," he said. "I'm sorry I didn't call you sooner, but I've been in the same meeting since five o'clock. I don't think I'm going to make it out there in time for dinner."

"Shoot," I said. "Do you think you'll be able to get out here at all tonight?"

"I wouldn't count on it. But I'll call you as soon as I know what I'm doing."

"No problem," I said. "I'll be here."

"Thanks for understanding. Bye."

"Bye-bye."

We hung up.

Shit.

I was absolutely devastated. Crushed. Désolée. I knew he was telling the truth and I know things come up and there's nothing you can do about them and I know that mature people recognize that fact and accept it and let it roll off them and move forward. But. Shit.

I smeared some green chili pesto onto a tortilla, rolled it up, and looked out the window while I ate. Then I refilled my whiskey glass, put some popcorn in the microwave, and stored the salad in the icebox next to the Scottish salmon steaks that were so fresh you could still smell the icy water of the loch. That's always my first reaction at the first sign of trouble: Eat and drink, as much and as quickly as possible. Remember after President Reagan was shot and Nancy Reagan got extra thin? She said, "I've just been too nervous and worried to eat." Oh, what I'd do for that kind of reaction.

I made three more rolled-up tortillas, put them on a tray next to my drink and popcorn, went up to my room, restoked the fire, and got in bed and watched television. I turned off the lights and went to sleep about ten and then, sometime during the night, Richard crawled into bed next to me and we snuggled up and I was so, so happy.

Wednesday morning

We wakened at five-thirty. Stars carpeted the black sky and the lone sound in the cold frosty air was the Wind River flowing majestically in the distance, but you had to listen very carefully to hear its smooth murmur. We lay in bed and, unwilling to break the spell, whispered, even though there was no one to hear us. When we got up and pulled on our riding clothes, we tiptoed down the stairs and out the door into the exquisite, magical world before dawn. The air left us breathless and shivering inside our heavy sheepskin jackets.

The horses' hooves made sure, solid sounds on small rocks in the road as we guided them past the mowed hay fields, spotting the outline of an occasional forgotten bale in the moonlight, toward the upper meadows where, a few days earlier, the wranglers had begun the annual ritual of assembling the herd. By the time we crested the hill and paused to look down into the open, gentle valley, dawn had begun and a still morning mist had lain down on the wide backs of the inky-black cattle, soothing them. The brilliant red-orange flames of the cook's fire reflected off the lake. Illuminated cutouts of cowhands moved around the fire's warmth. We could hear the youth and confidence, the sureness and strength and masculinity of their voices but not their words.

It was a scene I'd been a part of since the day I was born—the open space, the patient, well-trained cutting horses and creaking saddle leather, the friendly cowboys, the coffee that smells good and tastes awful, the big sky. Life's backstage has always appealed to me more than the spotlight, and dawn at the roundup is in the same exclusive brotherhood as the squad room at three-thirty in the morning.

What was different about this scene on this particular morning was that I was sharing it for the first time in my life. Richard seemed to fit in everywhere. He was as relaxed and comfortable and properly fitted beside me, gazing over the meadow, as if he were one of my brothers or my father and had been sitting there forever.

"Do you like to camp?" Richard said.

"I absolutely hate it," I answered.

He laughed. "Let's go get a cup of that terrible so-called coffee your so-called cook makes. Then I've got to head to town."

We descended the hill slowly and quietly and helped the wranglers devour thick, crispy slices of Circle B bacon and fried eggs and steaming hot, golden baking-powder biscuits with butter and strawberry jam before continuing on our daily tasks. They to the roundup, Richard to the opera, and me to mulch my rose bed for winter. Better late than never.

Mid-morning, Celestina called up the stairs as I was getting out of the shower. "Señorita Ellen Butterfield es en el teléfono."

"Gracias!" I yelled back and picked up. "Ellen?"

"Hi. Can you have lunch?" Her voice sounded whiny.

"I'd love to. Where?"

"Let's go to Michel's. I'll meet you there at noon."

"Great," I said. "Are you okay?"

"Oh, yeah," Ellen said. "Same old this and that. I'm sick of every-one. Especially men."

"That kind of lunch."

"Let's get drunk."

Michel's, a small French café off First Avenue near the country club, never went out of favor or style. Jean-Michel Fleury had been at the same location for twenty-five years and knew his market and his customers well—while the big-cheese men of Roundup lunched and plotted and made deals in the Men's Grill of the Roundup Country Club, the women lunched at Michel's. I don't believe it had quite yet dawned on the men that while they plotted and dealt and designed Roundup's future with bank presidents and CEOs and lawyers and judges, the women did the same thing down the street with bank presidents and CEOs and lawyers and judges and much better food. Actually, no one seemed to mind the arrangement and Roundup rolled along with the women's juggernaut rolling a little faster every day.

I looked forward to going there, to seeing a lot of old friends and acquaintances, and I dressed with particular care in my old "Reagan Red" Chanel suit because when you come up against a bunch of women who have weekly massages and manicures and regular face-lifts, and can go to a place like Michel's and just taste a little of each course, finding the conversation the real meal, you can never look too good. By the time I left the ranch, I had put myself together quite su-perbly, as well as I could at any rate, and that's why when I arrived at Michel's little Provençal cottage with its charming fabrics and cordon bleu cuisine, and saw Ellen Butterfield sitting at the power table in the bay window, I couldn't believe how awful she looked.

Her black gabardine suit had faded white stains on the skirt and the lapels of the jacket, the kind of spots that come from dropping toothpaste or something like that and trying to rub it off, which everyone knows never works. You drop toothpaste on your clothes, you might as well just forget it and change because whatever you do will just make it worse. She had on a white blouse with a jabot tie which was loose and askew and her black kid pumps were scuffed and run down. Her hair was filthy and, as usual, she wore no makeup.

She scarcely acknowledged my arrival, and after I had been seated and asked Jean-Michel for a glass of wine, Ellen spoke.

"How's it going?" She was already halfway through her first martini.

I shrugged. "So far, all I have is a lot of information but I wouldn't say any strong suspects have emerged." I decided not to confide in her about my appointment as U.S. marshal. "Why didn't you tell me your father had a mistress?"

"You mean Miami?" Ellen tossed off the rest of her cocktail and signaled for another.

"Yes. Why didn't you tell me?"

"She wasn't at the party, so what's the difference?"

"How do you know she wasn't at the party?" I was quite certain that I was the only one who knew about Miami's quick visit.

Ellen looked at me as if I had lost my mind. "Are you crazy?" she said. "Pamela and Miami in the same town is bad enough, but Miami in Pamela's house? They'd kill each other." She lit a cigarette and inhaled deeply. "You saw what happened at the funeral."

"How well do you know Miami?" I asked. "Thanks." I smiled up at the waitress who put my wine and Ellen's second martini on the table.

"Not well at all. I just know her. Everyone knows Miami. I wouldn't be surprised to hear that she had killed my father. I think they were truly in love, but they used to have huge fights."

"Oh?" I said.

"One time"—Ellen started laughing—"she gave him a black eye. A real shiner. It was really funny. He even thought it was funny. I mean, I think she really beat him up."

"I saw Christine yesterday."

"Oh?"

"She's in bad shape."

"I'm really kind of sorry for her," Ellen said.

"I wouldn't be too sorry," I said. "She's getting a lot of help. I'm more interested in how you're holding up. You look exhausted."

"I know. This has been the most horrible few days. First my father, then Christine, and then this mess with Greg. I don't think I'm ever going to find anybody." She inhaled deeply and shook her head. "You know when you think, 'This is it'? This is really 'it'?"

"Uh-huh." I finally did.

"Well, that's the way I feel about him." Her voice wavered. "Shall we order? Are you in a hurry?"

"Not especially," I said.

"Let's order," she said. "I know you're busy. I don't care if I eat or not. I don't care if I ever eat again."

We both ordered the salade niçoise.

"What happened?" I said.

"We started going out about three months ago. He'd just left his wife."

"Does he have any children?"

"Little ones. Two and six."

Instead of my saying, "Of course it didn't work, you idiot, a guy with two babies who's just left his wife, talk about a hopeless situation," I said politely, "Has he filed for divorce?"

"Not yet. There's this big mess with his wife. She refused to let him see the children." Ellen paused and shrugged. After a long moment, she continued. "Anyhow, he moved in with me and I felt like I was living in heaven. I know I've said this before but, Lilly, I was sure this was it. Everything was perfect. He'd even had a vasectomy, so I didn't have to take the Pill for the first time in twenty-five years."

"How old is he?"

"Thirty-three."

I started to laugh.

"I know, I know." Ellen looked sheepish. "He's twelve years younger than I am, but we fit together so perfectly. I never noticed any age difference and he said he didn't either."

I wouldn't let a thirty-three-year-old man see my body for a million dollars. Not even a blind one.

"Did you ever meet the children?" I asked without interest. I'd heard this story before. "Usually, once these guys can see their children the lover goes to the bottom of the list."

Ellen nodded. "I know, but we were so close I didn't think it would be a problem." She blew out a long stream of cigarette smoke and then ran her fingers through her hair and leaned her head on one hand. "After lots of thrashing around, the children were coming to visit for the weekend. Greg still hadn't gotten his own apartment because his lawyer told him not to establish residency anywhere until the thing with the children was worked out."

"Oh, brother," I said. "That's the biggest load of crap I've heard in ages. How did it go?"

"All right. Well, actually I'd say that of the four of us I did the least well."

Ellen went on to describe for me how, in addition to storing all the breakables in her apartment on high closet shelves that the children couldn't reach, she had slept Friday and Saturday nights on the perfectly puffed rose silk couch in her perfectly puffed living room, because he didn't feel it would be proper for her and Greg to sleep in the same bed with the children present. Ellen said she'd agreed with that and, "Besides, the children hadn't seen their father for eight weeks and they wanted to sleep with him."

I'm not saying that I'm such a totally great, totally together person, but come on. Here we were, forty-five years old, and she was still humiliating herself with men who weren't worth two cents. Depending on them. Needing their abuse. I abandoned that trap at age twenty-five when I told one of my lovers that I loved him. "No, you don't," he'd said. "You just think because we're sleeping together and you like it, you should love me. Learn to take this for what it is: great sex." Since then, I've had a ball from one end of the country to the other. I sipped my wine.

"So the next weekend, when they were coming over again, I told Greg that I was going to be out of town on Friday night." Ellen chewed up her olive and looked down into her empty long-stemmed glass. "I think I'll have the tie-breaker." She signaled the waitress for a third drink. "I mean, Lilly, I don't mind spending *one* weekend on the sofa but I absolutely refuse to spend *two* ever again."

"Where did you go?"

"Oh, I just checked into the Grand."

I felt horribly sad. "Ellen, I can't even believe that you've been sleeping on your couch or checking into a hotel while your lover sleeps in your bed with his children. Where do you think you are? Russia?"

"I know." Her eyes filled with tears. "Greg said it'd probably be a good idea until we all got to know each other a little better. I thought he was right. It gets worse," she blubbered. The martinis had taken their toll. "He just went back to his wife," she sobbed. "She's pregnant."

"I thought you said he'd had a vasectomy."

Ellen nodded and blew her nose.

"Are you pregnant, too?" I said.

"No."

There was little to say and I looked out the window. Then, because I felt I ought to say something, I asked her what Greg did for a living.

"Well," Ellen took a breath and cleared her throat, picked up her fork, tried to gather her nonexistent dignity, which didn't work, so she excused herself and went to the ladies' room. "I'm really sorry," she said when she got back. "I'm a complete mess. Where were we? Actually we probably ought to change the subject."

"I just asked where Greg worked."

"Oh, right. Well, this is where it gets a little sticky and why I couldn't decide whether or not to tell you about him because I was afraid you'd get mad at me."

"Why would I get mad at you, Ellen?" I said. "I'm not your mother."

"Greg works for the paper."

"For *your* paper?"

"Yes. And when I went to work this morning he wouldn't even talk to me. And I'm his boss."

That did it. Life's too short. I stood up and put a twenty-dollar bill on the table for the lunch I hadn't eaten. "Grow up, Ellen."

I stopped and greeted a couple of friends on my way out of the restaurant but I was too mad to stop and chat for long. I drove as fast as I could downtown and arrived twenty minutes early for my meeting with Ellen's nemesis, Roland Tewkesbury, the Butterfield family attorney and publisher of the *Morning News*.

Chapter Twenty-six

Wednesday afternoon

The Butterfields' *Morning News* high-tech high-rise had a very snappy uniformed guard who sat low behind a high counter and in front of a wall of thick glass blocks, probably bullet-proof, through which only vague movement could be discerned.

"May I help you?" he said politely.

"I'm Lilly Bennett and I have an appointment with Mr. Tewkesbury."

"One moment." He picked up a phone from the communications center concealed beneath the counter's ledge. Who knew what all he had hidden back there. An Uzi, maybe, and a couple of smoke bombs. That's what they wanted you to think, anyway. It was probably just a bologna-and-cheese sandwich and a bag of chips. "Hello, Tommi? This is Gordon downstairs. Miss Lilly Bennett is here to see Mr. Tewkesbury." He listened and nodded. "Fine. Thank you." He hung up, handed me a visitor's badge. "Take the elevator to the third floor and Mr. Tewkesbury's secretary, Tommi, will meet you."

I looked around while I waited for the elevator and noticed that no one seemed too broken up over the recent loss of the owner and publisher.

Tall and slim, with shiny honey-brunet hair pulled into a soft roll and subdued makeup on her lightly freckled face, Tommi epitomized the quintessential executive secretary. "Miss Bennett." She shook my hand warmly when I stepped off the elevator. "I'm so happy to meet you, I've heard so much about you."

Tommi guided me with unhurried efficiency down a silent paneled hallway that had portraits on the walls. I'm quite sure they were purchased ancestors, since Walter Butterfield came from nowhere. A door stood open at the end.

"Mr. Tewkesbury will be just a minute. Just as I was leaving, a call came in that he had to take."

"No problem," I said.

"May I bring you some sort of refreshment? Coffee or Perrier?" She glanced at the phone, where his light was still illuminated.

"I'd love a bottle of Perrier."

"Don't you love sparkling water?" She pulled open a pair of doors to reveal a bar. "I find it so refreshing, especially in the afternoon. Would you like a slice of lime? Oh, good. He's off now." She squeezed the lime, dropped it in and handed me my glass. "Let me tell him you're here." Tommi knocked softly on the door to Tewkesbury's office, opened it, ducked through and clicked it closed softly behind her. I admired and appreciated her professional poise and courtesy. She was one in a million.

Roland Tewkesbury's office was as stately as he himself was courtly. Paneled. Casement windows. Shelves and shelves of leather-bound books and framed, autographed pictures of himself with a string of U.S. Presidents, starting back with Jimmy Carter. Other frames held photos of him welcoming various of the world's luminaries to Roundup, such as Pope John Paul II, Mikhail Gorbachev, Mikhail Baryshnikov, Douglas Fairbanks, Jr., Sylvester Stallone. There was also a colored photographic portrait of Queen Elizabeth II in her Opening of Parliament regalia. A large oil portrait of a man in judge's robes hung above a red leather sofa.

Roland Tewkesbury put down a manila file, rose, and slid around his desk to greet me. I realized his desk was slightly downsized so that when he sat behind it, the illusion became a big man sitting at a big desk. He was expensively dressed in clothes that would look more appropriate in England than Roundup—a navy suit with big chalky pinstripes, a Turnbull & Asser shirt in wide red, white, and green stripes, and a seafoam-green, shiny silk Countess Mara tie. His dyed hair had a slightly orange cast in the daylight and in spite of a heavy coat of white powder, a web of broken capillaries bloomed across his face. I understood what Eli had meant by Miss Havisham's wedding cake. Roland Tewkesbury seemed decayed. Decadent. Effete. And I would not have been surprised to hear him burst into high-pitched hysterical giggles the way Tom Hulce did as Mozart in the movie *Amadeus.*

"Miss Bennett," he said in his odd, soft accent. "What a pleasant occasion."

"Thank you for making time for me, Mr. Tewkesbury. I know how busy you are." I played the game because of course one does, although from the looks of his desk he'd not been busy for quite some time. But for the manila file, a copy of *Who's Who in America,* and a collection of a dozen or so porcelain statuettes of Pekingese dogs whose bulgy little eyes so resembled his own, the mahogany masterpiece that served as his desk was as clear as the day it was hand-planed in what looked probably to be Philadelphia in the late 1700s.

"Not at all. Not at all. Please, make yourself comfortable." He indicated one of two oversized red leather armchairs.

"Thank you." I perched on the forward edge of one and took out my notebook. He settled himself across from me and leaned forward, a placid look on his face. He clasped his hands loosely on the desktop. "I won't take up a lot of your time, Mr. Tewkesbury," I said, "but you may or may not know that Ellen asked me to look into her father's murder. She's not convinced that Christine did it."

Roland shook his head slightly and smiled in a patronizing way I'd not seen since the mid-seventies. "Poor, poor Ellen. She takes everything so personally, doesn't she?" he said. "It's quite clear that Christine did it. Pamela told me that she heard Christine and Walter having an enormous row during the evening and that Christine shouted that she would kill her father."

"I see," I said. "Why do you suppose she said that?"

Roland widened his eyes, pursed his lips, and then frowned a little to indicate his ignorance. "I know that Walter had talked about cutting off her funds. He felt the drugs were out of control and told me several times that he felt the only way he could help his daughter was to quit supplying her with the means."

"So you think that he told her during his birthday party?"

"Possibly. Walter had a unique sense of humor and timing."

"Do you know if Christine is skilled with weapons, hunting guns?"

The question didn't surprise him. "Quite skilled enough, I should think. We frequently go shooting with the Royal Family. She always holds her own."

"You mean the royal family Royal Family? Like Queen Elizabeth and Prince Philip?"

"Yes." Roland tilted his head back ever so slightly. "Naturally."

"Wow," I said. "Not many people in Roundup hang around with the Queen of England. Are you British?"

"Quite." Then, as if anticipating my next question, he continued, "Walter Butterfield and I served together in the OSS during World War Two. I had always wanted to visit the American West, and after the war was over he invited me to come and visit. I was not able to take him up on the invitation until fifteen or so years ago, but then it became an annual expedition I undertook happily every summer. Four years ago, when Walter began to consider retirement, he asked me to come and fill in until his son was of age. I moved here at that time."

"Sort of a Regency-type of situation?" I said straight-faced.

The analogy clearly pleased Roland.

"Has it been common knowledge in the paper's management that you would be regent until Wally assumes control?"

"Certainly. That was one of the stipulations of my agreeing to come. And, Miss Bennett, I'm not a regent. I am the CEO."

"Did he ever consider making Ellen CEO?"

If Tewkesbury had been from Roundup, he would have scoffed directly, but he was too well-bred. He curved up his lips and frowned and shook his head. Little chips of powder drifted from his face to his lapels.

"And your wife, Mrs. Tewkesbury, how does she like it here?"

Roland's lips pulled back in a tight smile, revealing perfect little teeth. "She commutes between London and New York and Roundup. Perhaps you know of her? She's one of the world's premier divas. Dame Regina Weeks."

"Really," I said. Never heard of her.

"You've heard of her then?"

"Of course. What does that mean, 'Dame'?"

"It means Her Majesty has declared her a British National Treasure."

"Gee," I said. La-di-da. People like Roland give me an attitude problem. The more pretentious they get, the more cowgirl I get. If this guy kept it up, he'd have me spitting on his floor before long. "Where's she singin' now?"

"In Vienna this month, doing *Rigoletto*. She performs mostly on the Continent."

"Has she ever appeared with the Roundup Opry?"

"No. No. She goes next to do *Bohème* at the Royal Opera."

"I'll be darned," I said. "That's something. I love that picture of the queen."

"Oh, yes, thank you. Her Majesty sent it to me for Christmas last year."

"How very lovely," I said. Sometimes when I get around Brits, I start talking like them. Have you tea? Have you this? Have you that? I'll inquire directly. And so forth. "Well, back to more mundane matters, Mr. Tewkesbury. It's possible there are other suspects in Mr. Butterfield's murder."

"Oh?"

"Well, before I go any further, just as a matter of procedure, where were you when the shooting occurred?"

"On the dance floor."

I wrote that down and said, "Thank you. I have just a couple more questions. What can you tell me about Walter Butterfield's relationship with Miami McCloud?"

Tewkesbury tightened. He regarded his lapels, frowned, and then brushed them off. "Miss Miami McCloud and Walter were acquainted, but beyond that, I have no knowledge of any sort of relationship."

"She wasn't his mistress?"

"People in visible spots, such as Walter, are always susceptible to gossip and certainly there was gossip about them, but it was only that." His nostrils flared with disapproval.

"Miss McCloud was mentioned generously in his will and she certainly was upset at the funeral," I said. "More than the actual widow, Pamela."

"Walter's loss is incalculable to many of us." Tewkesbury's expression remained bland throughout this exchange, a true, loyal friend to Walter Butterfield. "And frankly, Miss Bennett, why would you be surprised that a woman of Mrs. Butterfield's breeding and elegance and public poise would possess more self-control than a circus performer?" The phone rang and Tewkesbury picked it up without speaking, listened, said, "Thank you, ask him to wait a moment, please," and hung up.

"I understand that Ellen was extremely angry last Friday when her father removed her from the Foundation Board of Trustees and appointed you in her place."

"I don't know where you're getting your information, Miss Bennett, but Walter put me on the board when Ellen resigned."

"Over what?" I said.

"Who knows with Ellen? Her father tried to get her to change her mind but she was adamant."

I put my book away and stood up. "Making Walter Butterfield sound like a saint must have been part of your job description."

"Hardly. But he was a fine man, very misunderstood and unappreciated. He'll be greatly missed," he recited. "Is there anything else you need?"

"No. Thanks for your time, Roland. I understand you'll be at my parents' before the opera opening Thursday night."

"I'm quite looking forward to it. Your mother is such an accomplished hostess." He stood up and escorted me to the door.

"Gee, I'll be sure to tell her you said so. Coming from someone like you, I know she'll be tickled with the compliment."

Roland preened. He thought I was serious.

We shook hands and once I was in the hall I thought about his collection of porcelain Pekingeses and how I never could relate to a dog that could sneeze its own eyes out.

Yuk.

Chapter Twenty-seven

When I got back to the RG&E van up on Wittier Gulch Mesa, Elias had on earphones and sat hunkered over his console. He held up a finger to indicate that I should be quiet. Baby peeked over his arm and wagged her tail. "Nope," he said, laying the headset on the counter. "Help yourself to a drink. There's some Cakebread sauvignon blanc in the icebox."

"You spoil me, Elias," I said and took out a bottle of my favorite white wine.

The truck hummed like a launch control room in a silo missile site. A bank of reel-to-reel tapes, each for a different part of the house, stopped and started randomly as the inhabitants, Pamela and her staff, moved around.

"What's up?"

Elias flipped a switch so that we could talk and if anything remarkable happened it would come over his loudspeaker system. For an assembly of jerry-rigged hardware and software, Elias's creative and complicated spy apparatus seemed effective.

"Couple of interesting things. Let me show you." He swung open the truck's double back doors so we could see the Butterfield house nestled below us. "See how the hacienda lays out inside the walls?"

The classic design of the Mexican compound, with a few twentieth-century touches, was elegantly simple. Thick adobe walls encircled the main residence, the stables, garage, swimming pool, tennis court, a number of large mulched flower and vegetable gardens, and an apple orchard.

The air was cool and fragrant and household sounds drifted up to us: the drone of a vacuum cleaner and the sound of the cook chopping in the kitchen.

"And then down there by the river"—Elias pointed—"is the caretaker's cottage."

"Right," I said. "Dwight Alexander."

"I didn't wire his place but I will later tonight."

"Oh?"

"Pamela just got back from there. She left the compound on her horse about two hours ago, rode over that way until she was out of sight of the place, and then cut down by the river and circled back to the cottage. She stayed there for about an hour and a half and then exited by the same route."

"Well." I shrugged. "As Dwight told me, 'What does a boy from Grosse Pointe know about digging ditches?' There has to be some use for him and Pamela picked the same one I would. When I met with him on Monday," I told Eli, "he claimed that he was out with the counter waitress from the Golden Nugget and got home about the same time the police arrived."

"Do you think he did the shooting?" Eli asked.

"Possibly, but not likely. By his own admission, why would he mess up a good thing? Which is certainly what he has. He doesn't seem to me to be the type who'd want to fight for his girl or settle down out here with Pamela. What did you find out about him?"

Elias went into the truck and sat down in front of his computer console and punched a few keys. Words scrolled across the screen. "Nothing, basically," he said, tilting his head back to read through his half-glasses. "His background is about as clean as it can be. No tickets, an occasional bad check, little stuff. Nothing."

"A lover, not a fighter?" I said.

"Exactly," Elias agreed. "Pamela's doctor is coming over at five-thirty."

He flipped another switch and the doctor's voice filled the air. It sounded familiar. Soothing. He called her darling. I'll be there at five-thirty, darling, he'd said.

"Tell me where you are now." Elias squeezed past me to the kitchenette counter and mixed himself another Bacardi and Coke and refilled his popcorn bowl. He handed me a bag of pretzels.

"Thanks." I settled back into my director's chair and crossed my legs, certain that, in my chic short wool suit, I looked like Lauren Hutton's short, and short-haired, twin. "First," I said, "starting with the premise that hating Walter was a motive common to all the suspects, so something more precipitated it, Ellen is right there at the top. And I can't tell whether or not she's telling the truth about anything."

"That doesn't especially surprise me," Eli said. "The last few years she's gotten sort of 'desperate,' I guess would be the best word. You know what I mean? Anxious for friends. She doesn't take care of herself at all, she looks like hell, and she laughs extra loudly. One minute she's your best buddy and the next a complete bitch. It really makes me sad because she's so smart and she could be so pretty, really be an asset to some guy, but she doesn't care and her eyes have that weird look, kind of like someone who's had shock therapy. You know, intense."

"I know exactly what you mean. *Now.* But I don't know why I didn't see that last Friday when she came out to the ranch. She seemed so together, so rational about protecting her interests and then that evening she told me that her father had bumped her off the Foundation board and put Tewkesbury on. And she had a good sense of humor about it. I mean, she was angry but I remember admiring her composure. She should have been irate."

"That's not so unusual," Elias said. "She's always been tightly wrapped."

"But get this," I said. "This afternoon, Tewkesbury told me she'd *resigned* from the board, that's why Walter asked him to step in. I think she's completely nuts."

We both sat quietly and contemplated that possibility for a moment. I decided not to mention to Eli Ellen's latest fiasco, her thirty-three-year-old employee/lover with the nonexistent vasectomy and pregnant wife, and instead let the Cakebread fill my mouth and flow down my throat like sweet round velvet.

"I don't know," I finally said. "Because of the timing of the murder, whoever shot Walter Butterfield had to be knowledgeable and quick. Ellen was holding the gun but she had a wobbly grip on it. My initial inclination was she didn't do it. But maybe she's a crack shot and could have done it and maybe even did. Can I use the phone?"

" 'Can' I use the phone? Or 'may' I use the phone?"

I laughed. "Just give me the phone."

Richard was at the final dress of *Lucia,* so I left a message for him to call as soon as it ended.

"Who's next?" Eli refilled his drink and popcorn. I never knew anyone over the age of eighteen who loved rum and Coke with such a passion as Elias. The inside of the truck smelled like a 7-Eleven. He poured more wine into my glass.

"Tell me what you found out about Rosak and Gryczkowski," I said.

Eli put his glasses back on and punched another button on his keyboard. "Interesting stuff. Carl Rosak was an MP in the Army. Dishonorably discharged for beating up a female suspect. Since then, in Roundup, police have been called two different times to motels on Buckskin Boulevard where Rosak has roughed up prostitutes. On both occasions, he's been drunk. Also on both occasions, charges have never been filed and he has not been arrested. He was arrested once, it was last June, DUI. Paul Decker got him off."

"Same lawyer that's representing Christine?" I asked.

"Yes."

"Expensive."

"Definitely." Eli keyed up another file. "Michael Gryczkowski. He looks okay to me. Average student at Billy the Kid, worked his way through Roundup State University, and then started at the bank as a trainee. He has a good work record. Has a wife, Donna, and six children. And a brand-new Corvette."

"You're joking."

"Nope."

"Well, isn't that interesting," I said.

"Yup."

"How much does a Corvette cost?"

"About thirty thousand."

"A bank junior vice president in Little Budapest with a wife and six children and a new Corvette."

"Yup."

"What about Miami?"

"More interesting stuff." Eli beamed. "Miami's real name is Brad Johnson and he's from Big Creek, Texas, where he was a high school football star. He and two of his friends, also big football jocks, had some sort of public altercation after a game on a Friday night and the next day the two other boys were found hanging from a tree. Brad was accused of murder, tried, and acquitted. The next day he disappeared and hasn't been back to Big Creek since. Miami McCloud surfaced four years later at the rodeo in Fort Worth, but he didn't actually have the surgery until twelve years ago, about six months before he came to Roundup."

"Excellent," I said. "How did you get all this information?"

"Other computer hackers. We have a worldwide network," Elias said. "You know, Lilly, once you have someone's Social Security number and if you've got hacker friends at the IRS and a couple of banks and police departments, you can find out virtually anything about anyone."

"I know," I said. "And it gives me the creeps. Ellen told me that Miami and Walter fought and one time, that she knows of, Miami beat him up. Maybe Miami pulled the trigger and all the conversation about blackmail and family members voting stock is coincidental. Walter's murder had to do with love and passion, and he and Miami had plenty of both."

Just then a white four-door Buick Regal turned into the Butter-fields' road and came to a stop at the front door. A man got out.

"Doctor Feelgood to the rescue," Elias said.

"Carl Rosak," I told him.

~ *Chapter Twenty-eight*

Early Wednesday evening

*B*uenas tardes, Dr. Rosak," Maria the maid said.

"Buenas tardes. Está la señora aquí?"

"Sí, está en su cuarto. Permite me."

'No. That's all right, Maria, I can find the way."

"Bueno."

Rosak went up the stairs two at a time and down the hall to Pamela's room, where he knocked loudly and Pamela opened the door.

"This is great, Eli," I whispered, although they could not hear us.

Rosak went in and shoved the odious little Mitzi out into the hall with his foot where she yapped and circled a couple of times and then took off toward the kitchen, where we could hear something sautéing while the cook continued to chop. She must have been fixing something Chinese.

"Why the hell didn't you call me?" Rosak growled. "What did you think? That now, with your old man gone, you'd give me the old heave-ho?"

"No. Of course not, Carl," Pamela's controlled voice seemed to be trying to force some humor and assuagement over a little edge of nervousness or maybe fear. "I thought it was too soon. I thought you'd be lying low."

"Lying low? Why the hell would I be lying low?" Pam had a number of llama rugs scattered on top of the glazed Mexican tiles on her bedroom floor which made Rosak's footsteps alternately ring out and thud as he crossed the room in her direction. "Look, sister, bumping into you six months ago after thirty-five years was the greatest thing that ever happened to me in my life. If you think that you're going to give me the shaft again, you'd better think about it. Hard." He grabbed her.

"No, Carl. Not now." Pamela shoved him away. "I can't believe you killed him. You're just as stupid as you always were. He was the only one I didn't want to find out. But you shot your wad, sugar. You're up shit creek in a chicken-wire canoe. You're history."

"What are you talking about?"

"Because you shot him."

"What?! Me?" Rosak laughed loudly. His laugh was sharp, like a barking dog. "That's a good one. That's really a good one. No way, Queenie, you're going to foist this off on me. You pulled the trigger, just like you've been saying you wanted to. You think you're going to get me to take the rap for killing your husband? That's good. Really good. I'm havin' a vodka. You want something?"

"Carl," Pamela said, "I didn't kill Walter."

Ice tinkled into glasses, followed by vodka. "Don't play that innocent crapola with me, Queenie. You're a tough, cold-hearted, ambitious old bitch and you know it. That's one of the reasons I never stopped loving you. You got spit." He handed her her glass and moved away. The sound of pants being unzipped was unmistakable.

Rosak took them off and tossed them. The belt buckle clinked and grated and skidded on the tiles until it ran into one of the soft fur rugs.

In the van, the phone rang. Eli answered. "Get out here," he said. "It's just getting good." He quickly relayed directions to Wittier Gulch Mesa and hung up.

I looked at him.

"Richard," he said. "He's in his car."

"What the hell difference does it make who shot Walter, anyway? Now we can be together, just the way we agreed." He jumped in the air and landed on his back in the middle of her bed with its six-foot-high, tufted gold velvet headboard. The image of Carl Rosak lying in such a bed, wearing a shirt and tie, shoes and socks, and no pants was revoltingly delectable. "I mean, when we bumped into each other, you said you'd been wanting me back all those years and you'd do anything to get rid of your husband. So relax and enjoy it, Queenie. Your dreams are coming true."

"Don't call me Queenie." The vodka had given Pamela confidence.

"That's what I've always called you, ever since you had pimples. Oh, look at the 'lady,' " he laughed. "I insulted her by saying 'pimples.' Who are you? Mrs. Fancy-Pants? Don't waste your breath trying that crap on me. I know you right down to your potato pancakes."

"You shut your fuckin' mouth, Carl." Pam poured another drink.

"Is that how ladies talk? Your 'fuckin' mouth'?" He barked out another laugh. This one sarcastic. "Don't think after all the bullshit I've been through with you that you're going to say ta-ta to me. Little Queenie Gryczkowski. Everyone thinks I'm your doctor and I'll come here whenever the hell I please. Now get the hell over here, Mrs. Big Shot. I feel like fuckin'."

"Wait a minute."

"No, you wait a minute. I told Gisela I wanted a divorce. I'm gonna be the chief honcho of Rancho del Sol." He got off the bed and refilled his drink. "Gimme your glass. You need to calm down. You need to let old Mr. Magic take care of everything."

"Listen to me, Carl." Pam's voice was strong. "This is serious. I don't know if you murdered Walter or not; if you say you didn't, okay, you didn't. But that nut-ball Ellen has hired this private investigator friend of hers, Lilly Bennett, to find out who murdered Walter because no one's buying Christine's story for a second—what a fluke that was, having her confess—and I don't want any Bennett, or anyone, for that matter, looking too deep into my life. The whole thing stinks and I don't want her getting the idea that *I* murdered Walter because of you and Mike. Do you understand?"

"Oh, yeah, her, real tight-ass," Rosak said. "She already came to see me."

"What? Who?"

"That Lilly Bennett."

"OH, JESUS." Pam moaned and sat down heavily as though she had collapsed. "Why didn't you tell me?"

"Because I knew you'd get upset and there's no reason to get your tits in an uproar. I set her straight, honey. I told her that you'd left the neighborhood over thirty years ago and no one knew where you were and that was the end of it. She believed me. I could tell. I told her it was all ancient history and that she'd best not come back because innocent people's lives were at stake and she'd better watch out where she was messing."

"HA. HA. HA." Pam sounded a little hysterical. "Where do you live? In a tree? You think Lilly Bennett is scared of you? That you set her straight? Lilly Bennett eats people like you for breakfast every day."

"Wooo," Elias whistled. "Harsh."

I smiled and flexed my biceps.

"Honey. Honey," Rosak said, trying to calm her. "Let me get you another drink."

"Honey! Honey!" she yelled. "Is that all you can say? This is a *disaster.* I've spent my whole goddamn life getting away from Little Budapest. From my mother. From you. And all the rest of the pathetic little losers in that dump. And now," she sobbed, "it'll all be out. No one will ever believe that all the stuff I do secretly for Mike and the kids is because I love them," she blubbered. "They'll think it's blackmail. Blood money. Oh, Jesus." Pam sobbed deeply and Rosak put his arms around her. "You son of a bitch."

"It'll be all right, Queenie. You'll see. I'll take care of everything. I'm in charge now."

Pam cried as though her heart were broken and I felt sorry for her. I don't know what she thought I was going to do with the information.

Put it on the front page of the paper or something. I didn't care who she was or where she came from and I wouldn't tell a soul unless it had a direct bearing on who murdered Walter.

Richard knocked softly on the van door and Eli let him in. He sat on my chair and I sat in his lap and poured him some wine.

"You smell good," he said into my neck. He smelled like Old Spice.

"It sounds like Mrs. Tewkesbury's quite the diva," I said to Richard as we all listened to Carl Rosak soothe and calm Pamela. "And I've never even heard of her."

Richard laughed. "Who? Regina Weeks?"

"Yes. 'Dame' Regina."

"Is that what he called her? He knows better than to do that. She's not a Dame and she never will be. Dame is a recognition of a British National Treasure."

"I know what a Dame is, Richard," I said.

"She's a solid mezzo. Mostly on the European circuit. But she ain't no Dame." Richard laughed and shook his head. "Tewkesbury is totally self-impressed. He cracks me up."

Things were heating up in Pamela's bedroom. She was beginning to respond to Carl Rosak's caresses. We all were. I understood why she kept him around. After all, in spite of his arm-flexing and threats, when it got right down to it, she was ultimately in control. So what if her past came out? She still had all the money. And people are willing to overlook anything when money's involved. Especially in Roundup. He had nothing. But, to his credit, he had managed to get her onto the bed and just as things were getting really good, car lights swept the main road and headed toward the hacienda. A navy-blue Jaguar sedan turned into the compound and stopped at the front door.

"I don't believe it," I said, watching through binoculars. "I can't believe Ellen is that stupid."

Ellen got out of the driver's side, and even before her passenger climbed out and turned to face our direction, I knew who it was going to be. Christine.

⌒ Chapter Twenty-nine

Wednesday evening

*T*he ringing of the front doorbell at the hacienda echoed through the truck and Baby started barking, thinking it was our door, and Mitzi barked over the speakers. The noise was deafening.

"Who in the hell could that be?" Pam said.

"Won't the maid get it?" Carl groaned.

"Of course the maid will get it," she snapped. "But what if it's for me? Get off. You're crushing me. Get your pants on. Hurry up."

There was a loud *thud* as Pamela pushed him off the bed onto the floor.

Downstairs, Mitzi barked herself into a frenzy and upstairs the sound of clothing being pulled on hastily had replaced the heavy breathing. Pam's footsteps scampered to her bathroom, where she slammed the door and I thought about the Chinese proverb of being careful about what you want too much—you may get it—and I thought about how disoriented Carl Rosak must be. For six months he'd been cruising along in the catbird seat because Pamela had wanted to conceal him and their son Michael from Walter. But now, boom, Walter's dead and she's treating him like some kind of low-class stranger. Carl Rosak had no clue he was simply one stud in Pamela's stable, and now that she was free, he would never, ever, make the cut. All he knew was that he was on a rope suspension bridge over a deep gap and the pleasant crossing, with the other side in sight, had turned bad: A hundred-mile-an-hour Chinook had begun to blow and the rope handles were snapping like snakes in his hands.

I continued to watch through the binoculars while Christine and Ellen waited for Maria to open the door. Christine looked very sleek. Her platinum hair was slicked back and she wore a smart-looking black suit and dark glasses and in both gloved hands she held a small package, about the size of a book, wrapped in red paper with a white ribbon. In twenty-four hours Christine had changed from a down-and-out junkie to a chic, self-assured-looking sophisticate and I re-called what Mack Cleveland had said about multiple-personality disorder, and that it was possible Christine suffered from it because frequently individuals with her experience did. This was not like any Christine I'd ever seen.

Ellen, in the same suit she had on at lunch, asked her sister about the package. I couldn't make out what Christine said but whatever it was, it was hostile and Ellen responded angrily and tried to take the package away. They yanked it back and forth a couple of times until the front door swung open.

Maria's big brown eyes widened slightly with surprise. "Señorita Christine. Señorita Ellen. Bienvenido."

"Gracias, Maria." Christine indicated her overnight case, gar-ment bag, and suitcase to the maid and walked through the door in possession of the package, leaving Ellen to consider whether or not to follow.

Ellen wavered. "I'm going back to town, Chris. Call me if you need anything," she finally said. Then she turned, still indecisive, and climbed back into her car and, after a moment, started the engine and drove away.

"What an asshole," we heard Christine say.

"Who is it, Maria?" Pamela called from the upstairs landing as the maid lugged Christine's gear into sight. "Oh, my God, Christine, dear. What're you doing here?"

"Welcome home, Christine," she parroted back sarcastically, her British accent impeccable, totally unlike the half-Roundup, half-Anglo enunciation she had used at the cocktail party or at the hospital. "How are you? Can I get you anything? My, but it's lovely to see you too, Pamela." Christine stopped at the top of the landing. "What am I doing here? Well, I finally, as they say, came to my senses and realized I never shot my father, I simply wanted to. So, after some interminable heart-to-hearts with that simpering psychiatrist Cleveland and his merry band of do-gooders and the ghoul of a shrink the state sent over, I convinced them that I was a danger neither to myself nor to society, such as it exists in this desolate, godforsaken spot of earth, and that I should be set free pending et cetera, et cetera, et cetera. So"—she drew in a deep breath—"the judge turned me loose on my own recognizance and about a billion dollars' worth of bail. Ellen and Uncle Roland signed for me. Honestly, it was horribly humiliating. Like I was a child or something."

"Well," Pam said, "good. I'm so glad you're home. How are you really, dear? You look fabulous. MITZI! Stop that barking right now." The little thing scooted up the stairs and jumped into Pamela's arms.

"Heavenly," Christine said, "as you can see. I'm sober. Detoxified. Deloused. Tranquilized. And tranquil. If I were any better, I'd be dead. How're you? I see the doctor's come to call. Are you sick?"

"Oh, no. Nothing like that. I'm just exhausted. I asked him to come by and check me out and then give me some sleeping pills." Pam became flustered and giggled nervously. "I don't mean I'll take them all the time. Just once in a while."

"It's okay, Pam. I know what you mean. You won't take them like I do. By the handfuls. Well, I'm going to take a bath. I feel like I'm drowning in a sea of disinfectant. See you later."

"Yes," Pam said. "Let's have dinner together. I'm sure Maria is cooking something special and delicious. What's your favorite? I know she'd love to fix it for you."

"You're lovely to offer, Pam. But I think I'll just have a tray in my room tonight. I'm awfully tired. I hope you'll understand."

"Of course I do, dear. Let Maria know if you need anything."

Christine's high heels stopped at her bedroom. "Oh, Pam," she said. "One more thing."

"Yes?"

"Your hem's stuck up in the waist of your panty hose," she said and closed her door.

"Shit." Pam pulled her skirt out of her waistband and stomped her way back down the hall to Carl Rosak. "You'd better get out of here," she told him, slamming the door. "Christine's home." Pamela picked up her hairbrush and began to run it through her hair. "Gosh, I thought that when you murdered someone they kept you in jail for more than five days."

Rosak made a faint attempt to recapture their lost ecstasy but Pamela would have none of it. Nor would Mitzi, who growled as Carl approached.

"Not now, Carl. You've got to go. You've been here for over an hour already. What will Gisela say? You'd better go home and try to make up with her."

"You know I don't care what she says. She says what I tell her to say. Can I see you tomorrow night?"

"No. It's opening night of the Opera. I'm going with Roland. Oh, God." Pamela sounded flustered and besieged, an act of helpless femininity for Rosak. "Cocktails at the Bennetts' first. Oh, God, I hope Lilly isn't there. Oh, I know she will be. What will I say to her? Maybe I'll tell Roland that I can't go to cocktails."

"What about Friday?"

"I don't know. Look, I'll call you tomorrow when I see what's what with Christine. Okay?" She opened the bedroom door and called, "BYE-BYE, DOCTOR," as Carl Rosak descended the stairs. "THANKS FOR COMING. I FEEL MUCH BETTER." Then, with Mitzi cradled in her arms, she watched out the window as he drove away. "Poor little Polack," she muttered. "I think I'd better change the phone number to something unlisted."

Moments later, Maria yelled, "Teléfono, señora. Señor Tewks."

"GRACIAS." Pamela picked up. "Hello, Roland," she purred.

"Good evening, Pam. I hope I'm not catching you at a bad time."

"No. I was just staring out the window."

"Oh, fine. I'll pick you up tomorrow evening at five-thirty."

"I really don't think I'm going to go, Roland. I mean, do you think it's right, with Walter being dead only a few days? Don't you think people will think I'm awful?"

"Certainly not!" Roland exclaimed. "Quite to the contrary. They'll find you plucky. You'll be the most beautiful woman there, and be-sides"—his voice dropped to a conspiratorial whisper—"you don't want to send me off to spend an evening with all those shitkickers by myself, do you? I'd expire! You'll liven things up."

Pamela laughed.

"And look at it this way: The opera will be insufferably long, as they all are, and you'll get in a good nap."

"You're terrible, Roland." She laughed again. "Okay. I'm sure you're right. But look, I'll have Dwight drop me off at the Bennetts' at six. That way, you won't have to come all the way out here."

"Are you sure? I don't mind. I can send my car."

"No. No. I'll just meet you there."

"Fine," Roland said. "Six at the Bennetts', then. But I'll take you home. I don't want you going into an empty house alone. Isn't Thursday Maria's night off?"

"You're right. I forgot. You might have to stay and protect me."

"That's two on Pam's doorstep with casseroles," Eli said, after they'd hung up. "Rosak and Tewkesbury. Not much of a choice."

"Where does she get the energy?" I said.

"Did you hear that?" Richard said, ignoring us both. " '*Sleep* through the opening night'? '*Shit*kickers'?"

"Yeah, what's wrong with her?" Eli said. "No one can sleep through *Lucia*. Too much yelling."

"And we've always been shitkickers, darling," I said to Richard.

That evening, Richard and I watched a tape of June Anderson and Richard Emerson in *Madama Butterfly*. Puccini's story in all its vari-ous, overexposed incarnations had never affected me, maybe because I've never cared for children. But this time, Butterfly loved B. F. Pinkerton so deeply, so innocently, so trustingly, and she died with such dignity, it brought me to my knees. I sobbed like a baby in Richard's arms.

A little later, I asked him if he believed in love at first sight, and he said he never had, but now he wasn't so sure.

"Me either," I said.

We didn't talk about it anymore. I think we were both afraid to, it was so big. Instead, we went for a quick walk and it was almost as though the whole day had not happened, as though we were right back where we'd started at dawn that morning. The same black sky, the same blanket of stars, the same silent chill, the same frosted blades of dried grasses crunching beneath our feet. And the same feelings of sureness and serenity and security, respect and comfort.

Chapter Thirty

Thursday morning

I had planned to spend all day Thursday primping, since the opera season opened that evening, and not only did I have a beautiful gown to wear—that was nothing new—I had a great escort for a change which was, as my mother said, A Miracle. I wanted to look extra good and achieving that condition took hours at the minimum. I should have started days ago.

But there was something I had to find out, so as soon as Richard left for town, I pulled on my jeans and boots and drove into Bennett's Fort and sat in a booth at the Golden Nugget Café drinking coffee and reading the paper until the Butterfields' foreman Dwight Alexander sauntered in to flirt with the counter waitress. Once he'd ordered, I approached him.

"How about dropping by my office before you head out?" I said.

He gave me the same sensuous appraisal as before and touched the tip of his tongue to the corner of his lips. "I'd like that, Sheriff," he said.

"I'll be waiting," I answered. "Don't take too long."

His mouth curved into a smile and he turned back to the counter and sipped his coffee.

As usual, it was a beautiful day, saturated in sunshine and blue, blue sky, and I wandered up the Old West wooden sidewalks of Bennett's Fort and looked in the hokey old storefronts. It was too early for any tourists to be there, so I had the rock shop and the photo studio where you could dress up as Billy the Kid or a dance-hall girl and get your picture taken in an authentic setting and the salt-water-taffy shop and the western curio shop and art gallery to myself. What a bunch of junk Cousin Buck made his living off and it didn't even bother him. I unlocked the Marshal's Office, let up the window shade, and turned on the heater.

The only mail the Marshal's Office received was catalogues from the local feed store and the Orvis fishing camp in the Wind River Mountains. Apparently the U.S. Department of Justice felt the district was either so top secret or so useless it didn't bother to communicate with it. I didn't even have any "Wanted" posters dated later than 1910, so, since there wasn't much corporate housekeeping to do while I waited for Dwight Alexander to show, I picked out a new graphite Orvis fishing rod and waders, spun around in Marshal Earp's chair a few times, and opened the top drawer of his desk where I'd had a modern telephone installed and called my answering service, which had no news, and hoped Dwight would be able to enlighten me somewhat; otherwise the time I could have spent with deep pink goo on my face was for naught.

Finally, faded jeans stretched so tight around his fanny and front and legs he might as well have been naked, Dwight strolled in and perched on the edge of my desk. As before, he rolled and twirled and twisted a piece of paper between his fingers and swung one leg languidly back and forth. "What's up, Sheriff?" he said.

"I need your help, Dwight."

"That's one of the things I'm best at. Helping out ladies in distress. What do you want me to do?"

"Start by sitting in the chair on the other side of the table."

"How come? I like it here by you," he said to my breasts.

"Because I said so."

"Yes, ma'am. Always happy to please." Dwight swung himself off the desk and plopped himself down in one of the two wooden armchairs across a scarred oak worktable from me.

"The main road in and out of Rancho del Sol is in plain view of your cabin," I said.

"Uh-huh."

"So when you're home, you see everyone who come and goes."

"Sometimes."

"You claim to have gotten home just before the police arrived early last Saturday morning, when Walter was shot, which means you may have passed the murderer heading the other direction on the road."

Dwight considered what I'd said for a couple of seconds. "I suppose that's true."

"Try to remember if you passed any other cars between here and the Butterfields' on your way home."

Dwight stared at his folded hands on the tabletop and then up at the ceiling. He shouldn't have been called upon to think. It did not become him. If his beautiful dusty blue eyes were not concentrated on sex, they became flat and empty as they shifted from side to side trying to remember something. Anything.

"Yeah!" His face lit up. "I did! I passed another car."

I waited for him to continue. He did not. He was as stupid as a starlet. "What kind of car?" I finally said.

"Just like mine. A red 'Vette."

"A red Corvette?"

"Yeah. I've seen one like it out there before, but never late at night. Usually in the afternoon. I figured it was one of the birthday-party people going home. You figure that was the getaway car?"

"Did you see any other cars? A white sports car, for instance?"

"Oh, sure," Dwight said matter-of-factly. "You mean Miami's Lamborghini? I saw her going back to town. Boy, that thing hauls. She must have some major cake to get a car like that."

"Was that before or after you saw the red Corvette?"

"Let me think," Dwight said and the painful process began again. "I don't remember," he said presently.

Michael Gryczkowski had a red Corvette.

"Will you do me a favor?" I said.

"Maybe. What do I get for it?" He turned on the slow grin.

"Nothing but my thanks and the good feeling that you've helped in a murder investigation."

"Oh, come on, Sheriff. You and I like each other. Can't you offer me *something* a little special? I'm a man who needs motivation."

I pretended to give his request serious consideration and then said, "How's this: I won't call your father and tell him that you're sleeping with Mrs. Butterfield and are a suspect in his old friend Walter Butterfield's murder and then maybe your father won't cut off your trust fund. How's that for motivation?"

The game was over.

Dwight ran his tongue across his teeth and whistled. "Pretty good. What do you want me to do?"

"I want you to keep an eye on the road and report who comes and who goes. And keep it confidential. Official business. If you do a good job, maybe I'll make you a deputy."

"Yeah?" Dwight said enthusiastically. "That'd be cool. You're a hard woman, Sheriff. But I like you anyway."

"And one more thing, Dwight," I said.

"Yeah?"

"I'm a marshal, not a sheriff. Get it straight."

Chapter Thirty-one

Thursday afternoon

I knew I had to go into town and try to meet with Michael Gryczkowski. My beauty time dwindled through my fingers like deep sea-green bath salts.

At least the Little Budapest branch of the Roundup National Bank sat at a busy intersection near the freeway, so I zipped down there without having to get snarled up in the downtown traffic. It was a new brick building with large trees in the parking lot and a surprisingly good collection of early-twentieth-century western art in the open lobby and around the banking floor. The receptionist came from central casting: semi-smart, semi-pretty, semi-respectful, downtrodden, eager, and sweet.

"I'd like to see Michael Gryczkowski, please," I told her.

"May I tell him who's calling?" she said. Her assessment of me reflected her disappointment that I had not made more of an effort with my appearance before I visited their fine institution which I did not tell her my family owned.

I wanted to tell her that I hadn't planned to come to town today and apologize for my faded Levi's and muddy boots and baggy canvas jacket. I did have on makeup and earrings, so I also wanted to tell her that it could have been much worse, but I only said, "U.S. Marshal Bennett," and showed her my badge.

"Ooo." Her eyes brightened. "I'll tell him you're here. I'll bet you're working undercover." She picked up her phone and punched in his intercom number. "The sheriff is here to see you, Mr. Gryczkowski. I'll send her back."

"Marshal," I told her over my shoulder once she'd indicated the direction. "Not sheriff. Marshal."

Even though it was only to be used judiciously, I decided to go ahead and say I was a U.S. marshal because, number 1: I was; and number 2: I hadn't thought up any other way to get information from Michael Gryczkowski. Besides, if you're The Law and talking to a law-abiding citizen, it helps cut through the crap in a hurry. And I was definitely in a hurry. I hadn't done my nails yet and it was after lunchtime.

A flick of recognition traced Michael Gryczkowski's eyes when he saw me but he could not place the quick glimpse we'd had of each other at his front door three days earlier. He looked so much like Pamela Butterfield and Carl Rosak, it was uncanny—Pamela's carved-granite face and Rosak's strong size and build. He appeared solid, dependable, unflappable.

"Sheriff?" he said and offered me his hand which I accepted.

I took out my badge and flashed it quickly. "Federal Marshal Bennett."

"Please sit down. Would you like a cup of coffee or tea?"

"No, thank you." Two Scandinavian chairs covered in a bright blue tweedy fabric were placed side by side in front of his desk. Children's drawings covered one of the padded walls of his cubicle and family photographs sat on the credenza. His desk was clear but for an adding machine, a telephone, a paper-clip holder, and a stand with two ball-point pens.

I took my notebook out of my jacket pocket and flipped it open to a clean page. "I'm investigating the murder last Friday night of Walter Butterfield."

"The publisher of the *Morning News?*" His face reflected no special emotion.

"Yes."

"Is there some connection with the bank?"

"No, Mr. Gryczkowski, it appears there may be some connection with your car."

"My car?" His surprise was legitimate. "How?" He frowned.

"Where were you last Friday night?"

He thought for a second. "We all went over to the Rosaks' after the game. My kids are on the Little League football team. Uncle Carl, that's Mr. Rosak, is the coach. We had a big barbecue."

"What did you do after that?"

"Well, Donna said I'd had more beers than I should've, so I left my car at Uncle Carl's and rode home in the van with her and the kids. My car's too small to haul the kids in anyway."

"What time was that?"

"Gee"—Michael Gryczkowski ran his hand across the bristly top of his crew cut—"I don't know. Couldn't have been too late, though. The kids are usually in bed about nine. So I guess it was probably eight-thirty or nine."

"And you went back and picked your car up on Saturday morning?"

"Yeah. I had a lot of running around to do, so I walked back over and picked it up about eight."

"Was the car in the same place you'd left it the night before?"

"I guess," Michael said. "I really don't remember. I suppose it was. Why do you think my car was involved? There are a number of red Corvettes in Roundup."

"I know. We're questioning all the owners," I lied. "I just have a couple more questions."

"No problem. I'm happy to help."

"Did you happen to notice if the gas gauge was the same as the day before?"

Finally. Pay dirt. "That's right! I always fill the 'Vette up on my way home on Friday afternoon in case Donna and I want to get away from the kids for a while and go for a drive in the mountains over the weekend. It was down by about a quarter of a tank. That's right. Gosh."

"Does anyone have keys to your car but you?"

"No way. No one touches my 'Vette but me." His frown had returned and he was clearly baffled and upset.

"My next question is not pejorative or meant to imply any wrongdoing on your part, Mr. Gryczkowski, and you do not need to answer."

"Shoot," he said. "I've got nothing to hide."

"A bank vice president does not earn an especially high salary and it is expensive to have six children."

"You can say that again."

"The last time I checked, a Corvette was going for about twenty-eight thousand dollars. How did you afford it?"

"Oh, that's easy," he smiled. "I had an older sister, Ramona. Never knew her. She was killed in a car accident just after I was born and through her job she had a double-indemnity life insurance policy. Anyhow, she'd designated me as beneficiary since she wasn't married and didn't have any kids of her own. The principal went into trust for me until I was twenty-one. It's a nice little nest egg for Donna and me and kicks out about fifty thousand a year. I don't know how our trust officer does it but that account makes money no matter what the economy's doing."

"Sounds great." I laughed and closed up my book. "Maybe I should move my money. What bank is he at?"

"Roundup National Trust Department. Downtown. Grover Pendington. What about my car? Do you think it was involved?"

"Possible. Why are you so certain about the gas gauge?"

"Positive. Just like I said, I filled the car on my way home on Friday, same as always, and on Saturday night I remember saying to Donna that I'd have to get the engine tuned because it was using too much gas. Now I remember the gauge was down by a quarter Saturday morning, but nothing else was different."

"I appreciate your help, Mr. Gryczkowski." I stood to go. "We'll be back in touch with you if necessary. One more question. Have you ever met Walter or Pamela Butterfield?"

"Me?" Michael Gryczkowski laughed. "We don't exactly travel in the same circles."

"But have you met them?"

He shook his head. "Nope."

I didn't think he was lying.

⌐ Chapter Thirty-two

W hat's up?" I asked Elias over the phone.

"It's been pretty quiet," he said from the truck. "Where are you? It sounds like you're talking in a barrel."

"I'm lying in my bath of pink bubbles with a mud mask on my face," I said. "The opera opens tonight, you know."

"I know. What time are we leaving? I still have to get my hair cut."

"Five-thirty," I told him. "You've got a while yet. Besides, you don't have that much hair. Has anything gone on around the Butterfields' today?"

"Pretty quiet. Pamela left for the beauty shop at about ten and said she wouldn't be back till three-thirty. Christine hasn't come out of her room and hasn't turned off her TV set since she got home yesterday afternoon. She placed one call. That was to her husband in London but he was out and hasn't called back yet. She's let Maria in with trays. And that's about it from here."

"Anything from Rosak?"

"He's called three times. Each time he sounds a little more desperate. I feel kind of sorry for him. I mean, she has been going along with him for a while and he's really getting jabbed as far as I'm concerned."

Elias had been getting jabbed by women since he was big enough to remember, so he was really an expert on the subject.

I told him what I'd learned from my conversations with Michael Gryczkowski and Dwight Alexander. I could feel the strings of the net gathering together, upping my adrenaline a notch.

At five-thirty, Elias and I climbed into Christian's Alouette with him and his wife Mimi, for the ride into Roundup. Like Christian, Mimi was long and lean, and her black silk jersey sheath and smooth blond chignon gave her the air of an exotic serpent. Mimi makes our family look good. She looks the way a woman with her money and position should. Glamorous and sleek. She and Christian should run for president.

I had on my favorite evening gown—cobalt-green taffeta with a heavily embroidered, jewel-encrusted, golden heraldic emblem on the bodice and tight long sleeves. The full skirt poofed around me in the chopper's small seat, so I appeared to be sitting on a lily pad. Mimi's and my perfume replaced the smell of stale cigarettes in the cabin.

We flew over Pamela's big Mercedes as it joined the stream of limousines and luxury sedans and four-wheel-drive vehicles and pickup trucks that funneled onto the blacktop from the ranches around Bennett's Fort heading into town for opening night at the Roundup opry. Strictly a dress-boot affair. In the distance, the setting sun silhouetted Roundup's skyline like a peculiar golden cutout against the deep purple Wind River Range.

Christian passed out champagne in bright yellow plastic mugs and the four of us laughed and yelled over the engine's loud noise and had no idea what the others were saying, and fifteen minutes later we descended over the park in front of my parents' home. I loved their house. It was stately and solid and maintained Roundup's architectural standards, being part-Tudor, part-Gothic, part-Edwardian, and part-French. A high rose-red brick wall surrounded the tree-filled estate and its two large trout ponds. Mother's magnificent formal rose garden, a greenhouse, a newly constructed lap pool, and an orangery completed the grounds. Thick vines and roses, perfectly sculpted in brass and wrought iron, ornamented the two grand black wrought-iron gates that sat in the wall at either end of a curving driveway. Wide granite steps led to the front doors, massive wooden things set back in a deep carved stone archway.

The house, the same rose-red brick as the wall, had two wings spreading out from a central staircase tower. Carved stone framed each leaded window and the chimneys rose majestically in double and triple octagons. My grandfather had built the house in the thirties in the worst of the Great Depression to keep the local craftsmen in work, and since they came from all over Europe, the structure had many small personal touches, mementos of homelands left behind. Family initials and scenes appeared in the stonework and a frieze of Porto Santo Stéfano ran all the way around the house in the wood trim beneath the eaves.

Mimi couldn't wait to get her hands on the place.

As the helicopter hovered, I spotted Richard, tall and relaxed in his white tie and tails, standing behind the windbreak at the helipad. I felt like a princess climbing out of a royal coach.

"I didn't expect to see you until we got to the opera house," I said.

"I'll go down a little early. Maybe you'd like to come with me?"

"I'd love to if I won't get in the way."

"Not a chance."

"Are you tired?" I asked him. He looked tired to me.

"Word's not in my vocabulary."

I took his arm and he guided me through the gates and up the drive and I suddenly had butterflies, the same silly, giddy feeling I used to get when a date called for me at my parents' house. Ridiculous.

Chapter Thirty-three

Thursday night

Opening night of the opera season traditionally began with a cocktail party for patrons hosted by my parents. They'd given the party for over thirty years or so and it had become an albatross for them. Well, for my mother, actually. It had always been an albatross for my father, who had always been of the opinion that opera singers should be shot and put out of their, and particularly his, misery. Mother was doomed to frustration, as only a westerner who has been educated at a Philadelphia finishing school can be. She knew, absolutely and irrefutably, all the proper things to do about everything, how to handle every conceivable social situation with courtesy, grace, dignity, and aplomb, but in Roundup, it was hard to find people who appreciated those distinctions and/or gave a damn.

Mother insisted on hosting the opening party because "it must be done properly and it makes me shudder to think what someone like Fanny Gaines or that awful Italian woman would do with it, and believe you me, they're dying to get their hands on this party. Over my dead body. The evening must be done with a sense of propriety and so

we must do it. We must set the tone. But, Lord knows, I'm sick of it."
She had made the same speech to me for thirty years, and when I lived
in Santa Bianca, she'd given it over the phone long-distance.

"Maybe I'll do it next year," I'd said to her that afternoon over the
phone from my bathtub.

"Be my guest," she said. But I knew she didn't mean it. Transfer of
power of this party would be over her dead body, literally. I imagined
Mimi would get the party the same day she got the house.

Mother and Daddy stood in the entry hall, the staircase arching behind them, to greet their guests. She looked quite regal, I thought,
decked out in the Bennett diamonds, a dazzling Art Deco display that
glittered and twinkled from her ears and neck and wrists and fingers
and the bodice of her slate-gray chiffon gown. She was tall and slim
and her gray-blond hair curled softly around her face and her bright
blue eyes scanned me quickly for imperfections, but her pleasure at
my being with Richard Jerome and her unwillingness to do or say
anything to screw it up apparently prevailed because all she said was,
"How beautiful you look, Lilly dear," before passing me along to my
father, who stood beside her trim and compact, handsome in his
evening clothes, anxious for the ordeal to be over. He smiled and
kissed my cheek and passed me along to their butler, Manuel, who
stood at the end of the line with a trayful of champagne.

Richard and I passed through an archway and down a set of steps
into the sparkling swirl of guests who filled the living room. It
smelled deliciously of cigarette smoke and expensive perfume. Roaring fires blazed from the hearths at either end and above one mantel
hung a portrait of my great-grandmother painted just before she and
Great-Grandfather were married. She'd been an Englishwoman and
the painting emphasized her creamy skin (accentuated by a string of
perfect luminous pearls around her throat), blushy cheeks, lustrous
dark brown hair that was pulled up into a Gibson-girl-type knot,
large black eyes, and full red, laughing mouth. She wore a pale pink
satin evening gown and her little West Highland white terrier sat
among the folds of opulent fabric on the floor. The whole painting

seemed backlit, illuminative, rich, and deep. She had a great sense of humor.

Great-Grandfather, standing in front of one of his locomotives, faced her from the opposite mantel. He looked exactly like my father and me. I don't know if he had a sense of humor or not, but one has to to get along.

A Persian rug covered the polished slate floor and red satin damask draperies bordered the tall windows. For the most part, the living room furniture was quite formal, eighteenth-century English pieces, the sofas and chairs upholstered in densely colored mustard and forest-green satins, and topping it all off, colorful regimental standards of cavalry brigades and various family cattle brands hung from a surrounding gallery. A lot of people would probably find the whole setup pretentious. Who cares? We loved it.

The first person I zeroed in on was Miami McCloud. In billows of white chiffon, she was reminiscent of a tall ship bobbing at anchor, standing patiently beneath Great-Grandmother and visiting with two of Roundup's most eligible bachelors, depending on your standards and desperation. Diminutive and very, very rich William Lethbridge III gazed up at her adoringly while the president of the Roundup Country Club, George Saint George, who was already completely—excuse my French—shit-faced, addressed an incomprehensible, slurry story to her basketballs. Miami pretended to find his every word fascinating.

Roundup attracts types of people who come west to escape whatever and then establish beachheads of whatever they left. George Saint George, for instance, a transplanted New England snob, a seedy, alcoholic Mayflower type, could not say more than four words without interjecting "Goddamn." He loved the country club, hated Roman Catholics, and respected Jews with equal fervor, was usually totally plastered and eternally clothed in threadbare evening clothes and black patent dance pumps evidently in case a debutante ball should be declared. His gray skin hung in droopy, jowly loops and I always thought he was a geek.

"Hi, Willy," I said to Will Lethbridge, and we kissed each other's cheeks. We'd grown up together and everyone always had thought how neat it would be if we'd gotten married since our ranches adjoined, we were approximately the same height, and his family owned the other string of banks. But our names precluded the match: too cute—Willy and Lilly—and besides, there simply had never been sparks between us.

"Do you know Miami McCloud?" he asked.

"Of course," I said. "Everyone knows Miami." She and I greeted each other warmly. "Good evening, Mr. Saint George," I said. "It's been a long time. You look just the same."

"Huh." His heavy-lidded, bloodshot, watery eyes regarded me without recognition. "I was just telling this young lady about, well, you know, I live just up the hill from that goddamned basilica, you know. So you know what I did? I telephoned the goddamned pope."

Miami laughed heartily. "Oh, George," she said. "You are such a naughty boy."

"You really think so?" He looked hopefully at her chest.

Once a geek, always a geek. I ached for Santa Bianca and friends whose lives had meaning.

Across the room, Richard had gone to work visiting with Mr. and Mrs. Van Hoorden, who had underwritten tonight's opening, and I ached for him. I wanted us to go back to the ranch and crawl into bed and pull the down comforter over our heads but I knew we couldn't, and wouldn't anyhow. I traded my champagne for Jameson's on the rocks and went off in search of Eli, but before I found him, Roland Tewkesbury entered the room and stopped down by Great-Grandfather. My spirits picked up.

Based on yesterday's overheard phone conversation with Pamela, I knew that tonight was probably the biggest night of his life. That a long-standing plan was about to be put into effect: The Seduction and Capture of Pamela Butterfield. But I couldn't tell if he felt the prize was worth killing for. He seemed nervous and distracted.

"Good evening, Roland," I said. "You look especially handsome tonight."

His face reddened and he patted his cheeks and hair. "Thank you. You're looking extremely elegant."

Pamela's voice, echoing through the entry hall, saved us from further embarrassment. She pranced into the living room resplendent in gold lamé from head to toe, looking, as she would say, "fabulous." But who wouldn't, I wondered, with all the sex she'd had in the last seventy-two hours?

She rushed over and kissed my cheek. "My God, Lilly! You look fabulous!" Her black eyes were wide and glittery. Her coal-black bouffant hair looked like it had been shellacked. "Did you like the funeral? Didn't I tell you it would be something? Roland, would you get me a martini, please? Straight up, very dry. Weren't the white roses exquisite?" I noticed she hadn't bothered to greet Roland. There were a lot of ground rules being laid down but he seemed fairly to swoon with joy at the command and buzzed off like a busy bee.

"Incredibly," I said. "Where's Ellen? I thought she was going to be here."

"Who knows?" Pam said. "She told me she had a fight with her boyfriend and I didn't even know she had one. I must say, after all these years and you girls still single, I've pretty much given up trying to keep track of your all's love lives. But, Lilly, I wish you could get her to do something about the way she looks. I don't understand why she doesn't take care of herself."

"Me either," I said. I looked around for Richard. He had wandered off to talk with the Widow Winthrop, who was very rich and could underwrite Richard's whole next season. She was blushing. Richard was a devil.

"Do you really believe that Christine shot Walter?" I said.

Pam was caught off guard. A flush darkened her cheeks and she looked at her hands. "I don't know," she said simply. "She said she did."

"How is she?"

Pam shrugged. "Who knows? Nuts, as usual. All locked up. No one can get in to see her."

"Why are you lying, Pam?" I said. "I know Christine's at home."

Tears quickly flooded her eyes. "I don't know. Roland said it would be better if people didn't know." Roland handed her a stemmed martini glass. "Oh, thanks, you're a doll," Pamela said. Her eyes were dry, as though the tears had been sucked right back into their ducts. It was weird.

"My pleasure," Roland said and then added, "Roland said 'what' would be better if people didn't know?"

"That Christine's at home," I said.

"Certainly it's better if people don't know." He took quick umbrage. "I don't want all the media out there with their helicopters and swarms. It isn't as though she's been set free. Her release is completely within the law. We had to put up an enormous bail and frankly, Miss Bennett, I don't see that it's any of your affair."

"Roland," Pam said, putting her hand on his arm to calm him down. "It's all right. Let's just change the subject, okay?" Pam had a lot at stake and she knew I knew it. The last thing she wanted was for Roland to antagonize me. "I knew I shouldn't have come this evening, Lilly. I really didn't want to. I think it's tacky for me to go out so soon after Walter's death, but Roland insisted. But I think I'm too upset to stay."

"A beautiful woman should never be left home alone on such a gala evening," Roland said. He dusted a speck of white powder off his black satin lapels. "And I'm quite sure Walter would agree."

"I'm surprised you'd call our opera opening 'gala,' Mr. Tewkesbury," I said. "Compared to the crowd you're used to traveling in, I'd think you'd think we were all just a bunch of shitkickers. Oh, look, here comes Ellen."

Ellen had gone downhill fast. I didn't think it would be possible for a woman our age to have skin so broken out, but she looked like the "Before" picture in an acne ad and had dressed in a gaudy, ill-fitting silk jacquard cocktail dress that, in spite of her thinness, accentuated a roll of flab around her back where her bra cut into her. Her feet were clad in the scuffed, run-down black kid pumps she wore with everything. She seemed just about to fall off the edge. There was always the possibility that she was truly mourning her father, but in my mind it was outweighed by the possibility that she shot him.

It took all my strength and self-control not to say, "Come on, Ellen, get ahold of yourself. Make a damn effort." There used to be a television commercial for something, I can't remember what, that said, "If you look good, you feel good, and if you feel good, you do good." I've always subscribed to that uncomplicated philosophy. Ellen obviously didn't. Well, I felt good, and I looked good, and I was tired of feeling sorry for Ellen Butterfield.

"I was just asking Pamela and Roland about Christine," I said. "How do you think she's doing?"

Ellen shrugged. "I don't know. I, uh, haven't seen her." Ellen was a terrible liar.

"Lilly knows that Christine is at home," Pam said.

Ellen looked at me sheepishly.

"Do you think Christine killed Walter?" I asked Roland.

"Well, after all, she did admit it, didn't she? Why? Who do you think shot him?"

"I don't know," I said. "There are four or five people it could have been, but I don't think it was Christine."

"Like who?" Ellen said.

"I'm not going to speculate. It's dangerous. But I can feel the tension building, can't you all? Something's about to give."

Pamela shuddered. "Gives me the creeps. Oh, my God. How in the world did *that* whore get in here?" she said, spotting Miami.

"I'm going to the bar," I said. "Your glass is empty, Mr. Tewkesbury. Let me get you another drink. Anyone else?"

Pam tossed off her martini and handed me the glass. "You're a doll."

As I left the room, I saw Elias and Ellen spot each other. They should get married, I thought. They've always been in love, why don't they just give up and do it? By the time I returned, Pamela and Miami stood practically toe to toe, but Miami was several inches taller and I wondered if she would start bumping and shoving Pamela backward with her chest and shoulders the way she probably used to bump football players when she was one.

"You are too cheap for words," Pamela spat. "And Walter would still be alive if it weren't for you. You're a home wrecker. You killed my husband just as much as Christine did."

"I don't understand this big interest of yours in Walter, Mrs. Butterfield," Miami said menacingly with a big tight smile that displayed her racks of white, white teeth. "You never had the slightest interest in him when he was alive. And you know what? If I weren't a lady, the temptation to come out there and shoot both you and Christine would be almost irresistible. You're nothing but a couple of lowlifes. Maybe I'd even drive stakes through your hearts."

The rest of the guests pretended the two women weren't even there.

Richard signaled me from across the room and I had to leave before the bout ended. But I imagine it was a tie. On our way to the opera house we stopped by Federal Express, where I shipped the two cocktail glasses I'd taken from Roland and Pamela to Washington. I was sure the information wouldn't add anything to what I already knew, to what my instincts were telling me, but for a twenty-dollar air bill, it would be unprofessional not to close the loop.

The opera was superb—not a soul slept, not even Pamela—and the dinner dance on the huge stage afterward was elegant and merry and lasted till the wee hours.

We rolled into the ranch at about four feeling no pain and fell into bed, and at seven o'clock, the phone rang. Richard didn't answer. He just picked up the whole phone and sort of tossed it onto me.

"Bennett here," I said smartly, not knowing which side was up.

"Wake up, Lilly," Elias said. "Christine Butterfield is dead."

ℭ Chapter Thirty-four

Friday morning

"**W**hat?" I had such a headache from all the booze the night before, I couldn't think where I was.

"I came back to the truck after the opera and fell asleep," Elias said. "Everything's been completely quiet in the hacienda until a few minutes ago, at about five of seven, Maria went in to take Christine her breakfast and found her body. She's been shot, I think. I haven't listened to the tapes yet but Maria's just called the police. Pamela told her to call Dr. Sheridan, 'Not,' she said, 'that goddamned Quack Rosak.' "

I could hear Pamela screaming hysterically over the speakers in the background.

"Okay. We'll be there in ten minutes."

"Drive carefully."

I handed the phone back to Richard. "Christine's been shot," I said.

"What?"

"Dead. She's dead."

We pulled on jeans and boots; I didn't bother to put on any

makeup. My face was so puffy from champagne, whiskey, cognac, and beer, it wouldn't have helped. I just hid the mess as best I could behind dark glasses.

Richard went directly to meet Elias at the Roundup Gas & Electric van at Wittier Gulch and I headed for Dwight Alexander's cabin by the creek. A beaten-up, putty-colored Mazda was parked in the lean-to next to his Corvette. I couldn't tell if my tracks were the only new ones in the hard mud going down the narrow road to his quiet, sleepy place.

From its low angle shooting straight across the prairie from Ft. Dodge, Iowa, the bright, clear morning sun threw clean white light over everything—the trees, the houses, the barns, the fields, and the distant mountains. I suppose it was pretty but I was just too excited to pay much attention. I jangled the rusty cowbell that hung on the doorframe and pounded on the door itself.

Dwight was still in bed and I could tell, when he finally answered the door, he was the kind of guy who, when you wakened him, liked to look rumpled. Like he was in a movie about a guy who lived on a ranch. Like he slept in his flannel shirt and jeans. Like his idol was Sam Shepard or Tom Cruise or Mel Gibson. The kind of guy who scratched his chest all the time and tried to look cool. That's how Dwight looked in the morning.

"What's up, Marshal?" He ran his fingers through his hair and licked his puffy lips and scratched his chest.

"I'd like to come in and talk to you, Dwight. It's official."

He made a face and stood aside so I could pass into his small, surprisingly tidy abode. "Want some coffee or something?" he said. "I can't do anything without a cup of coffee."

I didn't believe that he couldn't do *anything* without a cup of coffee but said, "Yes, thanks." I felt even worse than I looked.

Dwight put two earthenware mugs of tap water into the microwave, heated them up and then spooned teaspoonfuls of instant coffee into them. He handed me mine and then slouched back into a large, low easy chair where I imagined he and his ladies made love most of the time. It had that look about it.

He cleared his throat and regarded me over the rim of his cup. "Official?" He tossed his head so a long lank of his sandy hair would fly back from his forehead.

"Christine has been murdered."

"What?" Dwight looked blank. He actually sat up straight.

"Where were you last night?"

"Right here," he said in a rush. His eyes got wide like a little kid's. "Really. After I dropped Mrs. B. off at your family's place in town I came back home because she said Mr. Tewkesbury'd bring her back out. So I sat around and watched TV and had a pizza and a couple of beers."

"Did any cars go by?"

"Yeah. Ellen's."

"What time was that?"

"About nine."

"How do you know it was nine?"

"*Cheers* had just ended and I was in the kitchen and saw some car lights coming way down the road and remembered what you told me, so I went up the hill and watched her turn into the compound."

"Are you certain it was Ellen's car?" Ellen had been at the opera and at nine o'clock the first act hadn't ended—Lucia and the Lammermoor clan still liked each other. I didn't remember seeing Ellen at intermission but that didn't mean much since it had been a mob scene.

"Yeah. I know it was her car."

"How long was she there?"

"I don't know. I came back in and I didn't note what time I saw her taillights because a friend of mine came over and I got busy." He glanced at the closed bedroom door and grinned.

"Any other cars?"

"I didn't hear any until Mrs. B. came home. That was about two, I think. Mr. Tewkesbury just dropped her off and headed back to town."

"The police will be questioning you in a few minutes, Dwight. Tell them the truth."

"Yes, ma'am." Dwight was getting the hang of it. The old respect thing.

"Sorry you have to leave, Marshal. I hope you'll come back sometime and make it social." He hooked his thumbs into his belt loops and drummed his fingers on his fly and rocked up on his toes.

"Forget it, Dwight."

All the while we'd been talking, it sounded as though the entire Roundup Police Department had arrived at the hacienda and I could picture flashers and sirens and skid marks on the dirt road like an old Burt Reynolds and Sally Field movie.

Say what you will about the nonexistent ethics of the press, they move fast—faster than Jesse Owens or Carl What's-His-Name. That's probably part of their problem. If it took them longer to get to a story, they might give some thought to what it was about and what they'd do when they got there or even if it was worth going at all. Oh, well. That's another story. By the time I got back up to the road, the television and radio and newspaper people were gathered at the main entrance to Rancho del Sol. Unfurled antennas and raised broadcast towers adorned the tops of their vans and the crews were already huddled around cups of coffee that steamed in Wyoming's frosty autumn morning. Three Roundup squad cars, two unmarked cruisers, and the coroner's wagon jammed the driveway. I did a U-turn and parked my Jeep in front of the Channel 8 van, so I was first in line for heading back to town, and then I flipped my badge at the officer at the gate and entered the scene.

Jack Lewis, all turned out in a well-pressed brown whipcord suit and shiny reptile cowboy boots, had just arrived and was assembling his troops in the entry hall. A large chunk of turquoise topped the bolo at the neck of his starched white shirt. He looked more like a model at a photo shoot. His capped white teeth grinned at me scornfully and his voice was typically sarcastic.

"What are you doing here, Bennett?" he said. "Turning into an ambulance chaser? Can't retire gracefully? Here's an idea: Take up golf. Or, how about this: Fix your hair. You look like hell."

"Fuck you, Lewis." I smiled and showed him my badge. "Official business."

If he was surprised (I knew he wouldn't be impressed), he didn't show it. "This isn't a federal investigation, as far as I know."

"Too soon to tell," I answered. "Better not to take any chances. Besides, I might be helpful."

Lewis gave me a hard stare and then a grimace that might have been a grin and said, "You're right. You know your way around this bunch of rich assholes better than I do. Come on."

I followed him up the stairs to Christine's bedroom. What a mess. Clothes tossed everywhere. Bed unmade. Phone cord ripped out of the wall. Open makeup jars, smeared hair gel, and spilled powder. The doors out to the balcony stood open, dissolving the odor of death emanating from Christine's insides.

A single shot in the chest with a high-powered gun had driven her most of the way across her king-sized bed. Her head lay off the far side. She had been wearing a short thin cotton nightie trimmed with wide bands of hand-stitched lace around the hem and the capped sleeves. The lace trim on the front of the gown had been sucked into the huge hole where the blast had gone, like white water swirling down a drain. A pink satin bow lay half in and half out of the wound. Blood and tissue that had come out of her back along with the blast were spattered across the top of the bed table and the white silk lamp shade. The nightgown was up around her waist and her legs were spread-eagled exposing her fully. She'd been dead for a while. Rigor mortis was advanced, the spattered blood was almost black, and I knew if I touched it I would find it sticky. A marble-sized black swelling marked a fresh needle puncture on her left arm.

Jack and I walked around the bed and looked at her face. Her eyes were wide, wide open and her face had a frozen grimace of extreme pain which I found unusual because the gunshot would have been so big and so fast, there wouldn't have been time for her to experience any pain. I looked again at the bruise on her arm and realized she must have already been in the process of dying from an overdose when whoever shot her pulled the trigger.

Jack went into the bathroom and shoved around the packet of white powder and syringe with his ballpoint pen. "Huh," he said. "It always disappoints me that rich people are so dumb."

"Not all of us, Jack," I said.

"Huh," he said.

The center drawer of the dressing table stood open, so I rifled around in it and didn't find anything unusual but noticed, in the wastebasket, the red wrapping paper and gift box from the present she'd brought home. So it hadn't been a book. It had been a box of cocaine and all the trimmings. I stuffed the evidence into my pockets before Jack Lewis saw it. I intended to solve this case and I intended to cooperate, both approximately at the same moment.

"Anything over there?" he asked.

"Nah. Not really."

Jack gave the go-ahead for the technical crew to begin dusting for prints and the police photographer began snapping Christine from all angles. I don't think she would have cared that she looked gruesome, that her room was splattered with her insides, or that she was spread-eagled in a thin nightie so that they could take pictures even of her business. I knew that if Christine were watching from somewhere she couldn't have cared less what we did or what happened to her. I knew she would be glad her life was over.

"Any ideas?" Jack asked me as we went back downstairs toward the library where Walter had been shot six days before. Jack's young lieutenant had just finished questioning Maria, who I'm sure had forgotten every word of English she ever knew in her life. She left the library pale and shaking and he invited Dwight into the room. Jack and I stopped in the hall.

"Well, you're going to have to arrest Ellen Butterfield," I said. "But I don't think she did it."

"What are you talking about?"

"That young man is going to tell your young man that Ellen's car was out here last night at about nine o'clock, but I don't think she was driving it."

"Why?" Jack was way off balance. Good.

"Just a feeling. I think she'll be locked up for an hour, two at the most, and then a dozen people will come forward to say that they talked to her during intermission at the opera and you'll be back at square one."

Jack regarded me. "Are we going to cooperate?"

"Of course we're going to cooperate, Jack," I said. "I believe in cooperation. I just don't have anything to cooperate about at the moment. Besides, you know marshals only serve federal warrants and escort prisoners. We aren't *detectives.*"

"So?"

"So, I don't have anything for you but I would like to be there when you pick up Ellen."

"*If* we pick her up."

"You will. Why wouldn't you?"

"One more question, Lilly. How did you know about this? I'm sure you don't keep a police scanner on your bedside table."

"Phone call from a friend," I said. Not a lie.

~ Chapter Thirty-five

I drove back to the van and found Baby curled up in Richard's lap, asleep. Elias, still in his evening clothes, slumped at his console, his black tie untied and his shirt collar unbuttoned and his belly hanging over his tight cummerbund. They had just finished listening to the tape of Christine's murder and it had knocked the stuffing out of them. Both men were ashen, like they were about to throw up.

"Bad?" I said. "Oh, thank God for glazed doughnuts and coffee." I helped myself. They both looked at me with disgust.

"You won't be able to keep those down after you hear this," Elias said.

"You'd be surprised."

"Just listen." Elias pushed a button and the previous night's tapes began to roll and none of us spoke as we sat through Christine's last hours with her. We've made life so cheap. People live and die all day long on television, so when the real thing comes along it's like another show, but less exciting.

"I want to come home, Rory," Christine told her husband in London, where it was two-thirty in the morning, half past eight in the evening in Roundup. "No one here likes me." She sounded tired and vulnerable.

"Will the police let you come home, lovie?"

"I don't know. Why don't you come here? It would be fun. Especially now that Daddy's gone. We could have a good time. There's a track here."

"Bunch of broken-down cow ponies," Rory said. "When is that old bastard's will going to be read? I might come for that."

"I don't know. Pretty soon, I guess," Christine said, either forgetting the will had already been read or choosing not to tell her husband about it. "I'm staying clean, Rory. I haven't had anything for a week. I really feel good."

"Um, that's nice."

"Do you still love me, Rory? Are you even a little bit proud of me?"

"Of course I love you. You're my lovie. A week's a long time without dope. Isn't it making you nuts?"

"No, it's okay. Boring, though. I'm awfully bored. I have some tranquilizers that help. Well, I'm sorry I woke you up, but I just wanted to say good night. I'm going to go to bed now. I love you."

Rory laughed.

"What's funny about that?" Christine said.

"Nothing."

There was more laughter on Rory's end of the line, a woman's laugh quickly masked by a hand muffling the phone.

"Who's there with you?"

Rory took his hand away. "No one."

"Goddamn it, Rory! You've got someone there in my bed! You bastard!"

"No, I don't, sweet. I promise."

"You're lying." Christine slammed down the receiver and ripped the cord from the wall. She wandered furiously around her room picking up this and that. Turned up the volume on a Mary Tyler Moore rerun. Leafed through a book and then slammed it down on her bed table. Lit a cigarette. Pulled open a drawer, ruffled through some papers, and then said with some wonder, "Oh, my God. Will you look at that?" Her voice was scarcely audible over the television.

"Oh, I know I shouldn't," she said. "Don't be stupid, Christine, you've got a whole week invested in this this time. But maybe just a little won't hurt too much. Besides, I can stop again. I just did, didn't I? I've done it a dozen times before. It isn't that hard."

In the truck, the three of us listened, scarcely breathing, as glass and metal clinked on the porcelain of her bathroom sink. The cellophane ripped off the disposable syringe. The glassine bag of cocaine crinkled brightly and I could envision the white powder flowing into the teaspoon. Water ran. An eyedropper whooshed. A match flared. The cocaine dissolved and the syringe sucked it up. Rubber tubing snapped around her arm and she made a small noise as the needle entered her vein. The syringe clattered into the sink.

"Oh, yes. This is more like it." The drug worked quickly, sending Christine on a big last outing. As high as one can go while living. As powerful, invincible, euphoric as one can get.

It only took ten minutes to reach the end and when it started, it came fast. It would be a race with the gunman to see who got to her first. The bedroom door opened as Christine's chest pains began.

"Oh. You," she said, her voice a moan. "You can't kill me. I know all about you. Father told me everything about you and him and I've told everyone." Another crippling chest pain with just enough time to wonder what it might be. Just enough time for Christine Butterfield's last words to be, "ow!"

The gun exploded with noise. A spectacular parting shot for a life that hadn't ever amounted to anything and I wondered if whoever pulled the trigger would get off with a slap on the wrist. After all, with the right forensic work, a good lawyer might be able to prove that the only thing shot had been a corpse.

The television show ended and Mary Tyler Moore's theme song, "You're Going to Make It After All," was the only sound in Christine Butterfield's bedroom.

I pulled on my jacket. "Well, that's that, I guess," I said. "I'm going to Ellen's. I want to hear her version before Jack Lewis gets there. I'll call you from the car, Eli, because we need to make some security arrangements for her."

Both of their faces were completely white.

"Hey," I said. "Get a grip, you guys." I grabbed two more doughnuts on my way out but Richard's expression stopped me. He was looking at me as if I were a heartless ghoul. As if a monster lurked inside this person who he'd thought was fun.

"Look, Richard," I said. "I want you to understand something about me. One of the permanent conditions of policework is a blanket 'Sorry' for everything seen and heard, for all mankind. So although I'm sorry about Christine Butterfield's murder and death, I'm not particularly shocked. I'm more in a hurry than anything because Ellen is one of two living Butterfields, counting Wally, and she's in danger." I looked hard at him. "You know how much you love the challenge and excitement of what you do? Of finding all the millions of dollars it takes to get all that great stuff on the stage?"

He nodded.

"Well, that's how I feel about what I do. Or, as a wise man once observed, 'Like a dog to vomit.' Bye."

I stuck Baby under my arm, a doughnut in my mouth, and left. When I pulled onto the blacktop, it was just eight-thirty, and I was glad to see that I'd beaten the parade of police and press vehicles that would soon leave the Rancho del Sol. Only Channel 6 would leave a crew behind. That's why they were first in the news ratings—they could be counted on to show the body and usually were able to get everyone they interviewed to cry. Even people who didn't have anything to do with the story. Unreal.

❦ Chapter Thirty-six

*T*his is a surprise, Lilly," Ellen said, welcoming me into her elegant entry hall with its oval shape, mirrored walls, and white marble floor. Dozens of white tulips filled a sterling-silver tureen on an oval table in the center of the tiny chamber. I felt as if I were suspended in a beautifully glittering bright cloud. She was dressed in a pretty yellow satin negligee with deep ruffs of lace around the cuffs and neckline, which led me to believe that there was, or had been, a guest in the bedroom. The possibility that it had been Elias crossed my mind. "Come on in, I'll make us some coffee."

"That's okay, Ellen," I said. "I don't need anything to drink. I think we'd better have an honest conversation instead and we don't have much time."

"An honest conversation? What does that mean?" she said gaily, leading the way into the living room which was bright with morning sun. A crystal menagerie on one of the side tables magnified sunbeams into patterns on the carpet.

"Christine is dead."

"WHAT?" She turned quickly to face me. Her mouth dropped open in surprise, as I knew it would.

"She was shot last night during the opera and your car was seen entering the hacienda compound at nine o'clock."

"My what?"

"Did you leave the opera last night?"

"No. Of course not. Never." She shook her head. "Ask Elias. I was sitting with him. I was with him all evening."

"Where was your car?"

"In the main garage. I can't believe this. Did you say Christine was dead?"

"Tell me about the gift you argued over on Wednesday afternoon when you brought her home," I said.

"What do you mean?" Ellen took a cigarette from a porcelain box on the side table and lit it with an old-fashioned silver table lighter. "I didn't give her any gift."

"Ellen, please. I don't know whether or not you gave it to her, but I do know you and she had words about it. Come on, we watched the whole thing. We've got it all on tape, so tell me the truth, we don't have a lot of time. What was in the package?"

"Got it all on *tape*?" She laughed giddily. "What do you mean? Isn't that illegal?"

"Not when you've hired me to find out who murdered your father. We've had the house under surveillance for several days. We watched you bring Christine home. And we watched you have an argument with her about a gift-wrapped package." I pulled a clear plastic bag with the wrapping paper and box out of my jacket pocket and held it up. "Look familiar? What was it?"

"I don't know."

"I beg your pardon?"

"I don't know where she got it, and I don't know what was in it," Ellen said. "Honestly. But I know what I thought was in it. Drugs. It had that look about it and she had that look about her. It was like her little security box. She wouldn't even let me touch it. Really. That's the truth."

"I don't know whether to believe you or not."

"Why?"

"Why? Why should I believe you? You aren't stupid, Ellen, but you're acting like it. Your credibility with me is nonexistent. I met with Roland on Wednesday and he told me that it was against your father's better judgment to put him on the Foundation board but, because you'd resigned, and because a board meeting was coming up and with you gone there wasn't a quorum, he had no choice. Now, add that to the fact you've lied to me twice that I know of in the last fifteen hours, last night about Christine's going home and just now about the package, and you want to know why I don't believe you? I don't know whether you murdered your father and your sister or not, nor whether you know what was in that package or not."

I had not even raised my voice but Ellen's eyes filled with tears and she gaped at me as if I'd slapped her. "Lilly, believe me, I didn't kill them."

"Maybe. Maybe not," I said. "But Jack Lewis is on his way here to arrest you. So forget the tears, you don't have time."

"WHAT? Arrest ME?" She started to laugh. All the color drained from her face. "Why?"

"Come on," I said. "The niceties are over." I took her by the elbow and pushed her into her dressing room. "You're going to be arrested because your car was seen at Rancho del Sol last night at the time that your sister was shot. Now, get into the shower, then dress in something pretty, fix your hair and put on some makeup for a change because you're going to get a lot of attention and you want to look your best."

Ellen showered quickly and once she'd dried her hair and was swabbing foundation onto her mottled skin, I sat down on the edge of her tub and said, "Listen to me carefully: You'll be taken to the station, booked, and then possibly put into a holding cell while Paul Decker arranges your release. I called him from my car and he should be here any minute."

Ellen's hand started to shake. I didn't blame her, mine would have, too, under the same circumstances, and she hadn't even seen a holding cell. I'd seen plenty of them and they were horrible, filthy things usually full of horrible, filthy people who urinated and vomited all over themselves and everyone else. And what made the cells even worse was that keeping them clean was the inmates' responsibility, so you can imagine how clean they got. The only thing to be said on a holding cell's behalf was that if an inmate was withholding anything, she usually told it all, instantly. Anything to get out of there.

"If you're put into a cell, keep your eyes to yourself. Don't talk to your cellmates and ignore what they say to you. Stay cool. Stay calm. No matter what. Once you're released, leave the station immediately. Paul Decker will be with you and he'll take you straight to Elias's car. Get in and leave alone with him. Do not let anyone else accompany you. Do you understand?"

"No."

"Let's keep it simple," I said. "You're in danger. Your father and your sister have both been murdered in the last six days and, based on the trends I would say that, without protection, until we find the killer, your days are numbered in single digits."

"And Elias is going to protect me?" Ellen clipped on pearl earrings. She looked pleased at the prospect of being under Elias's wing.

"Yes, sort of."

"Why won't the police department do it?"

"They'll offer. Tell them that you've made your own arrangements. Now, while we're waiting for Chief Lewis, put a few things in a suitcase and I'll give it to Elias."

There was a knock on the front door and I went out and let in Paul, the giant Irish criminal defense lawyer whose phone number everyone carried around in his wallet in case of DUI. We greeted each other and he followed me back into Ellen's bedroom where she perched on the edge of her bed like a young girl leaving for boarding school. All packed. Ready to go. Waiting quietly until it was time to go to the airport. She looked all right. She had on a navy suit, pearls, makeup, and her security-blanket shoes.

"Ellen," I said. "Who knew that it was the maid's night off last night?"

"I don't have any idea. I didn't even know it. I didn't have that much to do with their home life."

"Have you ever heard of Carl Rosak?"

Ellen shook her head. "No."

"Michael Gryczkowski?"

"No. Who are they?"

I filled her and Paul in on Pamela's background and her relationship with Rosak and Gryczkowski.

"That sure clears up the blackmail question," Ellen said. "And it also answers the question about whether or not family members could serve on the Foundation board. She obviously wanted to put her illegitimate son on it and she wanted all of us out of the way so she and Wally and this Michael person could take over the paper. So you think Pam did it?"

"No," I said. "I don't."

"Well then, who did?"

"I don't know."

The doorbell rang and Paul excused himself to go answer it, closing the bedroom door behind him. Ellen's jaw was set and her lips were pursed into a tight line and her nostrils flared slightly.

"Don't be afraid." I put my hand on her shoulder. "This will be over before you know it. And don't forget, go straight to Elias's car as fast as you can. Do not talk to the reporters. Ignore them and keep your eyes on Elias. He's your target. And whatever you do, don't cry because that's what the TV people want, and besides, you really look pretty."

"I do?"

"Yes. Good luck, Ellen. You'll be fine."

"Thanks." She smiled and walked into the living room, where Jack Lewis read her her rights.

Once they had left, I took Ellen's suitcase down and put it in my car and then walked Baby in the park across the street. I took her leash off and she raced around while I watched her from a park bench. It was only ten o'clock in the morning but I felt like I'd been up for a thousand hours and was a thousand years old.

Maybe Ellen knew it was the maid's night off, maybe not, but several other people did. Roland Tewkesbury did. So did Pam and Dwight and possibly Miami and Carl Rosak. Pam was the kind of person who would want everyone to know that she had a cook; and people who want information like that known usually want everyone to know that they also give their servants days off. In the old days, maids always had Thursdays and every other Sunday off, a custom with which I would not expect Miami and Rosak to be familiar. And then there was the question of who took Ellen's car.

I pulled myself together and drove downtown to the main parking garage at Bennett Auditorium, a garage as big and drafty as the theater itself, and spoke with the young Mexican attendant who was reading a comic book, listening to rap music, and chewing gum. I reached past him and switched off the boom box.

"Hey!" he yelped. "You kin't do that."

"Were you on duty last night?"

"No."

"Who was?"

"How come?"

"I want to talk to him. It's personal. I'd like his name and address." I gave the young chap twenty dollars.

He took the money. "His name ees Mike Rodriguez. He libes in the projets by the ribber."

"There are probably fifty Mike Rodriguezes who live in the projects by the river. Exactly donde? Qué numero?"

"Ciento-ocho-cinco Wind Ribber Terraza."

"One-eight-five Wind River Terrace?" Incredible. Those federal housing project people really have a sense of humor when it comes to street names. Wind River Terrace. Why not Sutton Place?

"Sí."

"Qué es su nombre?"

"Antonio Valdez."

"Listen to me, Antonio Valdez." I handed him another twenty. "Don't tell anyone I was here. Okay? Not anyone. If you do tell, I'll know, and then I'll come back and you will be berry, berry sorry. Comprende?"

"Sí, señora."

"Adiós."

"Adiós, señora."

Mike Rodriguez swore to Dios, Jesús, and Santa Maria he never saw Ellen's car leave the garage during the opera, nor did he see it return. He was lying. But whoever he was lying for had given him more money than I had with me.

Chapter Thirty-seven

Friday afternoon

Down by the river, in front of the main ranch house where Elias lived, was the main ranch guest house, a small two-bedroom cabin, its logs chinked in white cement, empty flower boxes beneath its paned windows. The interior was simple—cedar floors with bright wool Navajo Indian rugs, polished pine furniture with comfortable cushions, and red-and-white-checked curtains. The living room, dining room, and kitchen were all one room. There was a large stone fireplace and the walls were lined with bookcases and crudely whittled portrayals of fourteen-inch-long rainbow and brook trout which the guests who did the whittling claimed got away. All lies. Because of our altitude, seventy-five hundred feet above sea level, any trout that grew as big as ten inches was a hero, got its picture taken and got returned to the creek. Names of famous men adorned the trout plaques—heads of state, secretaries of state, Fortune 500 CEOs—all friends and associates of my grandfather and father and brother. All succumbing to the Circle B mystique: Drink a lot of whiskey and tell a lot of lies. No harm. None of it meant anything outside the ranch anyhow.

The living room opened onto the porch, just twenty feet from the river where a guest could walk out and catch one of those big whoppers for breakfast. Getting guests to go home was a common problem at the Circle B and I was quite sure Ellen Butterfield would not be an exception, except that the fall roundup was wrapping up and the nearby stock pens overflowed with hundreds of lowing cattle and the air was full of dust and diesel fumes from the huge semis that rolled in to take them to market. I tried not to think about that part of ranching, that it was easier for me to deal with shooting a person than a steer.

"This is so beautiful," Ellen said as Elias carried in her small suitcase. She beamed at him. "I'd like to hide out here forever."

Elias blushed.

"I'm going home to clean up," I told them. They couldn't have cared less.

Once I'd pulled myself together and eaten a sandwich, I drove back out to the RG&E van to re-listen to Christine's murder, to see if there was any kind of sound at all afterward that might provide a clue as to the killer.

Christine's last words, "I know all about you. Father told me everything about you and him and I've told everyone," played over and over in my mind. ". . . everything about you. I've told everyone." Then the shot was fired.

No other words were spoken but it had sounded like the steps that went down the front stairs were a man's. They were heavy and not in high-heeled shoes, which all the women had been wearing that night. Obviously, the killer could have changed into flat shoes, but in any event, I was convinced that the killer was a man. A ten-gauge shotgun was usually a man's gun. Women tended more toward seventeen gauges and those just for sport. Women seldom killed with shotguns. Of course, Miami used to be a man and still had a man's footfall and had said right out she'd like to kill Pam and Christine.

I also believed that the same person had done both murders, the weapon was the same, for all intents and purposes, and it appeared that both victims knew the killer. To have two different murderers would be too coincidental.

The afternoon was mild and quiet at Wittier Gulch. The only sound came from a hawk that balanced on the very top of a pine tree nearby and screeched at the top of its lungs at whoever was interested in listening to him. Pencil-thin contrails appeared in the sky, spread, softened, and disappeared. People whizzing from L.A. to New York and New York to L.A. Out here it was silent. The van smelled like a Pizza Hut. Obviously the boys had gotten over their queasiness enough to change from glazed doughnuts to extra thick and crispy with pepperoni.

I poured myself a Jameson's and leaned back in my director's chair and put my boots up on the counter and flipped through the tapes of the day's activities at the Butterfield hacienda.

Pamela was in full flourish. The police technicians and coroner departed at about ten o'clock with what remained of Christine, leaving behind a security contingent of an officer at the front gate, one at the front door, and one at the door of Christine's bedroom.

"Why are you standing up here protecting an empty room?" Pam said to him. "I'm the one who needs watching, for Chrissakes."

"Yes, ma'am," he answered politely and stayed put.

Pam got on the phone and called Albert DeNunzio Celebrity Security Services in Los Angeles and arranged for a full menu of security options. Two personal bodyguards and two security men.

"I want 'em to have walkie-talkies, the works."

"Yes, ma'am," said Mr. DeNunzio.

Carl Rosak called but Pam told Maria to tell him she wasn't home and Roland called and asked her if she would like to go to dinner.

"I don't know, Roland. It's awfully sweet of you but I'm kind of afraid to go out after this mess with Christine."

"What mess with Christine?"

"You mean you haven't heard? Christine was murdered last night."

"Good Lord! How horrible."

"What do you mean, 'horrible'? She and her sister are like the twins from hell. As a matter of fact, Ellen's car was seen coming out here during the opera. I think Ellen shot her. And I think Ellen shot her father and I think they ought to fry her."

"Why didn't you call me?"

"What could you do?"

"I'm coming out directly," Roland said. "You shouldn't be left alone. Have the police provided protection for you?"

"Oh, sure, sort of. Two're outside and one's guarding Christine's bedroom door. I told him he should be guarding me. All he did was nod. But I'll tell you one thing, Roland, I'm scared to death. I mean, I can just feel it—I'm next. If they don't lock up Ellen, I know she's coming after me. I think I'm going to have a nervous breakdown." Pam started to cry.

"I'll be there in twenty minutes."

Pam blew her nose and sniffled. "No, it's okay. You don't have to come out. I'm sure I'll be fine. Why don't you come here for dinner, though? That would be better. Come at seven."

"I'll be there. But please, please, Pamela, if you need anything at all from me or you just want me to come out and be there, please call me. I mean it."

"I will, Roland. Thanks."

Maybe it was Roland Tewkesbury. He was a man. Sort of, I guess.

At one o'clock the Los Angeles security force arrived and did a comprehensive check of the grounds and house, concentrating on Pamela's bedroom, dressing room, car, and Dwight. They called the phone company and had the phone changed to an unlisted number that would take effect within hours.

"This is more like it," Pam said to no one in particular.

At four o'clock, she received a call from the Medical Examiner's Office inquiring as to what arrangements she had made for Christine.

"What do you mean, 'arrangements'?" Pam said.

"For her burial," the doctor said. "Which funeral home have you contacted?"

"Oh, for Chrissakes. You mean *I* have to do this? Oh, Jesus, let me see, who buried Walter?"

"I believe it was Ashbrook, Mrs. Butterfield."

"Well, why don't you give them a call?"

"Fine," he said, sounding abashed. "I suggest you call them as well."

"Fine. I'll do that," said Pam and hung up. "These girls are nothing but trouble, trouble, trouble."

She called the funeral home and told the funeral director she wanted Christine to be buried as soon as possible and asked him to handle everything else.

"Very well, Mrs. Butterfield," said Mr. Ashbrook. "Which minister shall I notify?"

"I don't care. Anybody but that windbag bishop. Just take care of it."

"Very well."

I switched off the volume on the tape machines and concentrated on what I knew and how it all linked together and listened to the information loll around in my mind. I guess I dozed off because the phone ringing at seven o'clock wakened me from a dead sleep. It was pitch-black in the truck except for the glowing digital dials on Elias's equipment. It was Richard.

"How're you doing?" I said.

"I'm dead."

"Me, too."

"Lilly, I think I'm going to stay in town tonight. I'd like to see the curtain up at eight and then go back to my apartment and get some sleep."

"I understand completely," I said. "I'll miss you but I'm going to do the same thing."

"I'll see you tomorrow," he said. "I'll miss you, too."

"Bye-bye," I said. I wanted to say "I love you," and I could tell he did, too.

We hung up and I just sat there for a minute or two, rubbing my eyes and running my hands through my hair. Baby jumped into my lap. She was warm with sleep and tucked herself back into a little ball. It was so wonderfully quiet and I knew that outside the sky was as black as coal and the moon would already have risen and be a distant, frigid disk far, far away casting a callous white light on the silvery prairie. I tucked my glasses into my jacket pocket and checked for my keys and then I heard it. A tiny click. A "click" with which I was familiar. The locking shut of a well-oiled shotgun.

Adrenaline coursed up my spine and my hair stood on end and I clamped my hand around the dog's muzzle and shook my finger at her to be quiet before putting her down, the only command she consistently obeyed. The rest of my movements slid familiarly through me like silk scarves through a magician's ring. I drew my .45 and, staying well back from the rear door, reached over and unlatched but did not open it, giving the gunman time to prepare himself for my oblivious exit. I pretended to call Elias on the phone. "Eli," I said, "what are you up to?" A broom leaned next to the refrigerator and I moved as far toward the front of the truck as I could and still reach the back door with the broom. "Me? Not much. I'm just leaving the truck." I was in position, three-quarters of the way to the front. "No, I don't think so. I think I'll just go home and go to bed. Thanks anyway. Bye." I counted to five and then shoved the broom handle against the back door. As the door swung open, a shotgun blast ripped it off. Chest-high. Where I should have been standing. I rolled out the driver's door and flattened myself on the frozen ground and crawled on my belly into the questionable protection of the large rear tires and peered around them. A second blast disintegrated the tires on the other side of the truck. The gunman's loads were gone.

"FREEZE, YOU SON OF A BITCH," I yelled, returning the fire around the edge of the truck, but it was too late. His running figure disappeared into the safety of a small rise and then into the black shape of a car. The door slammed shut and the engine started, tires spun quickly in the dirt before finding purchase and then he was gone. Whoever it was knew what he was doing because when the car door opened, no interior lights had come on and by the time I reached the rise, the car, guided only by pale parking lights, was well on its way, its taillights disconnected so I could get no sense of the make. It was a square-shaped sedan, which meant it could have been a Mercedes, a Buick, a Lincoln, a Cadillac, a Mercury, a Lexus, an Infiniti, or a BMW. I ran like hell down the road, trying to see more, but there was no way I'd gain on him and after about a quarter of a mile I gave up and walked back to the van. The dog raced out the blown-to-bits truck door, barking.

"You are such a chicken," I said and picked her up and gave her a kiss. The silence returned, save for a coyote yelping in the distance, its cry echoing across the mesa on the freezing air.

I called Elias from the car. "Is Ellen with you?" I said.

"Yes. We're having cocktails. Want to join us?"

"No, thanks. I'm going home to bed." I told Eli what had happened. "Send a couple of the boys out to keep an eye on the place tonight and then I'll go over at sunup and see if there are any tracks."

Getting shot at shakes me up. How long had the person been out there waiting for me to come out? Did I catch him off guard? Was he on his way into the truck to kill me? Was he a she? How did he know about our listening post in the first place? All I knew for sure was that it wasn't Ellen. But who had so much to hide, or so much at stake, or so much to gain, that it was worth killing three people?

I lit the fire in my bedroom and lay in the bathtub and had a couple more whiskeys and then Celestina's smiling face appeared at the door.

"Su comida, Lee-lee." She held a beautiful dinner tray with flowered linens and a pink rose in a sterling bud vase and delicately flowered china covered with silver domes to keep the dinner warm. Celestina had imparted to all of us her philosophy that if you have a good dinner and a good bed, you can accomplish anything. I think she's right and even if you don't accomplish anything, you've still had a good dinner and a good bed.

Once I had pulled on my oldest, softest flannel nightie, I wolfed down the huge steaming bowl of five-alarm chili and cheese and onions and warm tortillas and butter. Then I dropped into a sound sleep and did not move until morning.

☞ Chapter Thirty-eight

Saturday afternoon

*O*ctober is the most exquisite month of the year in the Northern Hemisphere. Have you ever met anyone from anywhere who didn't say his or her state or country or town or shore or mountain or leaves were perfection in October? "If you're going to visit, go in October, that's when it's at its finest," people say.

The same thing's true for funerals. If you're going to die, do it in October. The weather's divine and the ground's not frozen but it is cool enough, even on a warm day, for ladies to wear their furs and new fall suits and black kid gloves and dark stockings and suede high heels.

In my family, we seldom have formal interments. We generally sprinkle the person's ashes at the Circle B on wherever that person's favorite spot was or bury him quietly at the family cemetery up on a sunny hillside. It's nice. But we don't get all dressed up in city clothes for our services, which are held in the small Anglican church my great-grandfather built at Bennett's Fort, nor for the final disposition of the deceased's earthly remains. Since we wear our best ranch

226 Marne Davis Kellogg

clothes, it's not really what you could call casual. But I like dressy funerals, so I was happy to put on my best black suit and brown fox stole for Christine's service, which Pamela held on Saturday afternoon beneath the Arc de Butterfield at the Wind River Cemetery.

"The body's hardly cold," Propriety's Watchdog said when we got to the graveyard. "I thought only Jews buried theirs this fast. But with Pam, one never knows." Her back was straighter than usual. Disapproval lined her face. My father and I met each other's eyes, repeating a lifetime of looks of silent agreement, relief that we, for a change, weren't on the receiving end of Mother's Emily Post bombshells. As far as she was concerned, Miss Manners, the syndicated columnist, was a nouvelle, a nobody from nowhere. "Miss Manners," she would say, "isn't she Jewish?"

"Come along, Kate." My father guided her toward the Butterfield plot where Pamela, in a smart and simple black Adolpho trimmed with black velvet stood next to Roland Tewkesbury; a muscle man in dark glasses stood at attention directly behind them. He looked like a member of the White House Secret Service with his ear piece and handheld radio. There were two others just like him. First-class bodyguards. Mr. DeNunzio did good work.

I went over to say hello.

"God, you look fabulous," she said. "Where did you get that suit?"

"Santa Bianca."

"I should have known. You can't get anything like that in Roundup. Have you seen Ellen? She's vanished. Evaporated like smoke the second she got out of jail."

"Yes. I invited her to stay out at the Circle B. I think she's safer out there. She shouldn't run around out in public right at the moment until we arrest the murderer."

"What in the hell are you talking about? She is the murderer."

"I disagree," I said.

"Well, I'll tell you one thing," Pam growled. "This thing has got me scared spitless."

"You know," said Roland, "you really don't need to protect Ellen. The police will do it if you think she's really in danger. Or, I know she's welcome to move in with Pam until all this is over."

Pam gave him the eye over her Chanel dark glasses. "Let's not get carried away, Roland."

"Well," I said vaguely. "I'm sort of police. And besides, it's giving us a chance to catch up."

Down the lane, Miami's Lamborghini rumbled to a stop behind my car, and her legs, tightly wrapped in sparkly black Spandex, snaked their way out.

"What in the hell is *that* whore doing here? Hasn't she caused enough trouble already?" Pamela stormed.

"Do you want me to ask her to leave, Mrs. Butterfield?" the body-guard said.

"Hmmm," Pamela said and smiled. "Wouldn't that be something?"

Roland grinned.

"No," Pamela finally decided, "let her stay. It's a free country."

Dwight, who was leaning against the Mercedes and smoking a cig-arette and wearing mirrored dark glasses and a suit for a change, leered at Miami. His thumb absentmindedly stroked the cock of a six-shooter that was strapped to his leg in a fancy leather holster that hung from a fancy leather belt with a sterling silver rodeo champi-onship buckle.

I walked over to see him.

In Roundup, citizens could arm themselves pretty much anyway they wanted. Visible weapons. Concealed weapons. Didn't matter. Colorado had gone so far as to legalize some of the self-protection as-pects of the western life-style with its "Make My Day" Law that basi-cally said, "Yes, as a matter of fact, if a person breaks into your house or enters your property without your permission or against your will, you have a right to shoot." In Wyoming, the law was unwritten, but it was the law nevertheless.

"Do you have a license for your gun, Dwight?" I said.

"Sure do."

"Why exactly are you carrying it?"

"Mrs. B's scared. It's for her protection."

"Do you know how to shoot that gun, Dwight?"

"Yeah."

"I don't think so."

Miami stopped next to us. "Hi, honey," she said to me. She looked at Dwight. "Hi there, cutie. I'll bet you're one of Pamela's studs I'm always hearing so much about."

We started toward the grave to join the small group who showed up to say good-bye to Christine, leaving Dwight to consider how to answer whether or not he was. Jack Lewis and his aide stood next to their car. He and I waved to each other.

"I'm surprised to see you here," I said to Miami.

"You shouldn't be. I'm doing here what most of those other folks were doing at Walter's funeral: I'm here to make sure she's dead. Little no-good you-know-what."

"Did you shoot her?"

I loved Miami's laugh. It was as enormous as she was. "I wish I had," she roared. "But no. I was there in the doldrums with Lucia, fighting off that drunken jerk George Saint George on one side and holding hands with my fiancé on the other. But I'm eternally grateful to whoever did."

"Fiancé?" I said and she brandished her left hand. An enormous diamond blazed from her finger. "Miami," I said, "is that really an engagement ring?"

"Yes, ma'am. It is."

"Who to?"

"William Lethbridge the Third."

"You don't waste any time."

"I'm not getting any younger and you know Willy. He's a sweetie. He's been after me for years, and now with Walter gone, there wasn't any reason not to."

"Have you met his mother?" I asked. Mrs. William Lethbridge, Jr., was formidable. A Brahman battle-ax. I think one of the reasons Willy hadn't ever gotten married was because his mother just didn't think anyone was, or ever would be, good enough for him. Her son marrying Miami McCloud would send her toes-up and canary eyes.

"She'll get over it," Miami grinned, reading my mind. "Of course they don't know anything about my real background. My current one is hard enough for them to swallow, and I don't think even Willy, loving me as much as he does, could adjust to my being a transsexual even if I am all girl now."

"I am quite sure you're right," I laughed.

My mother shushed us to be quiet.

Jack Lewis stopped next to me as the minister, a young Lutheran pastor provided by the funeral home who stood at the head of the grave, indicated he was ready to begin. Christine's coffin was polished brown wood with brass handles, quite simple and tasteful. A spray of white roses lay on top.

I looked around. They were almost all there: Pamela, Roland, Miami, Dwight. Everyone but Ellen and Carl Rosak. And as I stood in the warm October sun, the clues and suspects floating through my mind, I studied them and asked each silently, "Did you try to kill me last night?" and waited for the answer. It would come.

About halfway through the ceremony, Pamela's face blanched. She had her eye on someone over my shoulder. I turned and saw Carl Rosak sitting in his white Buick. One of the bodyguards was making his way over to visit with him and after a minute or two, Rosak drove off.

Jack Lewis's boy wrote down the license number.

"Do you know who that was?" Jack whispered to me.

"No," I said. Look, he had a whole department. Besides, the U.S. Marshal Service needed a victory. Everyone thought we were just a bunch of boring geeks, too chicken to be real cops. Well, that's simply not true.

Jack leaned closer. "Why didn't you tell me that Miami McCloud threatened to kill Pamela Butterfield and Christine during cocktails Thursday night?"

"Jack," I said, "do you really think Miami could sneak anywhere, much less out of a full opera house?"

He tilted forward and peered around me at Miami and then shook his head.

Rosak's appearance had brought me back to reality as the service concluded with Christine being lowered slowly into the grave. We Bennetts all crossed ourselves and that was it. My mother watched, aghast, as Pamela, without a word to anyone, and the best-looking of her Hollywood bodyguards, ducked quickly into her limousine. Dwight floored it, and together with the station wagon carrying the balance of her security contingent, they roared out of the cemetery.

"Heavens," my mother said.

Jack and his lieutenant departed, leaving a huddled little group of people loosely connected to, and without affection for, Christine Butterfield. Since none of her family members remained, Mother graciously took it upon herself to conclude the sorry affair with a touch of propriety. "Would anyone like to come back to the house for sherry?" she asked Miami and Roland and me. "I'd hate to think this is simply the conclusion of that poor girl's life on this earth."

"How very thoughtful, Mrs. Bennett," Roland said. "I'd love to stop by for a minute."

"I'd like to but I've got some business to do," I told Mother.

"You bet," Miami said. "I'd love a drink. I'm delighted it's the end of her life on this earth. Christine Butterfield was no good. Besides"— she slapped my mother on the back—"maybe you can give me some pointers on etiquette and such, now that Willy Lethbridge and I are getting married."

"Good Lord," my mother said.

"What Kate means," my father followed up, "is best wishes and she's glad to do whatever she can to help."

That night, at about nine, Richard and I walked down to Elias's and had dinner with him and Ellen. She was more relaxed than I had ever seen her as she rustled around Elias's kitchen. I don't know where his cook, Marialita, was. Probably sulking in her room. She needn't have worried. By the looks of it, her career was not in jeopardy.

Ellen had roasted a chicken to beyond death, made lumpy mashed potatoes with lots of butter, lumpy gravy, and what looked like peas that had been cooked for so long they had pureed themselves. With lots of butter. Not the kind of dinner any of us ought to eat, except maybe Richard.

After dinner she and I excused ourselves and had a meeting in Eli's library. I had a long list of questions and her answers confirmed what I suspected. Finally, I was ready to proceed. Now it was simply a matter of strategy and timing.

☞ *Chapter Thirty-nine*

Sunday morning

Sunday morning, Richard and I went to early Communion in Bennett's Fort and then I fixed us a big delicious breakfast of apple pancakes and bacon and scrambled eggs and, at about eleven, he left for the office.

"Do you work every day?" I said.

"Yes, during the season."

"Opera is hard work."

"Very," he said and kissed me good-bye. "But when the curtain goes up, it makes it all worth it."

"Dog to vomit," I said.

"Yup."

The Roundup Opera Company does five performances a week: Thursday evening, Friday evening, Saturday matinee and evening, and a Sunday matinee. Monday, Tuesday, and Wednesday are "dark," but the administrative staff works seven days a week. A lot of people can't take it. Working in the performing arts is a lot like police work: No one's in it for the money. You're in it for love.

I took my coffee into the study and lit the fire. Outside, all the grasses had turned brown and lay flat on the ground, collapsed, surrendered to the wind. The river, where ice wouldn't begin to form for another month and a half or so, moved slowly and although the day was clear and sunny, the river's surface undulated like molten black glass. In the pasture, a few horses grazed quietly.

I sat down at my desk and took out a stack of heavy ecru note cards which had the Circle B brand engraved on them in bright red and began to put the strategy into play.

LILLY BENNETT AND RICHARD JEROME
REQUEST THE PLEASURE OF YOUR COMPANY
AT A STEAK-FRY
HONORING
DAME ELIZABETH ANDERSON AND HECTOR ARIAS
AND PRINCIPALS OF THE CAST OF
DONIZETTI'S *LUCIA DI LAMMERMOOR*
WEDNESDAY, OCTOBER THIRTEENTH
SIX O'CLOCK
CIRCLE B RANCH

R.S.V.P. 555-1724

The Circle B cards are so pretty, they can make any invitation sound appealing, even if it's to a hanging.

Then I addressed them: Pamela Butterfield. Roland Tewkesbury (I thought he might come just to visit with his only equal in Roundup: tenor virtuoso Hector Arias). Ellen Butterfield. Elias. Miami McCloud. Dwight Alexander. Carl Rosak. I also sent one to Jack Lewis, but changed the time to seven-thirty.

Celestina's son, Jesús, delivered them on Sunday afternoon.

⇒ Chapter Forty

Wednesday evening

Wednesday was a perfect day. The sun shone hotly from our endlessly blue sky and I rode Ariel through the valley to the big pens where Elias's wranglers loaded the last of the steers, fattened by summer's rich grazing, for market.

"Ellen and I'll be over right on time," Elias called through the dust. Ellen had been in the guest house for five days and Eli had been having all his meals there, which Ellen herself had continued to cook. Big meals which were making Elias bigger, but apparently neither he nor Ellen minded. Romance had seized the Circle B Ranch. I worried about Elias. Hoped he wasn't going to get creamed again.

I passed the afternoon reviewing and re-reviewing my strategy.

Right at six o'clock, as the sun settled on the mountains, Eli and Ellen arrived in a buckboard, for God's sake. It rolled to a stop at the bottom of the path that led to the patio where Richard and I, looking, I thought, sort of like Roy and Dale—he tall, rugged, and trim; me the opposite—waited to greet our guests. Elias hitched the team of gigantic Percherons to the hitching post. We walked down to greet them.

"Eli," I said. "Don't you think you're laying this on a bit thick?"

"What do you mean?" His feelings were hurt.

"Well, for one thing, you've got enough horse power there to drag a deadweight Sherman tank across the Continental Divide."

"So what?" He helped Ellen, who was dressed in a gingham skirt and blouse—sort of like Shirley Jones in *Oklahoma!*—out of the buggy. The only things missing were a bonnet and a basket of fresh corn muffins. We kissed each other's cheeks.

"Ellen," I said, "you look better than you've ever looked in your life." She did, too.

"Thanks. I feel like I'm living in heaven out here. I've never been anyplace so peaceful."

"You're welcome to stay as long as you want."

"Elias," Richard said, "I know you're having rum and Coke, but what can I get you to drink, Ellen?" He'd already handed me a large crystal tumbler of whiskey.

"White wine, please."

White wine? Ellen? This was getting serious. Next thing she'd be ordering club soda.

The thunder of a fast car cracked on the cattle guard and Pamela's Mercedes limousine, Dwight at the wheel, flew across the grounded steel bars down by the main ranch house. The bodyguards' station wagon followed closely behind.

"What's Pamela going to do when this is over?" Richard said as the man-made dust storm approached. "I've never seen anyone adapt so quickly to danger."

"I know," I laughed. "She loves it. But tonight is it. Curtains."

Dwight slammed to a stop, leaped out, the holster and gun still strapped to his leg, and ran around to open the door for Pamela and Roland. He'd be as disappointed as Pam when the killer was apprehended. The bodyguards fanned out around the house.

"Will you get a load of that?" Ellen said as Pam and Roland approached. "They look like a Ralph Lauren ad."

"My God, Lilly, you look fabulous," Pamela called out on her way up the path. "Where in the world did you get that belt?"

"Thanks, Pam," I said. "You look great, as usual. And I don't know how you do, after the ten days you've had."

"Lots of sex," she said as a joke but everyone knew it was the truth. "Vodka martini," she said to Celestina, who held a tray of bite-sized chili rellenos.

"Si, Señora Butterfield." Celestina smiled and turned to Richard, who was in charge of the bar, and said, "Bodka martine, Señor Herome."

"Gracias, Celestina. Roland, what can I get for you?"

Roland's checkered cowboy bandanna was tied so tightly around his neck, it looked as if his face was going to explode.

"Roland Tewkesbury should never be seen in outdoor daylight," Ellen muttered to Elias.

"Yeah," Elias agreed. "He doesn't look too good."

"I'd like the same, please." Roland turned to me. "You are so kind to invite us this evening. Hector and Mrs. Tewkesbury and I always have such pleasant times together, and naturally, Betts."

"Betts?" I said.

"That's what everyone calls Elizabeth Anderson."

"Ah," I said. "Stupid me."

"God, yes," Pamela said as though Roland had never spoken, "I'd think you'd be *sick to death* of all of us by now. Well, maybe I shouldn't say 'death' like that, there's been so much of it, but you know what I mean. God! Ellen! You really look fabulous! Where have you been? Maine Chance?"

"Lots of sex," Ellen answered.

"Oh, thanks, Richard." Pam took her drink from him and then turned to me. "You know, Lilly, you really should have your maid pass out the drinks. After all, that's what she's there for. Then that way, Richard's freed up to visit with the guests. Know what I mean?"

I caught Celestina grinning out of the corner of my eye. "I'll keep that in mind," I answered.

"I found your *Lucia* quite good," Roland said to Richard.

"I take no credit for the production. You'll have to compliment the director."

"I'll look forward to it." Roland glanced at his watch unobtrusively.

We had gathered at the far end of the patio near the large stone barbecue pit where Richard would cook the steaks a little later, once the business portion of the evening had concluded. Roland stood a few feet away as Richard shoved two more thick logs into the inferno under the grill. Even though the air grew chillier with the dropping sun, the sheet-steel cooktop shimmered with heat and kept us all comfortable.

Ellen and Pamela, who had on a buff doeskin skirt, a white cashmere turtleneck, and gobs of silver jewelry and a white cowboy hat with a turquoise-and-silver crest, and truly did look great, sat down at the round rawhide-topped table. Elias sat on the fence holding his drink, studying Ellen.

"Another hour or so," Richard said, admiring his fire and shoving his work gloves into his back pocket, "and it'll be perfect. Anyone ready for a refill? Ellen?"

"Not yet, thanks."

Heavens.

"Oh, there's Miami," I said. She had slammed to a complete stop at the cattle guard and commenced to drive the low-slung white sports car across one bar at a time. Ba-bump. Ba-bump. She seemed to stop with each bar and take a breath before conquering the next. It surprised me that Miami didn't know the faster you cross a cattle guard or speed bump, the easier it is on your car. This way? Well, the Lamborghini's oil pan scraped along.

"She'll be here in about an hour," Richard said. "Maybe I ought to take her a drink."

"My God, Lilly. I can't believe you'd have that cheap tramp—" Pamela stopped midsentence as Carl Rosak's Buick stopped behind Miami. He turned off his engine to wait her out. "Oh, my God." She looked at me as if I were Judas Iscariot and I was glad that I'd become invulnerable to that look over the years because she looked particularly betrayed. And rightfully so. "How could you?"

"Actually," I said, "it was hard convincing him to come until I told him you would be here and wanted to see him. He really loves you, Pam." I couldn't keep a straight face.

She shook her head with disgust and slumped back into her chair, a bundle of white-hot fury. She glared at me and she glared at Roland. "DO something," she ordered him.

Roland, who did not know anything about Carl Rosak, looked perplexed and said, "About what?"

"You are a complete, useless idiot."

I walked down the path. "Dwight. Won't you join us?"

The smile and the mirrored glasses. I think he was James Dean in *Giant* today and I tried to remember if James Dean had ever played a jailbird.

"Sure, Marshal," he said. "What'd you have in mind?"

"Cocktails and dinner and then who-knows-what."

"My kinda party."

"Next thing you know she'll be asking the *Mexicans* to join us," Pamela whispered to Roland.

"Who's that?" Ellen said as Carl Rosak walked up the path, out of place and uncomfortable. When he saw Pamela, his face lit up. Rosak had it bad for her.

"That," I said, "is an old friend of Pamela's."

Pamela gave me a death stare. "Bring me another martini." She handed Celestina her glass.

"Sí, señora." No back talk now.

Willy Lethbridge followed Miami into the patio and I imagined that when he misbehaved, she picked him up and stuck him under her arm the same way I did with Baby, and I wondered how the evening's revelations would affect their relationship.

"Miami." I kissed her cheek. "Welcome."

ᗒ *Chapter Forty-one*

Cocktails moved along smoothly, the tension mostly camouflaged by my guests' good manners. Celestina passed her *extra-caliente* jalapeño hors d'oeuvres and Richard kept the drinks coming. Elias and Ellen visited with Pamela and Roland. In spite of his animosity for her, Dwight could not take his eyes off Miami, who had on so much glitter she looked like a big silver star, but Miami couldn't take her eyes off Willy. Richard and I tried two or three times to strike up a conversation with Carl Rosak but he was intent on standing in close proximity to Pamela in case she needed anything, which she never would, at least from him. So far, she had ignored him completely.

When the last of the sun disappeared and the *candlearias* painted all our faces with gold, it got too cold to stay outside and we moved in by the living room fire, leaving the French doors open to the patio. I stood in front of the fireplace.

"I think it's a good idea to get the business part of the evening over with," I said. "So, if you'll each take a seat, we can end the suspense about who murdered Walter and Christine, and tried to murder me, and then we'll all enjoy ourselves more."

"This is a tawdry way to handle things," Roland said as Pamela pulled him down beside her on the couch directly opposite the fireplace. Rosak took a position behind Roland so he could keep watch, and Ellen settled herself and her skirts in the wing chair directly to my left. Dwight leaned against the bookcase in back of her and in the love seat to my right sat Miami and Willy. Richard and Elias hadn't settled and didn't look as if they would. "Inviting us all here under false pretenses," Roland huffed.

"Not at all," I answered. "The cast will arrive shortly, as advertised. Unfortunately, our killer will depart on the helicopter that brings them in and miss the festivities."

"That's absolutely ridiculous," Pam said. "No one here is a murderer. Except maybe you-know-who." She pointed over her shoulder with her thumb at Ellen.

These words were followed by a sharp, collective intake of breath as three of Elias's big Mexican wranglers, armed with rifles, slouched into sight and took their places unobtrusively—one outside on the patio, one by the front door, and the other disappearing into the kitchen. At the appearance of the comancheros, the assembled suspects looked less comfortable, one inevitably, but imperceptibly, less than the others.

Dwight, who was halfway through his third margarita, lost his composure completely. He gaped at the Mexicans and then at me with undisguised, slack-jawed, heroine worship. "Far out," he said. "Are you going to shoot the killer right on the spot?"

Pamela's face, already an inscrutable mask except for her black gypsy eyes that smoldered at me through her thick lashes, remained expressionless and she sat back, crossed her long legs, flashing her star-spangled Larry Mahan boots, waved her martini glass at Celestina again, and lit a cigarette. Finally she took her eyes off me and slid them over to regard the wranglers, figuring out how, if she felt like it, she could make good an escape, maybe instigate a shoot-out between her bank of bodyguards and Elias's ranch hands. But the guards had been clued in by me, U.S. Marshal Bennett, via a phone call I'd made earlier to their boss, Mr. DeNunzio in L.A., and they'd do what I said or lose their licenses.

"Forget it," I told her.

So Pamela turned her wrath to Roland Tewkesbury who looked

completely at sixes and sevens. "This is outrageous, Miss Bennett, and in very poor taste," he muttered as though he were speaking to someone, somewhere, whose job it was to write down and keep track of my indiscretions in a big book.

Get real, Roland, I thought. "Maybe you-all don't do things this way in England, Mr. Tewkesbury," I said to him, "but this is the way we do them in Roundup, and that's where you happen to be at the moment. I wouldn't get too smug, if I were you, because by the time we finish you will no doubt regret leaving the U.K., if in fact you've ever even visited there." He looked very put out at that last remark. Richard handed him a fresh drink.

Ellen hunched over in her chair and chewed off her nail polish. I knew Elias wanted to go over and reassure her but he restrained himself. "May I have a cigarette, please, Pamela?" she said. "I didn't bring mine. I've been trying to quit but I guess I'll try again later."

"What's going on here?" William Lethbridge III said. "I thought this was supposed to be an opera party."

"Me, too, Willy," Miami said. "But it looks more like a hanging or a shoot-out. I guess Walter Butterfield's killer is here and Lilly intends to grill him—or her—before Old Richard here grills the steaks." She laughed and patted Willy and said with resignation, "Che serà, serà. How 'bout a little more of that whiskey, Richard?"

"It'll be my pleasure."

A strong odor of English Leather, vodka, and sweat emanated from Carl Rosak, who moved back, slightly outside of the group, and remained quiet; the expression on his brutish face hardened. His big hand clutched a long-neck bottle of Coors and he never took his eyes off Pamela, who tried to pretend she was unaware of his intense scrutiny. She kept her eyes moving around, everywhere except to him, and I couldn't tell if she was afraid to meet his gaze or ashamed. A little of both, I imagined.

"Since we've got some time, I want to take this in an orderly manner," I said. I could see Richard across the room leaning against the sideboard and although he had no idea what was coming, I could tell he was proud of me. He just leaned there, his arms folded across his chest and his long legs crossed at the ankles, and grinned.

242 Marne Davis Kellogg

"Motive, opportunity, and capability," I raised my voice. "Those are the three basic elements that drive us to murder. Motive: 'Do I want to badly enough?' Opportunity: 'Can I set it up undetected?' And Capability: 'Am I able to pull it off?' Opportunity isn't really germane to our discussion, because there was ample and equal opportunity to contemplate and set up the murders. However, when it comes to motive, each of you has something to hide. Most of you are hiding REALLY BIG things. Real gut-wrenchers if they got out."

William Lethbridge III looked at Miami questioningly. "Not me, honey," I heard her whisper as she patted him on the thigh. The diamond on her finger sparkled brightly. "I am an open book."

"Everyone here hated Walter Butterfield," I said, "but not everyone hated Christine, and whoever killed these two people, and also attempted to kill me last Friday night out at Wittier Gulch—and it was the same person—really, truly hated them both. Despised them. Was mortally afraid of them. Christine's last words were, 'I know everything about you.' Which one of you was she talking about? Which one of you would kill *two* people, and attempt to kill a third, to protect a secret?" I let that one sink in for a couple of seconds as the air got heavier. Even Miami, who now must have realized that I knew about the hangings in Big Creek, Texas, began to look dismayed.

"Also," I continued, "look at the way he or she literally blew Walter and Christine to pieces. Not nice, clean shots, but shots of vengeance and hatred. Walter's head blown off. Blewee." I waved my hand past my head to demonstrate. "Christine's mid-section plastered all over her lamp shade." I watched Roland Tewkesbury look at his shiny cowboy boots with revulsion.

"Horrible," I said. "Also"—I sipped my whiskey—"the killer was very quick and capable with the guns. These murders were done like lightning strikes, blitzkrieg fashion. No conversation. Nothing. Just ba-boom and out of there, which also leads us to the fact that the killer was trusted by both victims. The killer was an individual who could go into Walter Butterfield's study, open the gun cabinet, remove a gun, probably carrying on a discussion with Mr. Butterfield the whole time, maybe even joking about shooting him, and then actually shoot him. Maybe they discussed business. Newspaper business.

Personal business. Family business." I made sure to establish eye contact with each one of the suspects, which had the result of making them all look and feel guilty. At that moment, if I'd wanted to, I could have gotten all of them to confess.

I turned to Dwight Alexander. His beautiful vacant eyes were wide and he licked his lips nervously and gasped for a deep breath. I could hear him thinking, Wow.

"Dwight," I said. He jumped at the sound of his name. "Now you could have hated Walter Butterfield enough to kill him. I mean, anybody could. Even I did. But of everyone here, your motives are the weakest. He gave you a job after a few wasted years of college. And he was a family friend. And I don't believe you would shoot him because you were jealous of any of Pamela's other lovers, since you have so many of your own who are closer to your own age. And I'm positive Pamela never promised you that if you murdered her husband she would marry you so you could become the Grand Vizier of Rancho del Sol."

Everyone laughed nervously.

Dwight blushed and looked at his boots.

"Jesus Christ, Lilly," Pam said. "What in the hell does my *age* have to do with anything? I'm in damn good shape."

"Whaddya mean, 'other lovers'?" Carl Rosak barked. "You never said anything about other lovers."

"Oh, shut up," Pamela said to him. "You really think you're the only man in my life? Me, Pamela Butterfield? You really think that out of all the men I can have in the world, I'd stick with some dumb Polack from Little Budapest?"

Rosak surged forward, fists clenched, but the biggest wrangler, the one with bandoliers wrapped around his big stomach and only one or two teeth, grabbed him and pushed him down into a chair where he fomented and fumed and growled like a big wild burly bear. "Slut," he said.

"Why don't you wake up and smell the coffee?" Pamela sneered at him.

I had to bite the inside of my mouth not to laugh and after a couple of seconds I continued addressing Dwight. "I don't believe that Christine had any direct effect on your life. You don't use drugs and she did, constantly. And on her rare visits to Rancho del Sol, aside from a couple of harmless 'leetle pokeys,' as Pamela's maid Maria calls them, you didn't have much to do with her."

"You were giving that psycho Christine 'leetle pokeys'?" Pamela roared at Dwight. "YOU, YOU . . ."

Dwight looked at her, raised his eyebrows slightly, grinned with one side of his mouth, and touched his tongue to his lips and she spluttered out like a candle. Raw sex on the hoof. "I didn't do it, Marshal," he said to me. "Really."

"I know," I said. "You have absolutely no gun sense at all. None. And I'm glad, for all our sakes, including yours, that that six-shooter has blanks. You are the perfect example of a man who is a lover, not a fighter, Dwight."

He smiled widely and chewed his gum. "I know. I'm a chicken. It's part of my charm."

Chapter Forty-two

"Motive and capability," I repeated. "Capability: That begins to narrow our field. Only three of you really are capable of firing those shots with a weapon that powerful. Miami. You're capable because of your profession. You're basically a gunslinger." Miami smiled and blotted a sheen of perspiration off her forehead with her hankie. "Mr. Rosak. You were a sharpshooter in the Army."

"I didn't kill those damn losers," he said.

"And finally, Mr. Tewkesbury. You claim that you go shooting frequently with the Royal Family. That's fast, good-shot company and slouchers aren't included. So I'm really just assuming that you're an outstanding shot."

"That's a correct assumption," Roland cooed, a slight blush in his cheeks hinting at his pleasure at being so singled out. He had retained his composure best of all of them. No sweat swamped his brow like Miami nor darkened his shirt like Rosak. Only a tiny line of moisture glistened from his upper lip.

"Miami, my dear," Willy said, "do you mean to tell me that you are a possible suspect in a murder?"

I wondered if Miami were accused of murder, if Willy would come to court every day like Christina Ferrari or Tammy Faye Bakker, the faithful paramour, and stare with vapid support until the bitter end.

"In two murders, apparently," Miami said.

Willy pursed his lips. I knew he was thinking, Yikes.

"By your own admission, Miami," I said, "you were out there the night of Walter's killing to give him his birthday present. That was confirmed by the wet print of your boot on the library carpet. But, if you had killed him, the print wouldn't have been completely melted when I saw it. There still would have been pieces of snow."

"Right." Miami squeezed Will's hand. "See? Everything's fine."

"Plus," I added, "your car is white, not red. A red sports car was seen leaving the rancho." Out of the corner of my eye I watched Carl Rosak's mouth go dry.

"You mean to tell me that that piece of trash was at *my* house visiting *my* husband during *my* party?" Pamela had moved to the edge of her seat to listen to the proceedings. Indignation straightened her back. "My God. What next?"

"Isn't that funny," Miami said. "I thought it was *Walter's* party."

"So that pretty much absolves Miami of any participation in the killings," I said to the air in case anyone needed to hear it.

"NO!" Pamela turned to me. "Lilly, what about Christine? Miami was practically dancing a jig at Christine's funeral. And everyone heard her threaten to kill Christine and me."

"Miami spent the entire evening at the opera," I said. "All of us were at the opera when Christine was shot. All except two. Carl Rosak and one other."

Pamela's hand flew to her mouth and she looked at Ellen and Roland and Rosak. "Get me another drink," she said to Celestina. "But cut him off." She indicated Roland. "He's going to have some work to do tonight, bailing you-know-who out of the slammer once again."

"Why don't you just shut up, Pamela?" Ellen said. "It wasn't me."

"Do you mind if I continue?" I said.

Pamela popped another relleno into her mouth and still her lipstick was perfect. She waved her hand and laughed. "Sure. Go ahead. We all know who did it. It was Ellen. I don't know why you don't just come out and say so."

Ellen shook her head.

"Carl Rosak and Pamela," I said. "Now there's an odd couple, on the surface anyway. For those of you who don't know, Pam's real name is Ramona Gryczkowski."

Ellen laughed out loud.

"So I changed my name," Pamela said to her. "So shoot me. Might as well, you've killed the whole rest of your family."

"And she and Carl Rosak grew up together," I kept going. "They were even the homecoming king and queen at Billy the Kid High School. I don't know precisely when you two reestablished contact but I believe it was recently and had something to do with blackmail for reasons I won't disclose at the moment."

"That's a lie," Rosak said.

"Will you shut up?" Pam said. "I want to hear what she has to say."

"Why, thank you, Pam," I said. "I think that after a while, because Pam is innately craftier than Carl, she turned the blackmail he controlled into a love affair she controlled by offering him her body and Walter's money if he'd be patient. All of herself, if he'd just hold on until Walter died, which she explained couldn't be long, based on his alcohol and tobacco consumption. Or perhaps you told him that you'd get a divorce just as soon as you could. People can carry on promises of divorce for just as long as the other person is willing to believe them. Sometimes years."

Pamela smiled at me like a conspiratorial cat.

"I think that Carl Rosak got bored with the blackmail. He didn't just want Pam's husband's money, he wanted Pam. So he borrowed Michael Gryczkowski's car on the night of Walter's birthday party and came out here to confront him."

"But I didn't kill him," Rosak said.

"Who's Michael Gryczkowski?" Roland asked.

I kept my mouth shut.

"Yeah. I did come out here that night. I knew where the outside entrance to Walter's library was and I was just going to sneak in and

put a birthday present on his desk and leave." Rosak aimed a revenge-
ful smile in Pamela's direction.

"What are you talking about, a birthday present? Are you *crazy?*"

"It was pictures of us."

I thought Pamela was going to have a convulsion. "Jesus Christ."
She stood up. "I'll kill you, you stupid bastard."

"Calm down, Pamela," Roland said. He placed his hand on her
arm. Although the room was cool, sweat dampened his face, leaving
small streaks in his makeup.

"Your mother was right, Ramona," Carl Rosak said to her. "You are
a slut."

"What happened, Mr. Rosak?" I said.

He gulped and ran his hand across his bristly hair. "It was snowing
hard and I was afraid that if I drove the Corvette all the way in, I'd
get stuck, so I left it at the bottom of the hill and walked. When I
went through the gate in the patio wall off Walter's library, I could
see him sitting at his desk. He was arguing with somebody. I couldn't
understand what he was saying but he was pounding on his desk with
his fists and then there was an explosion and most of his head disappeared. I took off."

"And?"

"And nothing. I got out of there." Rosak's hand shook as he lit his
cigarette.

The room was quiet.

"You've always been a wimp," Pamela said.

"Jeez," said Dwight. "His head disappeared?"

Chapter Forty-three

"As it turns out," I said, "Mr. Rosak is telling the truth. I saw his taillights. There's no way he could have gotten to the car that fast if he'd shot Mr. Butterfield. In fact, as the investigation has proceeded, the more the signs have pointed to Ellen as the killer. She was the first on the scene and she was holding the gun. Her car was there the night Christine was murdered and she knew I was alone at the surveillance van."

They all turned their eyes on her. Relief flooded over the group.

"Of course," Pamela said. "I've been telling you that all along. I told you so, Roland." She stopped for a moment and then said, "What surveillance van?"

I kept going, ignoring Pam's question. "But Walter's killer made one little mistake. Ellen, do you want to tell us what it was?"

"Wait a minute. HOLD IT," Pam yelled. "What in the hell are you talking about? 'Surveillance van'?"

"For the last week, Pam," I answered levelly, "I've heard every conversation conducted in your house and seen every coming and going and going and coming." I grinned at her.

"Holy shit." She tried not to laugh. "Is that legal?"

"Entirely."

That gave Pam something to chew on for a few minutes.

"Ellen," I said. "The killer's mistake."

She nodded and sipped her wine. "Lilly has spent the last few days helping me remember Father's library exactly as it appeared when I walked in. A hypnotist came out and finally I remembered that in addition to the patio door being open, the bathroom door was cracked open, too." Ellen looked at me and I picked up.

"The two biggest things that have bothered me since Walter's murder," I said, "are the speed with which the killer vanished, and Roland Tewkesbury's almost instantaneous appearance at Ellen's side. Richard Jerome was standing in the doorway trying to keep everyone calm and out of the way while I was on the phone calling the police. And when I turned back from the desk, there stood Mr. Tewkesbury next to Ellen. It never occurred to me to ask Richard why he'd let him through until Ellen remembered the ajar bathroom door and then Richard couldn't remember seeing Roland enter the room."

"Well," Roland said, "I quite remember his letting me pass."

"Mr. Tewkesbury," I said, "you shot Walter Butterfield. And then you ran into the bathroom to hide. You killed Walter and Christine Butterfield. And you tried to kill me."

Pamela gasped and shook his hand off her arm.

"I did no such thing."

"Where do you want me to start?" I said. "Christine's last words were, 'I know all about you.'"

"I beg your pardon?" Roland said. "I have no idea what you're talking about."

"You knew about our van because you overheard Ellen mentioning it to Paul Decker at the City Jail. We heard Christine tell you she knew about you and I have a feeling that if I were to take a large amount of cash and visit young Mr. Rodriguez, the parking-lot attendant, he would suddenly remember seeing you leave and return in Ellen's Jag during the opera. But I'd like to go back farther than that. Let me see, shall I start all the way back with West Virginia and Miss Rosalind Etheridge? Or shall I start with Ray Bartee?"

"West Virginia? I've never even flown over West Virginia, Miss Bennett."

I shook my head. "I'm really sorry, Mr. Bartee. But that's not what the FBI says."

"The FBI?" Pamela said. "You mean the Federal Bureau of Investigation?"

"You've been convicted of murder in West Virginia," I said to Roland. "You're an escaped convicted murderer."

"My God, Roland," Pam said. "You? How could you?"

Roland patted his lips with his cocktail napkin and then set it on the table. He stood. "If you'll excuse me for a moment."

A comanchero, a cigarette hanging out of the corner of his mouth, rolled casually around the edge of the French door behind me and leaned on the jamb with his arms crossed over his chest. The rifle rested comfortably in his grasp.

"I'm afraid not, Mr. Bartee," I said.

"My name is Roland Tewkesbury."

"Maybe it is now, but you used to be Ray Bartee and you robbed and murdered your employer, Miss Rosalind Etheridge, in 1960. Miss Etheridge's substantial assets are still missing."

"You're making wrongful accusations, Miss Bennett. You should be careful."

"Come on, Ray, give it up," I said. "We've got you dead to rights. If Jack Lewis and the Roundup Police can't build a case against you for the Butterfield murders, which I'm quite confident they can, well then, the West Virginia police are licking their chops and dusting off their electric chair, and quite frankly, sir, I'd a lot rather be in a prison in Roundup than in West Virginia. Wouldn't you?"

He and I stared at each other for a long minute.

"All we really want to know before Hector Arias and 'Betts' arrive, which should be shortly"—I glanced at my watch—"is how you and Walter made this all work; and why you shot him; and then, why you gave Christine the means to overdose and kill herself, and then shot her, too? And then tried to shoot me?"

"Christine! I didn't give Christine any such thing."

I opened a sterling silver cigarette box on the table next to me and removed the plastic bag containing the red wrapping paper and white ribbon and gift box. "This look familiar?" I dangled the bag in the air.

"It hasn't been DNA-tested yet, but when it is we're going to find you all over this paper, aren't we?"

That did it. All the puff went out. And like MacArthur's Park in the rain, all Roland's sweet, green icing began to roll down. He swallowed.

Chapter Forty-four

Roland, I am so *ashamed* of you." Pam scooted away from him by a
few inches and turned to me. "It's true, Lilly. He left the opera and
told me he had to go 'put the paper to bed,' so I never even gave it another thought. He and Walter were always going off to put the paper
to bed. But are you saying he came out to the rancho and shot Christine?" She looked at Roland. "Brother. Did you ever blow it big
time."

"Let's start with Walter," I said.

"May I have a drink, please?" Roland asked.

"Of course," Richard said. "Vodka martini?"

"Please."

"Better make him a double," I said. "I could use a refill, too. Anyone else?"

The room took on the effect of a commercial break during a television tabloid while Celestina and Richard refreshed everyone's drink.
No one wanted to miss a word, yet they all wanted to be comfortable
for Roland's remarkable dénouement. Miami excused herself to go to
the bathroom. Richard went outside and put more logs in the firebox
under the grill. The flames exploded from beneath the sheet steel out
into the air.

*　*　*

"Walter and I were lovers," Roland said.

Ellen, Pamela, and Miami choked in unison.

"That's the most ridiculous thing I ever heard," Pam said. "Get real."

"How did you meet?" I asked.

"I escaped from the Charlotte City Jail after my trial when they were transferring me to the prison in Gattling," Roland said. "I spent ten years with Miss Etheridge as her 'companion.' And I spent the whole time planning her murder and planning my new life." He shuddered. "She was a horrid, saggy old woman who wanted me to perform the full spectrum of sexual favors for her and on her and after a while I couldn't get near her without throwing up first. But I took my time and planned everything properly. And then I got caught. Screwed up everything. But then, like a miracle, the guards in charge of transferring me dropped the ball and I just walked away. Right out of a gas-station washroom and right down the highway in the opposite direction to Washington, D.C., where I had been depositing Miss Etheridge's 'substantial assets,' as you called them, for a number of years. Right to where my new life as Roland Tewkesbury was ready and waiting for me." He sighed happily with the memory. "As you all may or may not know, the Tewkesbury family was extremely revered in England." Roland's nostrils flared with pride. He sipped his drink.

"I had prepared a small, very elegant apartment in Georgetown, exquisitely furnished thanks to Miss Etheridge's large home and failing eyesight and, after my escape, I moved right in there as I had always intended."

He turned to white-faced Ellen. "I met your father in the bar at the Jockey Club shortly after he and Pamela had married, and we fell very much in love."

"Oh, my God, I think I'm going to throw up." Pamela tossed her hands in the air and let them slap down on her lap. "Walter? A homo? Now I've heard everything."

Miami had a big smile on her face. "Not quite," she said and winked at me. I winked back.

"Oh, please," Ellen said, completely disgusted.

"I'm sorry, but it's true," Roland said.

"Next he's going to tell us he and J. Edgar Hoover borrowed each other's dresses," Pam laughed.

"Why did you kill him?" I ignored Pam.

"Over the last few years, we'd grown apart. We were still very close friends, but not lovers." Roland turned his eyes on Miami. "Thanks to her."

She blew him a kiss.

"There was still our strong business link, but as the time for Walter to retire drew closer, he reneged on the agreement to have me stand in for his son, Wally." As Roland spoke, his accent became more identifiable as West Virginian and it sounded as though he was getting to know a comfortable old friend again after a long absence. His facade drifted away before us as visibly as the powder that filmed his checkered cowboy shirt and the lapels of his expensive doeskin jacket. "I don't think Walter ever really trusted me to carry out his grand plan if something happened to him." Roland blotted his eyes.

"Oh, for God's sake, Roland, get ahold of yourself. Be a man," Pam said and laughed loudly again. "Get it?"

Nervous laughter rippled through the group.

Roland could not stop. "On the morning of his birthday he told me that he had decided to appoint Ellen as publisher and chief executive and he was going to announce it that night at the party. He threw me a bone by saying that I could replace Ellen on the Foundation board. I couldn't let him do that."

"What?" Ellen said, sitting up straight. Finally. "Are you serious? My father was going to make me CEO?"

Roland nodded malevolently at her. His bulging Pekingese eyes had taken on an almost reptilian cast, lethal and flat, devoid of feeling or humanity, and I could tell she suddenly realized what enormous danger she had been in.

Out in the distance, the helicopter's light, tiny as a pinprick, appeared over the mesa.

"Miami had just left," Roland gushed on. "And he was in good spirits and said he was going to make the announcement and I told him if he did, then I'd make my own announcement. We exchanged words and he said he didn't think I'd do it. I had to slap him. I'd lost him and I couldn't bear to lose the *News*, too. He refused to change his mind, to see how badly he'd hurt me, so I shot him." Roland buried his face in his handkerchief and sobbed.

"Good God," Pamela snorted. "Compared to him, my background's like *Rebecca of Sunnybrook Farm.*"

"Why Christine?" I asked.

"I always loathed Christine. She and Miami were my only competition for Walter. She blackmailed me into going to Saint Mary's and signing the papers for her release. She told me she knew about her father and me. That Walter had told her years ago in a moment of weakness. So, for her, it was just a matter of time. I gave her the drugs, hoping the situation would take care of itself, but by the end of the day it became evident she was going to try to stay clean. My timing was just a matter of bad luck, wasn't it? If I'd just been five minutes later she would have been dead all on her own. You were next," he said to Miami.

"I'd squash you like a bug, honey," she told him.

"And you"—he turned his eyes on me. "You are a disrespectful, impudent busybody, a pain in the derriere. It would have given me great pleasure to kill you and your silly little dog."

"The gloves are off now, aren't they, Roland?" I laughed. "What would Her Majesty say about your behavior? I'm quite sure she'd swat you roundly."

I'll say one thing for Roland Tewkesbury, he hadn't lost the ability to look down his nose. "Mind your manners," he said.

Our laughter got lost in the sounds of the chopper as it landed. Jack Lewis and his aide followed the *Lucia* stars off while Carl Rosak took advantage of the confusion and left without saying good-bye, glad to escape with his skin. I didn't imagine anyone would hear much from Mr. Rosak in the future.

Roland, handcuffed, stopped at the bottom of the steps of the Alouette and asked, "How did you find out?"

I was holding Baby in my arms and she was growling at Jack Lewis because she knew he didn't like me. "Last Thursday evening at my parents' cocktail party when I saw the way you looked at Miami, I knew. I offered to get you a drink. Remember?"

"Yes." Roland nodded his head sadly.

"I sent the glass to Washington."

"You're a bitch," he said and climbed aboard.

That pretty much hurt my feelings. I handed Jack a cassette tape of Roland's confession. "This will be helpful as a road map."

"Thanks," he said, pocketing it.

"Sorry you can't stay for dinner, Jack. We're having rib-eyes and Jordan red."

"You are a bitch, Sheriff Bennett."

"Marshal," I said. "U.S. Marshal."

He smiled and touched his hand to his brow in a mock salute and the way seemed to be open for a more harmonious future between us.

The copilot pulled up the door.

The rest of the evening was a roaring success. And at about midnight, Pamela shoved the tenor, Hector Arias, into the back seat of her car. "Dwight will take you back to town a little later, honey," she told him. They roared off into the night with the bodyguards, whom Pamela had decided to keep, trailing in their wagon.

"Prob'ly going home for a 'leetle pokey,' " Richard said.

"Prob'ly so," I said.

Christian's helicopter, long returned from delivering Roland to the Roundup City Jail, flew away with the rest of the guests, and Elias and Ellen climbed into the buckboard and plodded away into the night down the road, leaving Richard and me alone.

He took my hand and led me into the starry black mountain night and we ended up sitting on a rock looking out over a small herd of dozing cattle. I thought about how much I was falling in love with Richard. I'd been back in Roundup only three months and maybe for the first time every part of my new life, now so changed, seemed to fit me perfectly.

I leaned back against him. He was so tall and strong, his arms folded me into him completely.

"I'll make you a deal," I said.

"Oh? What?"

"I'll stay in Roundup if you will. What do you think? Deal?"

"Deal," Richard said.

Oh, good.

Acknowledgments

Because Harry Smith, anchor, *CBS This Morning* and his wife, Andrea Joyce, sportscaster, CBS Sports, are such loyal friends and were willing to take a risk for me, BAD MANNERS has been published. I thank them particularly for their friendship, enthusiasm, and success. Without Harry's tenacity, Maureen Egen, executive vice president, Warner Books, and Sara Ann Freed, executive editor, Mysterious Press, would never have seen my manuscript.

I am extremely fortunate and grateful to have had the professional guidance of Denver psychiatrist William W. McCaw, Jr., M.D.; Thomas Haney, chief of investigations, and retired chief Jerry Kennedy, Denver Police Department; Chief U.S. Marshal Sid Goldberg, Denver Federal District; Sam Lusky; and Wayne Ude, professor of English, Old Dominion University, Norfolk, Virginia. Their counsel has been instrumental.

I also thank my friends Jane and Frank Batten; Susan Coe and Eloise Fasold—who read early drafts—and Gerri and Tommy Nicholson; Richard and Mary Schaefer; Gene and Mary Lou McGuire and Pam and Bill Wall for their confidence.

Most of all, for their love and positive energy, I thank those who mean the most to me: my wonderful husband Peter, Peter II, Hunter and Courtney; my parents and all the Davises; Peter's parents and all the Kelloggs. And finally, our wirehaired fox terrier Gussie, who is helpful and happy no matter what happens.

MARNE DAVIS KELLOGG
Denver, Colorado